THE INCIDENT

D F DORAN

BOOKS BY DF DORAN

The Copper Casket

The Candidate

The Incident

The Hostage

ABOUT THE INCIDENT

Thanksgiving 1964

An Armed Robbery Goes Bad. Wrong people are suspected. Can Jim Monaghan uncover the truth without losing his life?

Jim Monaghan's career is on the rise, but his personal life is in shambles. He's in love with a girl who is well above his station. At least, that's what her country club father things.

He needs a story to prove his worth so he can propose. This can't be it thought, can it?

PRAISE FOR DF DORAN'S JIM MONAGHAN THRILLERS

"A fascinating book, which certainly kept me reading right up to the end…" - Amazon review

"An Emotional Roller Coaster…" - Amazon review

"Jim Monaghan is a very interesting, multifaceted character with baggage…." - Amazon review

"Crisp writing and accelerated page-turning as funeral home intrigue encounters investigative journalism. Romance, murder, and 60's nostalgia…" - Amazon review

"It reads like a thriller, a classic "page turner" but with impressive depth…" - Amazon review

"Fast paced. Can't wait to start on ….Doran's next book…." - Amazon review

To my wife, Jan, without whose constant encouragement, this novel would not have been written.

To our children, Danya, Shannon, Bryan, and Kevin and your beautiful families — you are the wind beneath my wings.

1

"What do you want?" snarled the dapper man in a tailored blue suit. He looked ready to pounce.

"My name is Jim Monaghan and I am…"

"I know who the hell you are, Monaghan. Unfortunately, everyone in this town knows you."

Icy rain pelted Jim as Professor Harrison Fowler blocked the front door of his country club estate. Jim asked, "May I come in. I have something for Jenny."

"No, you may not come in. Jenny has no interest in whatever you have." Fowler snapped.

"Professor," Jim answered struggling to stay calm. "I have some photographs for Jenny. They are from the July Fourth parade. She asked me to bring her copies."

"My daughter talked to you? Disgusting," Fowler said shaking his head. "Look, Monaghan, my daughter has no interest in your photographs, nor does she have any interest in you. And that newspaper of yours had no right to publish her picture without asking me."

"Wait," Jim stammered, but Fowler interrupted.

"For God's sake, it's Thanksgiving. How dare you

show up at my front door asking to see my daughter with photographs from months ago. You are not in her class, Monaghan. If I see your face around here again, I will call Chief Buckner, and have you arrested. And you better not have parked that junk of a truck anywhere on my property," he barked as he slammed the door in Jim's face.

What an asshole, Jim thought. He shouted at the front door, "I don't drive the truck anymore. I have a new car, Jerk." He thought, *how could lovely, sophisticated Jenny Fowler have such a rude father?*

"Well Happy Thanksgiving to you, Harrison!" Jim shouted, extending his middle finger.

Jim steered his brand-new, red convertible into the circular driveway of Bernard Hill's palatial home at Lincoln's Country Club Estates three doors down from Fowler's.

Bernard, publisher of the Lincoln News Tribune and owner of a chain of daily newspapers, ten radio stations and two television stations, was behind Jim's purchase of the new car.

After work at the Lincoln News Tribune the day before, Jim walked to his battered black pickup truck with an unpainted orange door. The truck was damaged the previous year, in what police said was an accident, but Jim knew better. The accident killed Mary Ryan, the love of his life, and he never had the heart to repair the damage.

Bernard had appeared at the truck window and handed Jim an envelope.

"Congratulations on your second Associated Press Award," beamed Bernard. "I just got off the phone with Charlie Sloan, who told me you had won for your coverage of Governor Anderson's election. He also hinted he might try and hire you away, so I have decided to give you a bump in your salary, too.

"I am proud of you, son. When you come to Thanksgiving dinner tomorrow, come a little early. I have something to talk to you about."

Jim, stunned by Bernard Hill's unusual show of affection, thanked his publisher, mentor, and friend, averting his eyes to hide sudden tears.

"Thanks, Bernard, I really appreciate this."

Hill stood back and looked at Jim's battered pickup. "Jim, with the bonus and the bump in pay, you might be able to replace your truck. I know the truck means a lot to you, but it might be time for a new car."

After Bernard left, Jim thought of Mary Ryan. He knew she would want him to move on, and he drove to the Fiat dealership. He had often visited the dealership, admiring the new cars and anticipating the arrival of his dream car, a 1965 Fiat 850 Spider Convertible, red with black leather interior, five-speed stick transmission, whitewall tires, and a powerful rear-mounted, in-line, four-cylinder engine.

Jim signed over the bonus check and was able to pay the balance with his savings, even though it depleted his account. He didn't care. He had his new car.

Life is good, despite Harrison Fowler, Jim thought as he walked up to the Hill's two-story red brick home, white pillars bracing a portico on the second floor. The flagstone walkway paved the way to a solid oak door.

Grasping the gold-plated door knocker, Jim looked down the street at the Fowler estate *I should have brought the photographs when she called me after the Fourth of July parade,* Jim thought. *Now, any chance I had to spend some time with her is gone, thanks to her asshole father.*

Jim first met Jenny Fowler at the Fourth of July

Parade. She was on the Daughters of the American Revolution float and was dressed in a period costume. Jim's head was turned by Jenny's beauty and even more so by her warm smile and effortless self-confidence. But he never found the nerve to follow up and ask her out.

One late summer afternoon, News Tribune sports editor, Tyrone Thompson invited Jim to a woman's tennis match at Hamilton University. Unbeknownst to Jim, Jenny was captain of the Hamilton team and had won the individual NAIA title.

After the match, Thompson brought Jim along to interview the team. When Jim met Jenny, he was at a loss for words, and he was sure his incoherent mumbling had made a terrible impression.

Jim paused, noting the opulence of the neighborhood, and especially the Fowler estate. He thought, *probably doesn't make any difference, anyway. Tyrone told me she is out of my league. She is smart, beautiful, her father is a professor, and they are rich. She is way out of my league anyway.*

2

Thanksgiving Dinner was festive. Jim had been looking forward to this time with Bernard and his wife Jane, their daughter Audrey who was assistant publisher of the News Tribune, Judge McCallister and his new wife Alice, and Brad Hauser, the new managing editor of the paper, and his family.

Jim was particularly close to Audrey. She was the sister he'd never had, and he was the brother that Audrey, an only child, longed for. Though close personally, they made sure their professional life was separate. Audrey had recently filed for divorce from her husband, Jasper. His drinking and philandering had finally come to a head.

Everyone, even Audrey, was in a great mood. After a prayer of thanksgiving, Bernard gave a short speech about how grateful he was for his friends at the table.

Bernard toasted Jim for winning another Associated Press award, the election of Lucas Anderson as Governor of Ohio, and the growth of the Hill Family Enterprises. He said he was sad about Audrey's marriage ending, but with an end there was always a new beginning.

"1965" Bernard declared, "is going to be a good year." He urged Jim to concentrate on reporting and, hopefully, the authorities would continue pursuing corruption in Lincoln and Shelby County. He vowed Hill Enterprise media would keep the spotlight on the problems and racial attacks on the citizens in the public housing project, Simpson Village.

Jim said he had little confidence in Chief Buckner. "I know in my heart that Irene, Steve, and Mary were murdered. Their deaths were not accidents. And I know those responsible will make mistakes. I will always be looking out for that. For now, I am content to just be a reporter in 1965. And Bernard, I love covering politics."

Audrey insisted they leave the newspaper business alone and just enjoy the great dinner. Jane said she had broken tradition by roasting a prime rib instead of a turkey for dinner. "Bernard called Jim's brother Hugh and asked where he could get a good cut of beef for Thanksgiving. Hugh told us he had just butchered a black angus and would deliver a prime rib."

"You have to be kidding," Jim said, "Hugh is so tight, I can't imagine him giving anything away, let alone a prime rib. I am lucky to get a couple of pounds of hamburger when I visit," he joked.

After dinner, Judge McCallister put his arm around Jim and said he wanted to talk to him in Bernard's library. The judge had been an advisor to Jim in the copper casket investigation, until he learned he, too had been a victim. His wife's casket had been switched, and he had been defrauded.

The library was impressive. The ceilings were ten feet high and the room measured twenty feet by twenty-five feet. Three walls were lined with mahogany shelves filled with many first edition books. In the middle of the back wall, a four-foot high fireplace with a thick, scrolled mahogany mantel cast the room in a warm glow.

The ebony and gold clock on the mantel chimed the hour. Four brown leather chairs surrounded an antique mahogany table, and a matching sofa anchored the oriental carpet on the gleaming oak floor.

"Jim," the judge began, "my wife Alice knows I still love my first wife, though she has been dead for several years. And I know, that as a widow, Alice still loves her first husband. But that doesn't mean we can't love one another. You must move on, Jim. Mary would not only understand, she would want you to. Jim, do you think I love my first wife less, because, after she died, I have remarried?

"And do you think Alice loves her late husband less, because she is married to me? The answer is no. Once a loved one passes, you keep on living. I know you loved Mary Ryan. We all did. But she died. You have been making progress, but there is a large void in your life. You are still in love with Mary, and you can't get past the fact she is gone. I think it's time you gave yourself permission to see other young women."

"I did, Judge. I dated Anna Masters, but that didn't work out."

"So, what? Do you expect to fall in love with the next person you meet? That relationship ended. It's time you start looking again. One effort in two years is not enough."

Stunned by the judge's personal intervention, Jim looked down at his feet and then looked up at the judge and said, "Well, there is this girl, but I doubt she will go out with me. I just tried to deliver some photos of her

taken at the Fourth of July Parade, but her father
wouldn't let me in the door. He said she had no interest
in me. He told me I wasn't in their class. So, strike her
off the list of potentials," Jim lamented.

"Jim, you are an award-winning reporter. You are
courageous and persistent, and you're young and not
bad looking," the judge chuckled. "Are you telling me
you are afraid to ask a girl out because you fear, she will
say no? Or are you afraid of her father? I can't wait to
tell Audrey and Bernard about that."

"By the way Jim, who is this over-protective father?"
the judge asked.

"Professor Harrison Fowler, the new chairman of the
Shelby County Community Relations Committee."

"I know him," the judge said, "A bit of a pompous
ass if you ask me," he said smiling.

Encouraged by the judge's counsel, Jim decided, the
hell with Harrison Fowler, he would call Jenny. He
walked out to the living room and asked Audrey if she
had a Country Club member directory. He wanted to
call Jenny Fowler.

"Why don't you just wait for about an hour, Jim?
Mom and Dad always invite the neighbors over for
thanksgiving dessert. Mom's pumpkin pie is legendary.
Jenny and her parents are coming.

"By the way, Jim, I was surprised when Jenny called
me a couple of weeks ago. She asked me to be her
partner in the club's women's doubles tennis tourney. I
can play pretty well, but I am not in her league. She is a
champion. But, for some reason, she invited me. We
came in second, but she is so good, I know I held us
back. What surprised me, though, was after the match,
we were having a cold drink and she asked about you.
She wanted to know all about you. She asked if you were

dating anyone. Were you a nice guy? All sorts of questions.

"I was going to tell you, but with the divorce, I have been preoccupied.

"She might be receptive to you asking her out, Jim," Audrey said smiling.

Jim, stunned, poured himself another Bushmills. *Well, I'll be damned*, he thought.

3

Promptly at five p.m., the Fowlers and three other families joined the group for dessert.

When Jenny walked in, Jim felt he was struck by a thunderbolt. Wearing a light blue cashmere sweater, dark blue skirt, and polished black boots, she lit up the room with her deep blue eyes, creamy skin, shiny blond hair, and broad smile. All eyes were on her, except for her father. He was glaring at Jim.

Other than his brief encounter at Fowler's front door, Jim only knew Fowler by reputation. He was chairman of the Hamilton University History Department and people said he was smart, but snobbish.

Fowler took Bernard by the arm and said sternly, "Bernard, I am surprised you invited your hired help to your home on Thanksgiving. For goodness sake, that Monaghan is just a reporter. It doesn't seem appropriate."

Bernard, who had been briefed by Audrey, about the potential liaison between Jim and Jenny, ignored Fowler and called Jim over.

"Jim, I'm not sure if you have met Professor Harrison Fowler and his family. He is the chairman of the new County Committee. And this is his wife Martha and daughter Jenny."

"Yes, the Professor and I have met." Jim looked at Fowler directly. "I know the community has high hopes for the success of your Community Relations Committee," Jim said and extended his hand to Fowler.

Frowning, Fowler reluctantly and perfunctorily shook Jim's hand.

Jim stole a glance at Jenny. She was beaming at him.

"Hi, Jim, my name is Jenny. We have met a couple of times, but I don't think we have been formally introduced. And Dad says, if you haven't been formally introduced, you really haven't met," she said mischievously.

"And, if I recall, Jim, you were going to bring me photographs from the Fourth of July Parade." Putting her hands on her hips and appearing upset, she said, "Did you forget them and me?"

"As luck would have it, Jenny," Jim said, casting a glance at her father, "I have copies of those photos in my car. I will get them before you leave."

Jenny's mother, observing the dynamics between her daughter and Jim, took Jenny by the arm and told her they should visit with Bernard's wife. She was hoping to get Jane's pumpkin pie recipe. "I would like Cook to bake it for my Bridge Club on Tuesday."

When Martha and Jenny walked away, so did Harrison.

Bernard, smiling, said to Jim, "You might have a mountain to climb there, Jim. But put on your hiking boots. It's worth the climb."

For the next hour or so, either Mrs. Fowler or

Professor Fowler thwarted Jim's efforts to talk with Jenny, by steering her away. Jim was heartened when Jenny mouthed from across the room, "I'm sorry," then winked.

Finally, Judge McCallister whispered to Jim, "I think you need some help. Come with me." The Judge and Jim moved across the room and stood beside Jenny, who was visiting with one of her neighbors.

"Well, how is my first-year law student doing?" the Judge asked Jenny. The normally confident Jenny was slightly intimidated by her Dean and legendary retired federal jurist.

Before she had a chance to answer, Fowler walked in between Jim, his daughter, and the Judge. "What's going on here, Judge?" he asked.

"I was just about to have a chat with one of my students and Jim. I was thinking about having Jim talk to our students about investigations.

"As you know Harrison, Jim has just been awarded another Associated Press Award for his investigative reporting. I believe he is the youngest person ever to win one AP award and Bernard told me he has never heard of anyone winning two AP awards in consecutive years.

"I thought his insights on investigations would be of value to my students and I was about to run my idea past Jenny, who is an excellent first year student."

"Oh," said Fowler. "Not sure how a reporter could help law students, but you are the Dean.

"By the way, Monaghan, aren't your parents' farmers? Addressing law students at Hamilton is a long way from a farm," Fowler smirked.

"My parents are dead, Professor. They were killed in an auto accident when I was in high school."

Jenny gasped and drew her hand to her mouth and said, "Dad, you apologize to Jim."

"Sorry, Monaghan," Fowler said and walked away, slightly flushed.

"Jim, I am so sorry," Jenny said, "My dad can be a putz sometimes."

Jenny, the judge, and Jim continued their conversation until people started to leave. Martha told Jenny it was time to go as they had a busy day on Friday.

"I don't have anything going on tomorrow, Mom" Jenny said. "I would like to stay and continue my conversation with Judge McCallister and Jim."

"No, Jenny, you are going home with your father and me."

Frowning and rolling her eyes, Jenny said, "I'll be right there, Mother." Martha turned away, and Jenny grabbed Jim's hand and leaned towards him. "Don't lose this." She smiled at Jim and joined her parents.

Jim felt a piece of paper in his hand but kept his fist clenched until the Fowlers had walked out the door. Then he read the note.

"Jim, call me. This is my number. If anyone else answers, hang up."

Grinning, Jim turned and saw Bernard, the Judge, and Audrey all smiling back at him.

"This has been a great Thanksgiving," he sighed.

4

B ernard ushered Jim towards his library. "Jim, we still need to have our talk." Let's have our coffee in my library. We can have some privacy there.

Bernard sat in one of his oversized brown leather chairs. Jim chose a nearby chair and said, "Bernard, I can't thank you enough for the invitation to Thanksgiving dinner. My brother Hugh is celebrating Thanksgiving with his wife's family in Illinois. Edgar, Maybelle, and Haley went to Chicago to visit relatives. Without you, I would have had to go to O'Toole's and have Thanksgiving with Stavros. That would be sad.

"And what a treat to finally spend time with Jenny Fowler. Wow, it's been a great day. Thanks so much, Bernard."

"You are more than welcome, Jim, but I want to talk to you about your future. You probably don't know this, but I sit on Columbia University's Pulitzer committee. One of my best friends is Arthur (Punch) Sulzberger, publisher of the New York Times.

"I have been talking to him about you. You are very

young in the business to be a normal candidate for him, but your AP awards got his attention. Your coverage of the Governor's campaign, especially your stories on Lloyd Collier, were syndicated by the New York Times. Your stories have been in over five hundred newspapers."

"I can't believe Arthur Sulzberger even knows my name, let alone has been following my career. I am stunned and pleased," Jim said humbly.

"Well, as you know, since Punch has taken over as publisher, he wants to make some changes. He told me he wants to hire some young aggressive reporters. Does that sound like you, Jim?"

"Yes, Bernard, that does sound like me. But the New York Times? I'm just a farm boy from Dale. I'm not sure I could handle New York."

"Jim, for goodness sake. You were at the top of your class at Northwestern's Journalism school, one of the top J schools in the country. You were editor of the school's newspaper. Northwestern is in Evanston, a suburb of Chicago, which is the second largest city in the country. Now, don't tell me you couldn't handle New York."

"Ok, that was probably a stupid thing to say. But I am comfortable here in Lincoln, working for you. Brad Hauser is just a dream to work for and I am learning so much. Plus, Bernard, I feel I would be unfaithful to Mary, Irene, and Steve, if I moved and left whoever is responsible for their deaths to roam free.

"I just don't think I am ready for the New York Times. If it's ok with you, I would like to stay where I am. Oh, I should tell you, Charlie Sloan, editor of the Post-Dispatch offers me a job every time I run into him."

Bernard smiled. "Charlie and I are old friends. Every time I see him, he tells me he is going to hire you away. Jim, I will let Punch know you are not ready, and I will try not to gloat that we were able to keep you. But you should be prepared for several calls from newspapers throughout the country.

"I am grateful you want to stay at the News Tribune. I am giving Audrey more and more responsibility in running the paper. With you and Brad there, the news side is doing well, and Tyrone, while a pain sometimes, is a great sports editor. So, the paper is in great shape."

Jim and Bernard found everyone had left but Audrey. "Do you realize you two were speaking for an hour?" Audrey asked. "We didn't want to disturb you, so I hope it was important."

"It was, Audrey," Jim said. "Thank you all for a wonderful Thanksgiving."

As Jim walked to his car, he looked down the street at the Fowler home. When he first walked into the Hill's home, he feared he had no chance with Jenny. Now, he smiled as he thought, *Maybe, just maybe.*

5

J im started calling Jenny the next day. It took three phone calls before he finally connected with her.

They agreed to meet for dinner. "The only places I really know are O'Toole's and Harlow's Café," Jim offered.

"I haven't been to either place, so let's try O'Toole's. I will meet you there at six p.m. I will tell my parents I am meeting some classmates to study. They would never go to O'Toole's."

Excited about seeing Jenny, Jim was, however, concerned about the subterfuge.

His concern evaporated when Jenny walked into O'Toole's. Her blonde hair was pulled back in a ponytail, Her Hamilton University Law School tee-shirt was partially obscured by a Country Club windbreaker. She wore tight jeans and white tennis shoes. Jim was almost speechless.

"Sorry about being so casual for our first date, Jim, but this is what I wear when I study with my classmates. I apologize for meeting like this, but I am afraid my parents are not quite ready to know we are going out."

"I think you are beautiful," Jim said stumbling over his words.

"Thanks," Jenny said blushing.

Under the watchful eye of Stavros, owner and chief bartender of O'Toole's, Jim and Jenny slid into Jim's favorite booth in the back of the bar. Stavros had been one of Jim's best friends since he came to Lincoln. He was a source of comfort during Jim's many crises, and like Jim, was an avid sports fan.

"Why are your parents so uncomfortable with me?" Jim asked.

"Oh, it is that Boston Brahmin thing. Both mom and dad are from old time families in Boston. Both families go back to the American Revolution. They think they are better than the average person. They have it all planned out in their heads that I am going to marry into some well-established, wealthy family back in Boston.

"I know they are over-protective, but I am their only child, and they want what they think is best for me," Jenny continued.

"They were really upset I chose Hamilton as opposed to Harvard Law School. I was accepted by Harvard. They even offered me a scholarship."

"Well, why didn't you go to Harvard?" Jim asked.

"Judge McCallister. He is one of the brightest legal minds in the country. Do you know he was never reversed by the Supreme Court? I don't know of another Federal Judge who can make that statement."

Jim and Jenny both ordered cheeseburgers and continued their conversation. Jenny was fascinated that Jim was raised on a farm.

"I can't imagine having all that land. And all those animals. All we have is a cat and my dad hates it."

Jim asked Jenny about Law school. Did she know what kind of law she wanted to practice? How hard were the courses? And was it as rigorous as he had heard.

Jenny told him it was hard, but she was on top of it, and Judge McCallister counseled they should not make up their mind about the type of law they wanted to practice until at least the middle of their second year.

Stavros served the cheeseburgers and noted Jim had not touched his Bushmills, which was very unusual. Jim's full attention was on the young lady with the ponytail.

"Jim, said Jenny, "I had coffee with Audrey this morning. She called and asked me to go to the club. She wanted to tell me that you were an outstanding young man, a talented reporter, and a very good friend of hers and her parents."

"Yes, the Hills and I are close friends. They are my boss, but it goes beyond that relationship. It all started with the copper casket investigation. That investigation is also the basis for my friendship with the Judge," Jim answered.

"Jim, I read every word you wrote on that awful story. I knew Mary Ryan. She came to our sorority and talked to us about going to law school. As you know, not many women apply. She was smart and determined.

"You probably know there is a plaque in her honor at the law school. Judge McCallister says they are in the process of creating a Mary Ryan scholarship for law students who promise to go into public service. The rumor is the Hills are funding it."

"Yes, I know about the plaque. I was there when it was unveiled. And yes, the Hills are funding it," Jim replied

"Jim, after Mary Ryan died, one of her friends in our sorority told us the two of you were in love and were planning to marry. I am sorry for your loss. It must have been terrible, and I suspect it still is."

Stunned by Jenny bringing up Mary Ryan, Jim looked away. Jenny reached over and gently touched his hand.

"It's ok, Jim, I understand," she said gently.

Jim looked at Jenny and shook his head. "Jenny, to be honest, I have been a mess ever since Mary died. I know there are people who live in Shelby County who are responsible, and I have been trying to uncover evidence since she died.

"I know for sure the names of the two people who killed Irene Dunn, Steve Hampton, and Mary. But I know the story goes deeper than that. I am determined to keep turning over rocks until I find the individuals who ordered the murders, but I am not going to be a fanatic about it."

"I have dated one girl since Mary died, but we had very different values, and it didn't work out.

"I didn't realize we would be talking about Mary tonight and all that happened during the copper casket investigation. But Jenny, I might as well tell you something else about me. It may cause you to run home and ask your parents for the names of some of the families back in Boston."

"Don't be silly, Jim. I am fascinated by your stories. I didn't mean to upset you by talking about Mary, but I just wanted you to know I am sorry for the pain you must still be suffering."

"Thanks for saying that, Jenny."

Jenny listened intently when Jim told her of his relationship with Edgar, Haley, and Maybelle Johnson.

He told her they lived at Number Eight in the Simpson Village housing project, and they were Black. Jim told her about how supportive they were after his parents and Mary died.

He told her Maybelle was his substitute mother and Edgar and Haley were like a brother and sister. He told her he had spent many evenings at dinner at the Johnson's and had often slept on the sofa in the living room.

Jenny told Jim she couldn't wait to meet Maybelle, who sounded wonderful, and his friends Edgar and Haley.

They exchanged stories of their childhoods and noted that even though they had different backgrounds and led different lives, they shared a desire to help people and to make the world better.

Jenny looked at her watch and said she had to be on her way, as the law school library would be closing soon.

Jim did not tell Jenny about Christmas the year before, and his near suicide. *That can wait*, he thought.

Jim walked Jenny to her car. *Should I try to kiss her or just shake her hand*, he wondered.

They stood at the door of Jenny's car, a silver Mercedes sedan. They were holding hands.

"Well, are you going to ask me out for another date?" Jenny asked smiling, "Or do I have to send you another note?"

"I would love to go out again. But do I come to your house or do we meet somewhere?

"I think we should meet somewhere else for a while. I am free Wednesday afternoon, if that would work for you. Perhaps we can try Harlow's Café for a late lunch."

Jim immediately agreed. Jenny smiled as she opened the door and got in. "It was a fun night, Jim

Monaghan. I had a wonderful time." And she blew him a kiss.

Jim walked back into O'Toole's, sat at the bar, and ordered a Bushmills.

"You still hungry, Jim? You barely touched your cheeseburger. What the heck is going on with my friend Jim Monaghan?"

"Stavros, my friend, let me tell you an amazing story."

6

Jim and Jenny's relationship blossomed in the winter of 1964. They usually met at O'Toole's or Harlow's Café, with an occasional dinner at Judge McCallister's. They were always under the watchful eyes of Stavros, the judge, or Sgt. Major Harold E. Harlow, a decorated war hero from World War II and the Korean War, and one of Jim's friends, mentors, and father figures. Harlow would often sit on Jenny's side of the booth making sure the young duo ate their lunch or dinner.

"Why do you always sit with Jenny?" Jim once asked.

"Do you think I am stupid, Jim? It's either sitting beside you, you lunk, or this beautiful young woman. Easy decision."

Harlow became one of Jenny's favorite people, and he obviously enjoyed their conversations. She was intrigued by his stories. On occasion, Jim had to remind them that he was Jenny's date for the evening.

As Christmas approached, Jim insisted Jenny tell her

parents they were dating. "We can't keep sneaking around like this, Jenny. It's not right."

"I know Jim, I am working on it."

Jim wondered how committed Jenny was to their new relationship. Their physical relationship was modest and muted. Occasionally they would have an intimate embrace and kiss, but it was usually in the law school parking lot or in a downtown parking lot. They never had privacy.

They had no plans to be together on Christmas Eve and neither had talked about exchanging Christmas presents.

When Audrey asked how the relationship was going, Jim said. "Audrey, all we do is talk. We talk about everything, but trust me, all we do is talk."

Audrey, who was becoming fast friends with Jenny, knew the relationship was evolving. She knew Jim and Jenny were head over heels over one another. She encouraged Jenny to stand up to her parents, tell them about her dating Jim, and invite him for dessert on Christmas day, if not Christmas dinner.

On the day before Christmas eve, after dinner at O'Toole's, Jenny told Jim he was expected for dessert at her house on Christmas day. She told him to be there promptly at four p.m.

"Wow, what did you parents say when you told them?" Jim asked.

"Oh, they don't know it yet. They will be fine," Jenny said laughing.

7

The Fowler's Christmas tradition included morning church services at the First Presbyterian Church and a turkey dinner promptly at two p.m. The early dinner allowed their cook time to celebrate with her own family.

At dinner, conversations were polite but inconsequential. Finally, summoning up her courage, Jenny announced, "I have invited a guest for dessert. He will be here at four p.m."

Martha smiled and said, "Honey, is it someone from your law school? I so enjoy meeting your classmates.

"No, it is not someone from the law school," Jenny answered.

"From the club?" Martha asked.

"No, mother."

"Well, who is it?" Harrison demanded.

"It's Jim Monaghan. You both met him at the Hill's Thanksgiving party."

"No, I will not permit it," Harrison fumed.

"Absolutely not. No, Jenny. His type is not coming to our home on Christmas day. I will not permit it."

"What do you mean, Father, his type?"

"Well, he is a Catholic for one reason. Second, his family are immigrants from Ireland. Both his parents were born in that God-awful place. Third, he is a newspaper reporter. Fourth, he has no money. Fifth, I believe he is a Democrat. At least he is good friends with Governor Anderson."

"My goodness, Harrison, have you been investigating this Mr. Monaghan?" Martha asked.

"Yes, I have and, Jenny, he is not coming here today for dessert or any other day. And that's final," Harrison exclaimed.

"Father, you are being unreasonable. I have invited him for dessert and he will be here in an hour or so. And *that's* final," Jenny announced.

Father and daughter stared at one another across the table and finally Harrison blinked.

"And one more thing folks. Jim and I have been dating since the Friday after Thanksgiving, and let me tell you, I like him. I like him a lot."

Harrison threw his napkin on the table. "You have to be kidding me. There are so many fine young men at the club. And there are so many young men from wonderful and established families back in Boston, who would love to go out with you. Why, I heard from Walter Chaffee the other day and he said his son, Preston, who attends Harvard Law School, was inquiring about you.

"You should have gone to Harvard where you would have been with your own kind. This is just unacceptable."

"Oh, Father, you can't be serious. Preston Chaffee is an entitled ass. There is no chance I would even consider going out with him. I am a college graduate. I am twenty-one years old, and I can make my own decisions. I choose to go out with Jim Monaghan. And, I have invited him over for dessert.

"Listen to me young lady, as long as you live under my roof, you will do what you are told," Harrison fumed.

"I could move out. You know that, Father, so get used to it. I chose Hamilton because of Judge McCallister, who is a good friend of Jim's. Jim and I have been to the Judge's home for dinner a couple of times since Thanksgiving.

"And the Hills like Jim a lot. He is coming here, and I expect the two of you to treat him with respect."

Martha's lips formed a tiny smile of surprise and admiration. "We will treat your friend with respect, Jenny. Won't we, Harrison?" Harrison grumbled.

At ten to four p.m., the phone rang. It was the guard at the gate to Country Club Estates. Harrison took the call.

"Mr. Fowler, there is a Jim Monaghan here who says he is expected at your house, but he is not on any list of expected guests. Shall I let him in?"

"Let me talk to him," Harrison barked.

"Hello, Professor," Jim said.

"Monaghan, I didn't know my daughter had invited you and, frankly, I am not pleased. Unfortunately, there is nothing I can do about it. But I don't want that car of yours parked in my driveway. Park it outside the gate and walk to the house."

"But it is over a mile to your house from the main gate, Professor, and it is five degrees above zero. Why don't you want my car parked in your driveway?" Jim answered.

"Because those foreign cars leak oil," Harrison scrambled.

"You have three Mercedes and they are foreign cars. I doubt they leak oil and neither does my car," Jim answered.

"Monaghan, if you want to come to my house, park your car outside the gate and walk down." And Harrison hung up the phone.

That should take him a while, and he will be cold. Hope he has a coat, Harrison thought with a sarcastic smile.

The Grandfather clock in the living room struck four bells when Harrison turned to his wife and Jenny and said confidently, "Well, Jenny, it appears your friend is late. Are you sure he is coming?

As the chime from the clock began to silence, the front doorbell rang. Harrison jumped up and answered and was stunned to see Jim Monaghan.

"How did you get here so quickly? You did park your car in front of the entrance to our neighborhood, didn't you?" he asked.

"No, I called Bernard, and he let me park in his driveway. It's only three houses down."

Chagrined, Fowler escorted Jim into the dining room. Jenny jumped up, gave Jim a hug, much to Jim's surprise and her father's displeasure, while her mother said, "Welcome to our home, Jim." "Are you ready for dessert?"

Jenny and her mother both were attired in fancy dresses while Harrison wore an obviously expensive suit, crisp white shirt with French cuffs and a red bow tie. Jim felt underdressed. Clad in his only blue blazer, he wore a black turtle neck sweater and gray slacks.

The conversation over the baked Alaska dessert was as frosty as the ice cream. Later, Jim and Jenny relaxed on the sofa, while her parents sat in matching gold velvet wing chairs.

Jim tried to start conversations by asking Harrison about the County Community Commission, Hamilton University, and his ancestors in Boston. Harrison provided mostly one-word answers and never more than short sentences.

Finally, Jim asked why the Fowlers had moved to Lincoln, Ohio as opposed to staying in Boston. Jim noted the professor's BA, MA and PhD were from Harvard.

Martha perked up and asked, "Yes, Harrison, why did we move to Lincoln?"

Jim thought, for the first time, Harrison seemed flustered. Rather than answer, he turned to Jim and asked why he didn't go to Hamilton? "It's closer and obviously an excellent school."

"As I told you at Thanksgiving, my parents died in an auto accident. They were enroute to my high school graduation. I was valedictorian of my high school class and it was going to be a great evening. I had just heard from Northwestern's Medill School of Journalism and they were awarding me a full academic scholarship.

"My parents, my brother and I were going to celebrate, but of course we didn't. I chose Northwestern because they gave me a larger scholarship than Hamilton."

"Well, your school was rural, so that might explain being valedictorian. Not a lot of academic competition," Harrison sneered.

"Dad, that's not a very nice to say. You should apologize to Jim!" Jenny insisted.

"That's ok, Jenny, I get a lot of comments about being from such a small town. Only 150 people. Actually, my high school had more people than my town because it drew students from three towns and many farms. But Professor, my SAT scores were very high, top two percent and, as you know, that competition is nationwide."

"Enough, Harrison," Martha chided. "Jim, it must have been so hard on you to lose both your parents in an auto accident. I am so sorry."

"Thank you, Mrs. Fowler. I appreciate your concern," Jim said, surprised at Jenny's mother comment.

"Harrison, I think we need to give these young people some privacy."

Harrison's eyes widened and looked at his wife with shock.

"Jenny why don't you and Jim visit in the library? Jim, you might be interested in Harrison's collection of history books. Some are very old."

In the library, Jenny expressed shock at her mother's attitude. "I think you will be able to call on me at home in the future," she said hopefully.

"Well, I hope I can park in your driveway when I come the next time." Noting Jenny's confused look, Jim recounted her father's directive to park outside the main gate to Country Club Estates and walk to the house.

Jenny rolled her eyes.

8

Inauguration Day

F rom Thanksgiving through Christmas and New Year's Eve, Jim and Jenny's relationship grew closer. Jim's work at the News Tribune had settled into a routine. He told Brad Hauser he was getting used to working as a reporter without the drama. The only potential scandals on the radar were a theft in the city clerk's office and rumors of the city manager having an affair with his assistant, who happened to be Mayor Weir's daughter.

As the inauguration day of Governor-elect Lucas Anderson approached, Jim wrote stories of Anderson's background, from his modest beginning in a small town, to the Governor's mansion. Highlighted in his story was the dramatic conflict with his longtime chief aide, Lloyd Collier.

Jim covered Anderson's gubernatorial campaign the previous August. On his first night on the job, Jim observed Anderson entering a hotel room with a beautiful young campaign aide. Jim was certain he was onto a major story as Anderson portrayed himself as a family-values candidate. And the young woman was not Anderson's wife.

Audrey Hill and his editor, Willy Williams told Jim he was foolish to even think what he saw was true and was a potential story. Everything changed when the young woman, named Cindy Jenkins, was discovered dead the morning after Anderson visited her hotel room. The story was complicated even more, when Jim's reporting discovered she was a high-end prostitute working out of a condo in Columbus.

Jim's investigation uncovered Lloyd Collier, Anderson's chief aide, sabotaging Anderson's campaign. Collier was also involved in a physical assault on Anita Winston, Cindy Jenkins' roommate, also a prostitute.

Jim's work provided Anderson the information he needed to fire Collier. The dismissal turned ugly, and Collier pulled a gun away from a security guard, pointed it at Anderson, then at Jim who had heard the shouting and ran to the room. When a state trooper came to Anderson's aid, Collier swerved and aimed at the trooper. But before Collier could get a shot off, the trooper fired. Collier died at the scene.

Jim and Jenny had spent several evenings with the Andersons as the Inauguration approached. Anderson described his preparation for taking the reins of the governorship. Jim was impressed with all planning and study Anderson and his team were undertaking, and he was able to provide insight to his readers to the behind the scenes activities at the statehouse.

Jim had VIP tickets to the Inauguration and the Inaugural Ball. Reportorial duties for the day had been assigned to the state house reporters and Jim was looking forward to an off-duty evening and to spending time with Jenny at the festivities.

Harrison eventually relented on his demand that Jim park outside the entrance gate, so he pulled his Fiat into the circular driveway of the Fowler home. It was the biggest in Country Club Estates. The two-story home featured equal-sized wings connected by a colonnade of concrete pillars on the first floor and an expansive balcony on the second.

The brick exterior was painted white and had a gray slate roof and copper gutters. On each side of the portico, six large windows fronted the driveway on each floor. Jenny had told Jim her dad's study was behind the balcony.

Jim had not spent much time inside the house. Jenny's parents frequently had him wait at the door. He had never seen the back of the house, as he had never stepped onto the Lincoln Country Club golf course.

9

The Fowler estate, on half an acre, was meticulously landscaped, and backed onto the 11th fairway of the Lincoln Country Club.

A winter storm was building, and the temperature was well below freezing, so the Fowlers allowed Jim to wait for Jenny in the foyer.

Jenny was in a rare foul mood that day. She said she had been berated and criticized all morning by her parents, especially her father, for going out with Jim.

She quoted her father, "That's why you should have gone to Harvard, so you could be with people of your own class. Not this Catholic newspaper person, whose family amounted to nothing."

Jenny said her father was on his usual tear, pontificating about people who were born to lead, and Jim wasn't one of them.

"I am so sick and tired of it, Jim. My dad lives in his own world. Sometimes, I think he has no grasp of reality. He only talks to people who he thinks are on his social level. It's disgusting. I thought I had an ally in my mother, but she, too, said she hopes I find someone 'with a more substantive career.' I must do something, and I am able to do it. It's just going to take some time."

When Jim asked what she meant, she told him. "I will tell you more when I decide what I am going to do," she answered.

As they drove to the ceremony, a radio bulletin announced that, as one of his last acts in office, the outgoing governor had pardoned Alex Reid and Reverend Smallwood. Citing their exemplary behavior in prison and their service to the community prior to their arrests, he made their pardons effective immediately.

Jim nearly drove off the road when he heard the news. He recounted for Jenny the late morning in June of '63, when Irene Dunn, an elderly widow, called the obituary desk and told Jim her husband's copper casket had been switched to a plain wooden box.

The sixty days following that call were a blur in Jim's memory. Despite impediments from Willy, his cantankerous editor, Jim's investigation brought to light the wide extent of the cruel scam. As the trial approached, Steve Hampton, a Reid Funeral Home employee and key witness was found dead of an apparent suicide.

That same night, Irene Dunn died after a fall which broke her neck. And that same evening, Jim's truck was rammed by another speeding truck. He barely escaped serious injuries, or even death, but Mary Ryan was killed.

Jenny patiently listened, even though it was not the first time he had told her the story. She gently reminded him she had read every word he had written.

Jim fumed, blaming Reid and Smallwood for the three deaths. He was certain all three were not accidents and he told Jenny of working with Sgt. Major Harlow to uncover the truth. Two employees of Ronald Pugh, the largest farmer in Shelby County and the money behind many businesses, were fingered by another Pugh employee, who was with them the night of the murders.

Devastated by the pardon, Jim vowed he would find the real leader of the reprehensible enterprise. Patiently, Jenny told Jim, she had heard the stories before. She urged him to slow down his driving as the road was getting slick. He needed to calm down, too, she urged.

When Jim continued to rant and rave, Jenny exploded at him. "Look Jim, I know you are personally involved in all of this. I know the stories inside and out, because you talk about them all the time, especially when you are drinking. But for God's sake, slow down. Take a deep breath. There is nothing you can do about it right now." Jim's car fishtailed, and he grasped the steering wheel to correct the spin.

"S*low down*, Jim! The storm is getting worse, and the road is very slick," Jenny exclaimed.

Miffed at Jenny's criticism and angry at her lack of sympathy, Jim drove on to the state capital pouting, but he did slow down.

At the state capitol rotunda, Jim found soon-to-be Governor Anderson and pleaded he negate the pardon. Anderson told Jim there was nothing he could do about it. The Governor had the power to pardon, and Reid and Smallwood were probably already walking out of the Ohio State Reformatory in Mansfield.

Jim turned to walk away, but Anderson's question startled him. "Jim, do you know a Ronald Pugh?" Jim stopped in his tracks, spun around, and asked the governor why he asked.

Jim hated Pugh and was certain, though he couldn't

prove it, that Pugh was behind the Reid Funeral Home corruption and the deaths of Mary and his two friends.

"Ronald Pugh was in the Governor's mansion yesterday. He has been one of the Governor's biggest financial supporters. I know Pugh had a relationship with Alex Reid and Rev. Smallwood. But it seems like quite a coincidence that one day Pugh meets with the Governor, and the next day, the Governor pardons Reid and Smallwood."

"You know something, Lucas, politics suck. I am just sick about the pardon. Again, the bastards get away and justice is out the window." Jim walked away muttering. He took Jenny by the arm saying out loud to himself, "Where in the hell can you get a drink around here?"

The evening was a bust for Jim and Jenny. Jim was morose and drank too much. Jenny told him to take her home early as he was getting drunk and she couldn't drive the stick-shift Fiat. She chided him for drinking too much so often.

Jim told her a friend had left him a key to their condominium and they could stay there, if Jenny was worried about Jim's drinking.

"Get serious, Jim. Just take me home."

Stung by her criticism, Jim cradled a cup of coffee, and drove home, cautious on the slippery roads. Neither spoke during the thirty-minute drive, but at Jenny's door, Jim apologized, and they planned lunch for the next day. Jenny told him to go straight home and not stop at a bar.

When Jim arrived home, he found a message taped to his door. He read it quickly, raced down the stairs, and drove as fast as he could, skidding on the icy streets, back to Country Club Estates.

10

J im's mind raced as he pulled up to Bernard Hill's
home.

The note said, "Come to Bernard's home no
matter what time you get in. Audrey needs you." It was
signed by Judge McCallister. *What could it be?* Jim
wondered, but then realized, he was so into himself and
his reaction to the pardon of Reid and Smallwood, he
didn't notice that none of the Hills were at the
Inauguration or the Inaugural Ball.

This was unusual because Bernard was a close friend
and fraternity brother of Anderson's father-in-law at
Ohio State years before. Audrey, Lucas, and his wife Ann
were close friends. And Audrey and her parents were big
supporters of Lucas' campaign for governor.

A sheen of glistening ice almost sent Jim sprawling as
he jumped out of his car. He noticed Judge McCallister's
car parked in the circular driveway, and he was met by
Dr. Ross, the Hill's neighbor who had treated Jim on
Christmas Day in 1963. Dr. Ross's eyes were red, and his
face was somber.

"What is going on? Why are you and the judge here? It's ten at night." Jim asked. Ross just shook his head sadly and told Jim to go inside and see Audrey.

Jim found Audrey sitting on the sofa between Judge McCallister and his wife. Audrey was crying and rocking back and forth. Seeing Jim, she jumped into his arms and sobbed. She tried to speak but couldn't.

Jim, still unaware of what was going on, eased Audrey back onto the couch and knelt before her, holding her hand. Audrey's divorce had been finalized the previous week, but Jim didn't think it would have made her so distraught. Then he realized Bernard and Jane were not there.

"There was an accident, Jim," the Judge said quietly. "Bernard and Jane were on their way to the Inauguration when a driver lost control on the slick road, veered across the interstate median, and hit them head on. They were killed instantly. Audrey was about 10 minutes behind them in her own car.

"She was one of the first people at the accident scene. It's awful, Jim. Bernard was one of my best friends," the Judge said in a quiet voice, his chin quivering.

Jim was speechless. He had seen so much death in his 23 years, his parents, Irene, Steve, and, of course, Mary. Bernard was a rock in Jim's life. He was more than a publisher. He was a mentor, leader, and friend. Jim admired and respected Bernard and was grateful to him.

Audrey's teary eyes met Jim's. "Jim, I know how much my dad thought of you. He knew he could count on you, and I need you now more than ever. You are the brother I never had. Dad told me you probably have offers to go other places, but I need you.

"With the divorce, and now this, I am devastated. I

know I must run the family businesses, but I am not ready. Hell, I don't think I can plan my parents' funeral. Please, tell me I can count on you."

"Audrey, you have always been there for me. You can count on me being here for you."

The Hill's funeral was an event unlike anything Lincoln had seen. There were massive crowds at the visitation. When you own the major newspaper in town, a string of weekly newspapers, ten radio stations, and two television stations, you influence a lot of people. Everyone wanted to pay their respects.

An overflow crowd gathered at the First Presbyterian Church on Saturday, January 23. Both United States Senators were there as was most of the Ohio Congressional delegation and numerous members of the Ohio Legislature. Governor Anderson gave the eulogy. When he finished, there wasn't a dry eye in the church.

People were surprised at the couple in the front pew with Audrey Hill. Audrey was an only child, as were her parents. No uncles, no aunts, and no cousins. Jim had been a constant presence at the Hill home since the accident, and he helped Audrey plan the funeral arrangements. Jenny came over the day after the accident.

An only child herself, she and Audrey had become close friends since Thanksgiving. Audrey was a sounding board for Jenny as she tried to deal with her parents and their objections to her relationship with Jim.

Both Jenny and Jim were surprised and honored when Audrey asked them to sit with her at the funeral.

Veteran managers at the weekly newspapers, radio stations, and the two television stations expected Audrey to take some time off after the funeral. And because she was young, they expected her to be a hands-off manager.

So, they were surprised when she called a meeting three days after the funeral and left no doubt that she was going to be in charge.

Her first decision at the News Tribune, which caused some muttering, was to promote Jim to News Editor, with a substantial raise in pay. The muttering stopped when Hauser reminded everyone that Jim had won two national Associated Press Awards for reporting, and he didn't know any other reporter in the United States who could make that claim.

Jim had argued with Audrey that the promotion was too soon and not necessary, but Audrey reminded him she was the publisher.

11

A s the days slipped into weeks, then months, since Bernard's and Jane's untimely deaths, Audrey's passion for the newspaper business intensified. She called meetings, gave directions, and was a visible presence in all aspects of the business.

Everyone welcomed her involvement except for Zack "Willy" Williams, the executive editor, whose sole responsibility was the editorial page. And there, Audrey kept him on a short leash.

Jim was getting used to the routine of being the news editor of the paper. His responsibilities included being the chief reporter on all major news stories and management of several other reporters and copy editors. He seldom worked evenings, opting to spend time with Jenny and assigning other reporters to the evening events.

Most of the reporters were older than Jim, but they worked smoothly as subordinates, citing Jim's fair management style as the reason.

Jim and Jenny were frequent visitors at Maybelle

Johnson's home, in Simpson Village, usually on Sunday afternoon, and usually for her famous fried chicken or meatloaf. Jim watched with pride as Jenny made herself at home at Number Eight. She helped in the kitchen, pestering Maybelle for tips on cooking.

"You can't cook friend chicken, unless you got a cast iron skillet," Maybelle counseled. "And you only turn it once on each side."

Jim was especially pleased with Jenny's relationship with Haley. She talked to Haley about her work in the News Tribune photo lab and her plans for college.

"Maybe, you could get a scholarship to Hamilton," Jenny suggested while winking at Jim. Jim melted. He knew Jenny was kind and generous and he knew where the scholarship money would come from.

Edgar elbowed Jim in the shoulder and said, "Don't know how you did it, Bro, but you got a winner in Jenny."

"We are just dating, Edgar, just dating," Jim answered, and Edgar replied, "Sure you are."

Things had somewhat settled down in the neighborhood around Simpson Village. The trashing of the neighborhood had ceased. The last time a pickup truck filled with garbage came into the neighborhood, the occupants were met by the Stones, a group of young men from the neighborhood.

They pulled the two men out of the cab and pummeled them. Then they put them back in the cab and packed the garbage in the cab around the men. No one had seen a trash-filled pickup since.

Rufus was the Stones' leader, and he ruled with an iron hand. The previous year, after the two men who had assaulted and tried to kidnap Haley were set free, the neighborhood erupted. That evening Jim and his date,

Anna Masters, visited Reverend Jefferson's church only to be threatened by some of the Stones who had closed in around them. Rufus came to their rescue.

The Stones were the primary source of marijuana in the town and their main customers were the students at Hamilton University. Rufus allowed the Stones to sell the illegal drug, but never knew where the marijuana came from.

Two of the Stones met their source along the trees on the north end of Simpson Village where they were hidden from view. Their source always wore a facemask, and he was always accompanied by a bodyguard, who was armed with a pistol and was also masked. Once the transaction was complete, the source and his guard walked back through the trees and became invisible. The Stones would never be able to identify the dealers.

Some Stone members committed various minor crimes, but they mainly kept the peace in the neighborhood. Edgar's brother, Roger, was one of the original leaders of the Stones, but Edgar never joined. Maybelle wouldn't allow it.

But there was still harassment. Lincoln Police Chief, Billy Joe Buckner, had created a special squad assigned to the northeast section of town where Simpson Village was located. Frequently, the officers in that squad would detain young neighborhood men, question them, and then release them.

Pleas for police restraint by the Reverend Jeremiah Jefferson to Chief Buckner went unacknowledged. "If the young men have violated the law, arrest them, but please stop the hassling," Reverend Jefferson pleaded.

The hassling continued.

Jim assigned reporters to observe the neighborhood,

but every time Jim's reporters were present, inexplicably, the police were never there.

As summer approached, Jenny finished her first year of law school, ranked first in her class. Her relationship with Judge McCallister blossomed. He suggested she intern with one of his federal judge friends in Columbus, but Jenny turned it down, opting to take summer school classes, so she might graduate early.

"I have a feeling I am going to need to graduate early," she told Jim smiling. Jim completely missed her subtle message. Much to the frustration of Jenny's parents, Jim and Jenny found time almost daily to be together.

Though neither said it out loud, they both knew they were madly in love with one another. Their physical relationship evolved quickly. Often, they would spend hours at Jim's apartment exploring one another's body.

Jim, Hauser, and Audrey met at O'Toole's for lunch. As they discussed editorial and staff decisions, Jim twirled his pen and looked out the window.

Audrey said, "Jim, you seemed bored. Is the News Tribune too small a world for you? Are you thinking about all those offers from the Washington Post, Chicago Tribune, and, of course, your friend Charlie Sloan at the Post-Dispatch?"

"No, not at all. It's just that everything has become so routine. The occasional murder, armed robbery, and no elections this year. When I first got here, writing obituaries was exciting, because it was new. Then Irene Dunn called and for the next two years, nothing but intensity 24/7.

Now, since January, it has been mundane. I am looking for a big story. And I can't scratch the surface of Ronald Pugh's operation. Since his pardon, Alex Reid has been under the radar, and no one knows where Reverend Smallwood is. Reid won't return my calls, won't let me in his funeral home, and, as I said, no one knows where Smallwood is. I am just looking for some action.

"I just know if I ever came face to face with those bastards, I could shake them up and maybe, just maybe, bother one of them enough to crack."

"Be careful what you wish for," Hauser counseled.

12

———

Startled by a loud ringing, Jim jumped out of bed, grabbed the phone, and recognized the voice of his friend, Edgar Johnson. Johnson breathlessly told him the Lincoln Police Department special squad was intimidating his neighbors when the unthinkable happened.

"The police say it was an accident, but they just ran over Rufus Burton," Edgar yelled into Jim's phone.

"Slow down and start at the beginning," Jim said, "Tell me exactly what happened."

"You know about Chief Buckner's special squad. They have been harassing us for months now. Tonight, they were doing their usual crap of stopping guys and threatening to arrest them. If the kids said anything or even looked at the cops the wrong way the risked getting roughed up. Eventually the cops would release them. Rufus and the Stones confronted the cops. The Stones said that Rufus just wanted to talk to them. He wanted to ask them to leave the guys alone since they weren't breaking any laws."

"Slow down Edgar. Tell me what happened. How did someone run over Rufus?" Jim asked as he tried to dress and talk on the phone at the same time.

"The cops know Rufus is the leader of the Stones, and they hate him because they can't pin anything on him. The Stones, about ten of them, with Rufus in front, were walking towards the intersection of Fourth and Bradley, where the police squad cars were parked, when one of the cops, I think it was Crabtree, a thug, drove his car right at Rufus.

"Rufus got hit by the front of the car and he went down. The car didn't stop, and one of the wheels ran over his chest.

"Ken Simon's ambulance took him to Mercy Hospital, and he is in bad shape. I am trying to calm the Stones down. They respect Rufus, and they are beyond furious. They are sure that cop purposely rammed into Rufus, and they want justice.

"You need to get over here to the hospital. You need to write their side of the story. We both know what the police will say, Jim. You know who will get the blame, and it won't be a guy with a badge. Some of the Stones trust you and they want to talk to you." Edgar pleaded.

The Stones were milling around the Mercy Hospital emergency room, when Jim arrived. He spied Edgar talking with Sister Mary Mark, the hospital's administrator. When Edgar saw Jim, he beckoned him over.

"Jim, will you please assure Sister these young men are under control and she has nothing to worry about."

Jim and Sister Mary Mark were friends. She was with Jim when he was brought to the Mercy Emergency Room nearly two years ago, when his truck was T-boned into a utility pole and Mary Ryan was thrust through the windshield. Sister comforted Jim when Mary's family decided to remove the life support on Mary's battered body, and she prayed with Jim when Mary died.

"If Edgar says there won't be any trouble, there won't be," Jim promised.

"That's good enough for me, Jim, but please have everyone respect the other patients and let our team take care of Rufus," Sister Mary Mark said as she left the emergency room.

Jim turned to Edgar, "I have been writing this story over in my head on the way over and, Edgar, it's just not believable. No cop is just going to run someone over. What were Rufus and the Stones doing? Were they bothering the cops?"

"I've told you that's exactly what happened. I saw it all from our front window. The Stones were not doing anything. They were just hanging out in that vacant lot across from our house and Reverend Jefferson's church. There were three squad cars parked on Fourth Street.

"We call them Buckner's goons, because they are not part of Lt. Malcolm's regular eleven-to-seven shift.

"I watched Rufus walk up to the lead car. The cop looked straight ahead and didn't even look over when Rufus tapped on the car window. So, Rufus and the Stones started to cross Fourth Street to Reverend Jefferson's church.

"Then, the lead squad car didn't move, but the cop revved his engine. Everyone ran across the street, except Rufus, who just stared at the cop behind the wheel. The cop put it in gear and then gunned it.

"Rufus tried to jump on the hood, but he wasn't quick enough, and he went down, and the car ran over him. Then all the cops got out with shotguns, fired a couple of rounds in the air and the Stones just sat in the street.

"Mom called Simon's ambulance and I walked over to help keep everyone calm. The kids said Rufus wanted to talk to the cops. He wanted to ask them to stop detaining the Stones who had done nothing wrong. Once the ambulance took Rufus away, the cops left, and we came to the hospital. But, Jim, the Stones are furious."

"I understand why, Edgar," Jim said. "Here is Harrison Fowler's home phone number. You know he is chairman of the Shelby County Community Relations Committee. Call him, but for God's sake, don't tell him where you got the number. Tell him what happened. Tell him, you know he would be interested in police brutality. But don't tell him where you got the number."

Edgar smiled at Jim's caution. He promised the Stones would not be a problem.

Edgar took Jim over to where the Stones were gathered. He told them Jim wanted to hear their story.

Tommy, who had threatened Jim and Anna Masters the previous year at Reverend Jefferson's church, was the first to speak.

"It's those damn cops, Monaghan. They just ran over Rufus. They tried to kill him. We gonna get revenge, that's for sure."

"Easy, Tommy," Edgar urged. "You know Rufus would want you to stay cool. Now tell Jim what happened."

The Stones told Jim the story of what happened, and it was nearly identical to Edgar's eyewitness account. Jim promised the Stones he would report their side of the story, but he warned, the police would probably have a different perspective.

"You can't believe the damn cops," Tommy muttered. "They are all liars."

At four-thirty a.m., Jim left the hospital and drove to the newspaper office. *Not much sense in going back to bed. I will just write the story from Edgar's and the Stones' points of view, not naming anyone, and then go to the cop shop at seven and see what they have to say.*

13

It was Jack Wilson's favorite time of day.

With a steaming cup of Nescafe, he wandered around Wilson Sporting Goods store beaming with pride.

At 50-years of age, Jack was in good shape. Nearly six feet tall, he kept his weight at 180 pounds, only about 10 pounds heavier than he was as an all-state halfback at Lincoln Central High School, 32 years ago.

Jack had been recruited to Ohio State, but his football career ended at spring practice of his sophomore year when his knee collapsed. The result was an occasional limp, but Jack joked that the upside was the ability to forecast the weather when his knee ached.

Wearing khaki pants and a red Ohio State golf shirt, Jack walked around his store, occasionally checking his perfectly groomed hair in reflections from the glass display cases. Jack's appearance was important to him, which is why he showered and shaved every morning after his daily constitution of 100 push-ups and 100 sit-ups.

As Jack's eyes roamed his store, he noted everything was in place, neat and clean, not a trace of trash or misplaced product. On the north side were the long guns: the Winchester 70-bolt action, the new Winchester Model 94 30-30 lever action, the new Colt 22 single-shot bolt action rifle, and a variety of others.

All were secured by individual locks on the trigger guards and barrels. Jack thought, with hunting season approaching, he might want to increase his inventory.

While not a big hunter, like his father before him, Jack catered to the hunters of central Ohio. He amused himself at the difference between, as he referred to them, hunters and "hunters". The serious ones were meticulous about observing the rules of the short turkey and pheasant seasons.

They were careful about safety and the respective bag limits. They were always interested in the newest guns and scopes and whatever would increase their potential for success.

Then there were the other "hunters"; those that hunted crow, coyote, and wild boar. There were no bag limits on them, and only crow had a limited blackout period, April and May. Mostly, these guys were interested in a good time, or as one of his favorite customers told him once,

"It's a great time, Jack, you should come with us--lots of laughs and plenty of cold beer."

Not only was Jack the second-generation owner of Wilson Sporting Goods, he was also Deputy Mayor and City Councilman of Lincoln. So, most customers were constituents as well. And Jack treated everyone with respect, always willing to listen to questions about the newest guns or why garbage was not picked up at someone's house. The father of three boys, he was a popular and respected office-holder in Lincoln.

Jack surveyed the handguns and ammunition, under lock and key in the front glass display counters. Removing a few smudges from the glass, he made sure the counters were locked.

The balance of the store was divided into sections. Baseball gloves, bats, and balls were next to basketballs and footballs, all separated by shoes, jerseys, and other paraphernalia specific to each sport with equal representation of Ohio State, Hamilton University, Cincinnati Reds, and Cleveland Indians memorabilia. Jack rotated his inventory based on the sporting season.

Baseball season was ending, and football was about to start. He thought he should move the football gear to the front of the store, but he was in no hurry. Baseball was his favorite sport and his wife wondered if he made any money off the sport.

Jack was generous to a fault, donating bats and balls to various teams. His friend, Don Hansen, local businessman and long-time coach of the Lincoln American Legion baseball team, would often call and tell of a young man who needed equipment. If a player needed a glove or a bat, Jack found a way to get one to him, anonymously.

As the sun edged towards its 6:32 a.m. sunrise, Jack looked across the street at Harlow's Café and his friend, Sgt. Major Harlow. Harlow's café opened at six a.m., two hours before Jack's opening at eight. Jack waved as Harlow looked out his window and waved back.

The two friends had been waving at one another since Harlow opened his café years before. Jack couldn't wait for his young assistant to arrive at seven-thirty, so he could walk over to Harlow's and get a real cup of coffee and visit about the issues of the day.

The Sgt. Major had the pulse of the citizens of his town.

Strong morning winds announced a possible change in the weather. It had been hot and humid, typical for August, and Jack anticipated thunderstorms in the afternoon. The wind gusts were particularly forceful. Jack heard his aging building creak.

He knew he was behind on the maintenance of the building his father had built sixty years ago. The plate glass windows in front were single-pane and the bricks and mortar on the front of the store were deteriorating.

Jack bent over to inspect what appeared to be a scuff mark on the hardwood floor near his cash register behind the main counter, when he was startled by a loud, garbled, menacing voice.

"Don't move, or I will blow your head off."

Jack instinctively turned and faced his assailant, who was dressed in a camouflage jacket and pants. A black ski mask covered his mouth and nose left only his eyes visible.

A sudden blow to his head with the barrel of a sawed-off shotgun knocked Jack to the floor. He gasped as a heavy boot jammed into his back. Blood immediately started to pour out from the head wound.

Jack heard the assailant yell that the keys to the gun racks were in the second drawer. *How did he know that*, Jack wondered? As the seconds, which seemed like hours, ticked off, he heard glass breaking and low conversations about guns and ammunition.

His assailant's voice, muffled by the mask, seemed familiar, as did the camo outfit the man was wearing. His brief vision of the man was burned in Jack's mind. He was of medium height and appeared wiry in build. His camo outfit looked like the ones Jack sold in his store.

Jack heard someone yell, "We have all the guns and ammo. You want anything else?" The man with his boot pressing into Jack's back answered, "Shut up! We need to go." He kicked Jack and warned him to stay on the floor and not move.

Jack couldn't stop himself; he rolled over and asked, "Don't I know you?"

With that, the assailant pulled a 357-magnum handgun from his holster and fired two shots into Jack's chest. The cold, flat gray eyes were etched in Jack's mind, before it faded into darkness.

14

J im cornered his friend Lt. Everett Malcolm, commander of the eleven-to-seven shift. As usual at shift change, the cop shop was chaotic. The midnight shift and the day shift did not get along, but this morning, Jim noticed the tension was greater than normal.

"What do you know about Rufus Burton being run over?" Jim asked Malcolm.

"I don't know anything about it. It was the Chief's special unit. I don't know anything about that unit, and I don't want to, but let me tell you something. It's going to get bad if that squad continues what they are doing," Malcolm said grimly.

"What are they doing that has you so concerned?" Jim asked.

"Jesus, Monaghan, open your eyes, talk to your friends," Malcolm icily replied.

Their conversation was interrupted by a voice that silenced everyone in the room.

"I want the truth, and if this was police brutality,

there will be consequences, and I mean serious consequences!" shouted Harrison Fowler. Tall, slim, and decked out in a perfectly tailored, dark blue Brooks Brothers suit, crisp white shirt with French cuffs, and red bow tie, Fowler scowled deeply. His pale blue eyes darted around the room, obviously looking for someone in charge.

After the initial silence in response, the cop shop returned to its usual loud chatter.

"I am personally investigating, and if I find brutality, there will be hell to pay," Fowler declared even more loudly.

"There ain't going to be any damn investigation," shouted Police Chief Billy Joe Buckner. Buckner was a tall man, at least six feet five and over well 300 pounds. He was nearly bald, and Jim privately nicknamed him Bullet Head. Buckner had an unusually large nose and almost no chin. His stomach cascaded over his belt and his uniform shirt, despite the early morning hour, was wet under the arms.

His southern drawl was usually filled with expletives and he proudly identified himself as a redneck from Alabama. Attached to his black belt was his trademark three-foot-long Billy Club. His brightly polished silver belt buckle was engraved with a confederate flag.

Buckner was a surprise selection by City Manager Arlen Davis. Davis had plucked Buckner from a medium-size town in Alabama ten years ago and hired him as police Captain. Buckner was named Chief of Police a year ago.

Buckner and Fowler glared at one another, neither man blinking.

Their confrontation was interrupted by a radio dispatch that echoed through the cop shop.

"Shots Fired! Shots Fired! Code 12! Code 12! Wilson's Sporting Goods, Second and Main." Officers scrambled to their cars. Code 12 signaled an armed robbery and 'shots fired' raised the tension level.

Jim hopped into Lt. Malcolm's squad car, and together they sped the three blocks to Wilson's store.

Jim's heart was pounding. He knew Jack would be alone in his store at that time of the morning. Wilson was one of Jim's anonymous sources on what was really going on in Lincoln politics. As they pulled up to the store, Jim silently prayed.

15

J im and Lt. Malcolm waited as two officers, using Billy Clubs, broke the window on the locked front door of Wilson Sporting Goods to gain entrance, and together they rushed in to find the store in shambles.

Jim noticed the empty gun racks, shattered glass counters, and missing hand guns and ammunition. Even the team sports area was ransacked, especially the baseball department. Baseball bats lay scattered on the floor.

Jim kept yelling Jack's name, and his voice echoed in the silence. As he and Malcolm walked towards the cash register, Jim was the first to see the blood on the floor behind the counter.

Rushing behind the counter, he found his friend lying motionless on the floor, unconscious. Shocked by Jack's bludgeoned face and blood pouring from his chest, Jim screamed for medical help.

As he knelt beside Jack, Jim pressed his hands to Jack's chest wounds to stem the bleeding. Lt. Malcolm grabbed a jacket from the baseball clothes rack, folded it and placed it under Jack's head. Another officer placed a blanket over Jack, to prevent him from going into shock.

As they were working, Jim motioned, with a dip of his head, to a boot print in the blood beside Jack's body. It seemed like an eternity until Ken Simon and his ambulance crew rushed into the building and took over.

At the front door, Jim met Art Wilks, chief photographer for the Lincoln News Tribune. With his trusty Nikon F Photomic T camera hanging from a strap around his neck, Wilks, a former Army Ranger, was an imposing physical presence and was welcomed by the police officers. He often helped the police at crime scenes, snapping photographs, which were later used in investigations.

The Lincoln PD did not have an official crime scene photographer. Wilks was a friend of many of the police officers, taking family photos on special occasions and never charging the officers.

"How the hell did you get here so early?" Jim asked.

"I have a police radio in my house, and I heard the code 12 at Jack's place, so here I am."

"Jesus, Art, you got to get a life. Police radio in your house?"

"Yeah, Jim, but I am here, and you don't see any other photographers, here do you?"

"Get as many pictures as you can, but make sure you get a shot of the boot print in the blood right behind the cash register. I'm sure it's important."

"I'm on it," Wilks said.

Jim brought Wilks behind the cash register where Wilson lay in a pool of blood.

"There, do you see the boot print?" Jim asked.

"I can take it from here, Jim," Wilks countered.

Simon, a veteran medic from the Korean War,

finished up his emergency work on Wilson's chest after ripping open his shirt and tending to the open wounds.

"We need to get him to Mercy STAT," Simon yelled to his assistants.

Jim's heart sank as his friend, pale and unconscious, was placed on a gurney and rushed to Simon's waiting ambulance. Sirens blaring, the ambulance headed to Mercy Hospital.

Jim leaned back against the front plate glass window and watched as some twenty policemen roamed around the store. "Isn't this a crime scene and shouldn't someone be collecting evidence?" Jim asked Lt. Malcolm. Before Malcolm could answer, a bellowing voice shouted,

"Get that asshole reporter out of here!" Chief Buckner's face was red, and his eyes narrowed in anger. "You got no reason to be here, so get out now, or I will arrest you," Buckner shouted, glaring at Jim.

Jim crossed over to Harlow's café to see if his friend, Sgt. Major Harlow had seen or heard anything.

"'Bout time you got here. Of course, I know stuff. Who the hell do you think called the police?" Harlow replied, frowning deeply.

"It was around six-thirty or so when I saw Jack. He and I wave at one another just about every morning. He looked fine, and I was looking forward to him coming over for his usual cup of coffee after his assistant comes in.

"Then a few minutes later, I heard gun shots, three in rapid succession. I grabbed the shotgun I keep behind the counter and ran over. The front door was locked, but I could see the rifles missing from their racks on the north side of the store. I knew there was a robbery, and because I heard shots fired, I was afraid Jack was hurt.

"I ran back and called the police.

"Simon told me Jack is in rough shape. I hope the cops find the guy who did this, and if they do, there is no point in a trial. Jack is a former commander of the Legion and…"

Harlow's voice trailed off as he and Jim saw Chief Buckner exit Wilson's store.

"What can you tell us, Chief?" Jim asked.

"It's obvious isn't it? The Stones did it. Rufus, their leader, was involved in an accident with a squad car early this morning and this is retaliation for it. We are going to get them bastards and put them away. They are a menace."

"How can you say that Chief? You haven't even started your investigation," Jim countered.

"Monaghan, when you have been a cop as long as I have, you just know. Now, get the hell out of my way. I'm busy."

Jim watched the chief walk back to the front of Wilson's store, where to his surprise, Buckner shook hands with Harrison Fowler, Mayor Weir, and City Manager Arlen Davis. Together they got in the chief's squad car and drove away.

What the hell is that all about? Jim wondered.

16

The News Tribune was chaotic when Jim walked in and was greeted by an irritated managing editor, Brad Hauser.

Hauser stood five-foot-ten, slightly overweight, his blond hair disheveled, but dressed impeccably. He told Jim it was 45 minutes to deadline and Jim could have called telling him what the story was, so he could plan the front page.

As angry as Hauser appeared, he was flanked by a calm Audrey Hill in a tailored light green jacket with matching skirt. Her dark brown hair was pulled into a bun, and despite her hands on her hips, her deep blue eyes expressed a warm welcome for Jim.

"I've got the story down pat and can have it to you in 20 minutes," Jim promised as he sprinted to his desk, situated behind two file cabinets and next to the sports department. Before he reached his desk, Zach Willy Williams, executive editor of the News Tribune, came puffing into the newsroom.

"I've got the lead for the front page. The Stones did

it, and they are led by Edgar Johnson. The Stones did it. That's the lead and maybe the headline for the Wilson robbery and assault story."

All activity in the newsroom came to a halt, and the normal noise level, with less than an hour until the first deadline, ceased. The relationship between Willy and Jim had been the talk of the newsroom for the past few years.

Everyone knew Willy disliked Jim, and the feeling was mutual. Their low point came when Willy fired Jim during his coverage of the previous year's gubernatorial race.

"That's bullshit, Willy," Jim said. Immediately Hauser and Audrey stepped between the two. The comparison between Willy and Jim was stark. Willy was 60 years old, five-feet- seven, squat, with his hair losing the battle to baldness. His wire-rimmed glasses were perched on top of his head and he wore his typical scowl. Dressed in a short-sleeved dress shirt, clip-on stained orange tie, and wrinkled blue slacks, he glared up at Jim who, over a head taller, stared down with contempt.

Jim was an athletic six feet tall, wide shoulders, narrow waist, with muscular biceps straining his black golf shirt.

"I just talked to the chief, and he assured me they are well on their way to arresting Edgar and the Stones. So, that's the lead," Willy announced.

Turning to Audrey, Willy said, "I know you are doing your best since your father died, but he and I handled stories like this for years, and I know what I am doing."

Audrey rolled her eyes and replied, "Brad can handle it, Willy. Thanks." She and Hauser walked away, as Jim sat at his desk.

"Jim," Sports Editor Tyrone Thompson whispered from across his desk, "you have to be careful. Willy still has influence in this town. He has lots of friends, and Audrey is new to her position. You can't keep pissing him off."

Nodding agreement, Jim took the cover off his L.C. Smith typewriter and pecked out his story on the armed robbery of Wilson's Sporting Goods and the attempted murder of Deputy Mayor Jack Wilson.

Later, exhausted, Jim leaned back in his chair and dozed while waiting for the first edition of the paper to be delivered. Josh Wheeler, the summer intern shook Jim's shoulder and delivered the paper, fresh off the presses.

"You have another page one banner story," he said. "Do you ever get tired of writing the most important stories in the paper?"

Not wanting to be bothered, but knowing it was only a few years ago, that he himself was an intern at the Columbus Post-Dispatch, Jim quashed his initial reaction to ignore Wheeler.

He turned to the young intern, and told him that without news stories, there wouldn't be anything for a reporter to do. "I never get tired of reporting stories. It's uncomfortable sometimes, like today, when the story involves a friend. But, let's have lunch sometime this week and we can talk."

Wheeler beamed.

Jim found the article on Jack Wilson the lead story on page one under a banner headline. He looked on page one, then page three, for his story on Rufus being run over by the police. When he finally found it on page five, he yelled at Hauser, "Why the hell isn't the Rufus story on page one or at least on page three?"

It wasn't often Hauser was so blatantly challenged, and the newsroom again quieted. Hauser walked over to Jim's desk, pulled up a chair and said,

"Monaghan, you are a good reporter, and I will accept your question as wanting to learn about being an editor. The Rufus Burton story, while important, does not rise in importance to the robbery and shooting of the deputy mayor.

"We simply don't have enough solid and credible information about what happened to Rufus. That's your job. Nail down exactly what happened, and then we will reassess where in the paper the story should be placed. Now, I know you haven't had much sleep, and you probably didn't eat breakfast.

"Go to and get some lunch. And keep your mouth shut as you leave," Hauser concluded with a smile.

17

At O'Toole's Tavern, Stavros placed a Bushmills and water on the table as Jim slid into his favorite booth.

Jim checked his watch and smiled with anticipation. Jenny would be arriving soon from her summer school class. She would be excited and full of energy coming from Judge McCallister's seminar. She was rarely late, but sometimes she stayed after class to talk with McCallister.

"So much for having a special relationship with Judge McCallister," Jenny frowned as she slid into the booth across from Jim. "He nailed me today on my interpretation of a Supreme Court case. I admit, I didn't research it as thoroughly as I should have, but my goodness, he just ripped me to shreds in his usual calm voice. After class I told him I got the message and would never come to class again without being totally prepared."

Jenny explained she had spent too much time buying furniture and decorating her new three-bedroom condo and not enough time researching the Supreme Court case.

"I just don't understand why you need a three-bedroom condo, and I really don't understand how you could afford to buy it. Did your parents give you the money?" Jim asked.

"I bought a three bedroom because of resale. It's close to the University, so it would be great for a professor and his family. And it's close to the new golf course and country club being built around the Lincoln reservoir. The reservoir is becoming a popular place for boating and water skiing. The wrap-around balcony has a view of the reservoir, the new country club, and Hamilton University. And it was a good buy."

"Yeah, but how many law students buy condos? You told me your father was going to disinherit you if you continued to see me. Then you buy an expensive condo, and every time I ask you about it, you say, it's not appropriate to talk about it. When is it going to be appropriate?"

Smiling, Jenny said, "In time, Jim, in time."

Jenny's smile turned into a stern look. "How many drinks have you had? It's only two o'clock in the afternoon."

Frustrated by the criticism, Jim was pleased when Audrey and Brad Hauser joined them in their booth. Jenny and Audrey hugged and began whispering to one another. Their relationship intensified the day after Audrey's parents were killed. Audrey was comforting to Jenny when she decided to move out of her parents' home, because of their unrelenting criticism about her relationship with Jim.

After her parents' funeral and the finalization of her divorce, Audrey moved into her parent's home. One evening, after an intense argument with her father over Jim, Jenny knocked on Audrey's door. Audrey welcomed Jenny and helped her finalize her plans to purchase and move into her new condo.

As the women chatted, Jim asked Hauser, "How in the hell can the police be saying Edgar and the Stones robbed Jack's store and shot him? And what's this crap about Edgar being the head of the Stones? I know for a fact, he has nothing to do with them."

"Slow down," Hauser said. "Is there a chance your personal relationship with Edgar is clouding your judgement as a reporter? Edgar's brother was the leader of the Stones before he was sent to prison, and you know the Stones had to be hot after Rufus Burton was run over," Hauser challenged.

"I was at the hospital with Edgar and the Stones until four- thirty this morning," Jim replied. "For them to come to a decision to rob Jack's store, plan all the details, get themselves organized, and rob him two hours later is just impossible. Even coming to an agreement to do something is not possible for those guys. Without Rufus, they are leaderless.

"Besides, they all like Jack. I bet there is not one kid who lives at Simpson who hasn't benefited from Jack's generosity. Hell, Edgar told me Jack kept him in baseballs, bats, and gloves when he was playing ball. It's just not possible, Brad," Jim argued.

"Then get the facts and prove it, and I will put it on the front page," Hauser replied.

Jenny and Audrey were amused watching the two spar.

"Brad and I just came by for a quick drink and to remind you, Jim, we have an editorial board meeting this afternoon at four. I am holding it at the country club, so there won't be any interruptions. And if the meeting goes late, the News Tribune will buy you all dinner."

After Hauser and Audrey departed, Jim knew he had to ask Jenny a question.

He hated to ask, but he had been pondering what he saw outside Wilson's store all day and felt compelled to tie up what he thought was a loose end.

"Does your dad know Chief Buckner, Mayor Weir, and City Manager Arlen Davis?"

"Why do you ask?" Jenny replied cautiously.

"Early this morning, your dad walked into the cop shop demanding an investigation into the so-called accident involving Rufus. He and Buckner were glaring at one another. But at the crime scene at Jack's store, Buckner shook your dad's hand and, together with Mayor Weir and City Manager Davis, they got into the chief's squad car and they sped off. It looked like they were friends."

"I don't know about that. But ever since he was named to that commission, he has been going to meetings early in the morning a couple of times a week. I know it has nothing to do with the University. When I was living at my parents' house, I asked what the meetings were about were about, and he gave me the usual bull crap answer about certain people were born to lead. I just got sick of it and quit asking him questions.

"I'm glad you have the editorial board meeting this afternoon and I hope it goes late, since I have to study. Could you plan on spending some time at my condo this weekend? I need help rearranging some furniture and putting up some pictures. But not until this weekend, Jim. After my experience with the Judge this morning, I am never going to class unprepared again."

18

J im, Audrey, and Brad arrived at the busy parking lot of the Lincoln Country Club at the same time.

"Why don't either of you guys play golf? Judging from the number of cars in the parking lot, I would say there are quite a few golfers out today," Audrey asked as they walked towards the entrance of the rambling, single story, thirty-year-old building. The trim was painted white accenting the red brick structure. While impressive, it did not compare to The Members Country Club in Columbus, the most prestigious in Ohio.

"We don't play golf, Audrey, because our boss works us so hard, we don't have time," Jim answered playfully. He had played a few times, enjoyed it, but just never found the time to get out on Lincoln's public course.

Audrey, Brad, and Jim paused as six men came bustling out of the door. Jim stopped in his tracks and came face to face with Ronald Pugh, Chief Buckner, Mayor Weir, Manager Davis, Alex Reid, and Judge Lawlor. There, for the first time, Jim confronted the people he was certain were responsible for Mary's death. The two years of frustration, anger, and hurt ignited Jim's emotions.

"Well, what a motley group this is!" Jim exclaimed. "Where is Reverend Smallwood?"

Then glaring at Reid, he said, "I can't believe you got out of jail. How much did Pugh pay the Governor to grant you a pardon? I was hoping you would stay there forever and become some Bubba's boyfriend."

Jim felt Audrey's hand on his arm, and out of the corner of his eye, he saw Pugh wave at someone, but it was Reid, who faced him, with his chin not more than two inches away.

"Listen to me, you punk. I served my time even though I was convicted unfairly. And I settled the lawsuit. It was your friend Hampton who was switching all the caskets. I was an innocent victim in the whole episode. So, go screw yourself, Monaghan. I don't have to take any shit from you or that crappy paper anymore. Keep out of my business and stay out of my life."

As Audrey tried to pull Jim away, he turned to Pugh. "I know you are behind all of this crap that has been going on and one of these days, I will prove it."

Pugh tried to push Jim away, but as Jim pushed back. He felt two strong arms throw him to the ground and a knee thrust roughly onto his chest.

"Just keep the asshole on the ground while we leave," Pugh said to his number one employee, Slick Beck. Beck, a former Army Ranger, who received a dishonorable discharge for assaulting an officer, was of medium height wiry, and, strong. Jim's efforts to squirm out of the hold were thwarted by Slick's firm grip.

Audrey complained to the chief that Jim was being

assaulted, but Buckner just laughed and told her Jim started it, and she needed more employees like Willy.

"Willy knows the score, not like this piece of shit," Buckner growled. "He's lucky I don't arrest him for assaulting Ron."

Jim, still under Beck's firm grasp, turned his gaze to Judge Lawlor. He was the judge who gave Reid and Smallwood light sentences. And he was a last-minute substitute in Clyde and Buck's sentencing. He gave them suspended sentences for their kidnapping and assault of Haley Johnson.

"Hey, Judge, why did you give Buck and Clyde suspended sentences? You know they were guilty. Did Pugh tell, you to do that? How much did he pay you?"

Judge Lawlor sneered at Jim with venom and extended his middle finger.

"When Pugh goes down, Judge, you will go down, too, I promise" Jim shouted. The pressure on his chest intensified, and Beck slugged him in the kidney. Jim gasped for breath.

Reid and Pugh stared down at Jim with contempt. "We're not done with you, Monaghan," Pugh threatened. As Reid and Pugh walked away, Jim heard Reid tell Pugh, "I'll see you at the Eagle's Nest.

Everyone but Mayor Weir, went to their cars, and, finally, Slick took his knee off Jim's chest. Weir took Audrey aside and warned, "Monaghan is a problem, Audrey. You need to rein him in. His obsession with this Pugh conspiracy business is insane. Ron is very successful farmer and businessman, but most people don't realize just how powerful he is. His patience for Jim Monaghan is not limitless."

Audrey did her best to control her temper. She told the Mayor what she saw today was enough to hire additional staff to help Jim in his investigation. Weir shook his head and walked away.

Jim stood, brushing himself off. He glowered at Hauser. "Where the hell were you during all this crap?" Hauser pulled a small black device from his jacket pocket.

"I was recording it. I have every word. Once Slick got you on the ground, and I realized you weren't in danger, I hit the button and recorded everything. That is a suspicious group and, for sure, Jim, you are under their skin."

"Well, they are under my skin, too," Jim answered. "You two may not have heard it, but Reid told Pugh he would meet him at the Eagles Nest. Pugh calls his farm Eagle Incorporated, and now he is talking about an Eagles' Nest. Who the hell does he think he is, Hitler? That's almost as funny as the head of the KKK being called the Grand Goblin."

Audrey turned to Jim and frowned, "I think Ronald Pugh is far more dangerous than any of us ever thought. And I don't like it that Chief Buckner is with him. My dad always had concerns about Buckner, and he did some research on him. I must find that file. When I do, it might shed some light on that group. But what would Mayor Weir be doing with them? His father started this country club, and he has a very profitable home building business. So much of this just doesn't make sense."

19

It was all smiles at lunch at Number Eight Simpson Village.

"You know, Jimmy, we been through so much this past year. Those guys in their trucks throwing garbage, and then them kidnapping Haley. The garbage throwin' is pretty much stopped after some of the boys beat those awful men up. I don't approve of violence, but somethin' had to be done. It's so much better now.

"But with this police squad bothering our young men, I almost wish the garbage guys was back. The police just stop and hassle our young men. I know some of the boys isn't angels, but they shouldn't be arrested if they didn't break the law. Hopefully, it's gonna be over one of these days.

"I know it is hard, Maybelle. But every time I assign a reporter to be out here at night, the police don't show up. I don't have enough people to have someone here every night."

"Well," Maybelle sighed. "Rev. Jefferson says we just gotta prevail. We gotta stay strong. Reverend Jefferson quotes Dr. King and tells us we will overcome. He is reaching out to the young men, and I think he's getting' some of them to listen. Dr. King is making so much progress all over the country. So, let's say our prayers things will get better and enjoy this fine lunch Haley and I made," Maybelle said.

"How are the Stones reacting now, Edgar?" Jim queried. "They were boiling over at the hospital. Has someone been able to lead them? Tommy is a hothead, so I hope they don't start following him. And rumor has it that some of the Stones are involved in drug sales, especially marijuana. Do you have any idea, where they are getting the weed to sell?"

Edgar's grimaced, "The Stones are in disarray. Some of the guys are dealing drugs and some are committing petty crimes, but most of them are only members of the Stones because they are bored and want to belong to something. Tommy is trying to be the leader, but you are right. He is a hothead. Some are following him, but most are just hanging back. They are scared, Jim.

"I have no idea where they are getting the marijuana. Dewayne and Tyrell are the two who get the stuff, but they are tight lipped about where and from who. Dealers can be vicious, so I know they will never tell.

"The biggest problem is there is nothing for the kids to do. Too many have dropped out of school and they don't have steady jobs. Hansen hires as many as he can, but there are a lot of guys who stand around all day They can't find work and by nighttime they get a little buzzed up and it's not good."

Jim nodded. "You know, that new recreation building those business guys from Chicago are building on the east side of town is nearly complete," he said. "I talked to them a couple of weeks ago, and they told me they are ahead of schedule. They are going to hire recreation professionals, and because it's not too far from the neighborhood, it should help. Besides, they promised Audrey they would have an outreach to kids from this neighborhood. They are going to offer after-school and summer programs at low-cost. And some of the programs will even be free. It definitely has promise."

"Yeah, it does, Jim, but it is still two miles away. Only a few of the boys have cars, and unless the city routes a bus between here and there, not many kids will be able to use the facilities, especially in the winter.

We have that vacant block across the street. It is just weeds and dirt. The Park District owns it and they don't do squat with it. I studied the Lincoln Public Works budget, and they spend a ton of money on parks, ball fields, swimming pools, and a bunch of other stuff on the other side of town. Here in our neighborhood, nothing."

"Why are looking at the city's public works budget? I had no idea you were interested in that sort of thing."

"There is a lot about me you don't know, Jim, big investigative reporter. There is a lot."

Jim looked at Maybelle and Haley, who were all smiles. "What's going on that I don't know?" Jim asked.

"Tell him," Maybelle said to Edgar.

"Not yet, mom, maybe in a couple of weeks."

Jim looked from Maybelle, to Haley, to Edgar but got no response.

"Anybody home? I think I smell an apple pie baking," said Reverend Jeremiah Jefferson as he poked his head in the front door.

Everyone stood to greet the respected pastor of the Fellowship of the Disciples of Christ Church, located catty-corner across the street from the Johnson's residence at the intersection of Fourth and Bradley.

Jefferson, a veteran of civil rights marches, was a friend of Reverend Martin Luther King. He was also a friend of Jim's and was helpful to him after Christmas, 1963.

"Reverend, Edgar is involved in something, researching the Lincoln Public Works budget and I don't know what else. Can you fill me in on what Edgar is doing? No one here will tell me anything," Jim pleaded.

Reverend Jefferson's face broke into a huge smile. He walked to Edgar and put his hand on his shoulder. "I am so proud of this young man. He is an inspiration to everyone."

"Reverend," Edgar raised his hand, "I am not ready to tell Jim what I am doing. We were discussing the lack of opportunities for young people here in the neighborhood. We were talking about that vacant block across the street and how, maybe, it has potential," Edgar said.

"Ok, Edgar, I will keep mum, but it is strange you would bring up the vacant lot across the street," Reverend Jefferson said. "You all know Donald Hansen has been named president of the Lincoln Park Board. He and I have been meeting, and we have some ideas. Edgar, your work has been helpful to us."

Edgar stood up and warned, "Reverend, don't."

Jim looked askance at Edgar. "What have you been doing, and why won't you tell me?"

"In time, Jim, when I am ready," Edgar replied smiling.

20

On his way to Jenny's condo to help her move in, Jim stopped in at Ken Simon's ambulance service office.

Simon was a valuable source for Jim. They had been introduced by Sgt. Major Harlow, a fellow veteran. Middle aged, but still in good shape, Simon's curly hair was usually messy, and he typically sported a five o'clock shadow on his rugged face. His company was the leading ambulance company in Lincoln.

"Anything new in your world that I should know about?" Jim asked.

Leaning back in his chair and plopping his feet on his desk, Simon sipped a drink of coffee and spilled some on his white shirt, just missing his company's logo patch.

"Damn, I can't seem to keep my shirt clean." He looked around his cluttered desk searching for a rag to clean up his spill. As Simon stood, Jim noticed there were coffee stains on his white pants as well.

"I wouldn't worry about that stain on your shirt; it matches the ones on your pants." Both men laughed.

"Not a lot going on," Simon finally answered Jim. "Just the usual heart attacks, home accidents, and car crashes out on the interstate. The kids won't be back at Hamilton for a couple of weeks, so everything is quiet there. The only regular activity is up in the northeast end. We have been treating a lot of the young men from Simpson Village neighborhood for cuts and bruises.

"You mean, you get calls and you run your ambulance to Edgar's neighborhood?" Jim asked.

"No, I just keep one of my rigs in the neighborhood. It's only four blocks from the State Highway. I assign my new people there. It's good experience for them, treating all sorts of minor injuries. The guys tell me the number of times they treat the kids is increasing, though. I'm not exactly sure, what's causing the increase.

"Those families don't have any money, so we just give them some field care. It doesn't cost a lot, and I am glad to do it. I consider it on-the-job training. The moms out there really appreciate it, and I don't think my guys have bought dinner in months. Someone is always bringing them sandwiches or something.

My guys do transport anyone seriously injured to Mercy Hospital, where Sister Mary Mark makes sure they are taken care of, and those families never see a bill. Still mostly, they are minor bruises and cuts."

"How do the kids say they get the injuries?" Jim asked.

"Mostly from fighting, but not always with one another. They tell my guys the cops have been roughing them up."

"Lt. Malcom would never allow that," Jim said defensive of his friend.

"No, it's Buckner's special force of three squad cars with six patrolmen. They all carry Billy Clubs like the

Chief. They answer only to the Chief and they patrol only in Edgar's part of town. Although, occasionally, they go to Hamilton University and bust some of the kids for underage drinking.

"There are rumors that if you are caught at the University for underage drinking, you can slip a cop $20, and you will be released. But I don't know if any of that is true," Simon said.

With that, a call came in reporting an accident near the interstate and Simon was off.

Jenny's condo was five stories high with ample parking in front. The brown brick building featured large windows, sliding-glass doors and wrought iron balconies. Jim looked up to the top floor at Jenny's condo with its wrap-around balcony. It was the nicest condo in the building with an expansive view of Hamilton University, the new golf course, and Lincoln Reservoir. Plus being on the top floor, it had an open view of the sky.

As Jim approached the front door, he came face to face with Martha Fowler, Jenny's mother. His relationship with Martha was friendlier than with Jenny's father, but it was still cold. Their conversations were usually an exchange of one-word answers.

Martha was striding down the sidewalk and Jim stepped out of her way. She stopped, glanced at Jim and said "Hello, Mr. Monaghan. Are you here to help Jenny move furniture?"

"Yes, Mrs. Fowler I am. What do you think of Jenny's new place?"

"Well, it is a condo, which doesn't impress me. And, I don't know why Jenny bought it. She has her own room at home. She says she is closer to school, but for almost five years, our home was close enough."

Martha sighed, "But she is twenty-two years old, and

there is not much Harrison, or I can do about it. I am sure, you prefer calling on her here as opposed to coming to our home," Martha remarked with a wry smile.

Jim didn't respond. Instead he said, "Well, it was nice seeing you, Mrs. Fowler. I had better go and help Jenny."

"I appreciate your helping her out. I suggested she get some professional movers, but she said, you would be able to handle everything." Martha bit her lip, then turned and walked to her car.

"I ran into your mother on the sidewalk," Jim announced. "Wow, what did she say about your outfit?"

"I had a shirt covering up my bikini top. It's hot in here and the air conditioning is not working right yet. But she has seen me in these short shorts before.

"If you object Jim, I will change clothes," she said mischievously.

"No, you look great to me!"

"By the way, did you have a nice visit with my mother, Jim?" Jenny asked smiling.

"Actually, it was pretty civil. It may have been one of the longest conversations I have had with her. She didn't bark at me. So, that's progress."

"Well, she was reasonable with me. It was her first time at my condo, and after looking around, she told me she liked it. She told me she was beginning to accept the fact that I had moved out, but she said I had to make peace with my dad. I told her I was sick of his pontificating and his criticism of you. I told her he threatened to disinherit me, and I told him to keep his money.

"That's when my mother really surprised me. She said she was having some concerns about my dad's behavior lately, and she thought it was terrible he threatened me with disinheritance. It was something the family just didn't do.

"She also told me that my dad has a good Boston Brahmin name, but her family had the money. And I was not to worry. How about that, Jim? Mom rarely stands up to my dad, so what she said was interesting. She even brought me a plant for the condo. Kind of a peace offering."

"Well, that still doesn't explain how you paid for this condo. When are you going to tell me?"

"In time, Jim. More importantly, I think mother will eventually warm up to you. Now, where do you think the sofa should go?"

Jim stood back and watched Jenny move around the living room, suggesting places for furniture. He was mesmerized by her beauty.

"Are you going to help me or are you just going to leer at me," Jenny asked.

Jim walked over, picked Jenny up, and carried her to the bedroom. "I think we need to rearrange some things in here," he said.

Putting her arms around Jim, Jenny said smiling, "You do, do you?"

21

"Where's Monaghan?" boomed Donald Hansen as he and Reverend Jefferson entered the editorial conference room. Jim and Josh Wheeler, the young intern, were sitting at the conference table sharing a pizza from the new Italian café across the street. Jim had promised Wheeler some time, and, while he felt uncomfortable in the role of mentor, he knew Wheeler was eager to learn. And Jim remembered how lost he sometimes felt when he himself was an eager young intern three and a half years ago.

"We need to talk, Jim," Hansen said "And bring your bosses in, because this is big. I am going to need the full support of this newspaper." Hansen's frame matched his deep, resonant voice. At six-feet-five inches and close to three hundred pounds, Hansen was decked out in a navy-blue golf shirt, khaki pants, and cowboy boots. He was a force.

By contrast, Reverend Jefferson, was thin, almost gaunt. His shoulders were slightly stooped, and his thinning hair was totally gray. His short gray beard was neatly trimmed.

Knowing Audrey was at the country club for lunch, Jim hailed Brad Hauser to join them.

Hansen and Reverend Jefferson cleared a large space on the conference table, pushing overflowing ash trays, empty soda bottles, and a week's worth of newspapers out of the way. Hansen laid out a map of the city of Lincoln superimposed over the boundaries of Shelby County.

With a black marker, Hansen divided the city map into four quadrants. Northeast, Southeast, Northwest, and Southwest.

"What do you see, Jim?"

"I see the city drawn into four sections. Northwest is industrial; southeast is mostly Hamilton University; northeast is the poor neighborhoods around Simpson Village; and southwest is the Country Club area."

"I knew you were smart, Jim. Technically accurate, but what else do you see?"

Jim paused, looked down at the map, placed his hand under his chin, "Well, Industrial and warehouses; Hamilton University area; rich sections; and poor sections," he said pointing to each sector on the map.

"Black and white sections," Reverend Jefferson interjected.

Now look at this." Hansen directed, as he placed an overlay, with parks, swimming pools, recreation centers, baseball diamonds, basketball courts, and tennis courts, onto the map of Lincoln.

There was silence as Jim, Hauser, and Wheeler studied the map.

"All the recreation stuff is located where the rich people live!" exclaimed Wheeler.

"Who's the kid?" Hansen asked.

"He is our intern from Northwestern," Hauser answered. "He is from Urbana, Illinois and is not familiar with Lincoln. He has been here for only a couple of weeks.

"Well, it took him ten seconds to see the inequities of the Park District and where it spends its money. And, as the new president of the park board, I am announcing: This shit stops now!" His voice echoed through the room.

Reverend Jefferson, in a softer voice, added, "Donald and I have decided to have a community meeting at my church on Friday night. We think it will ease the tension in the neighborhood. Don is interested in getting input from the citizens as to what should be done.

"Across from our church, we have that barren square block at Fourth and Bradley, and there are so many things we can do there. But it will work best if we get input from the citizens before we do anything."

While Jefferson was talking, Jim, Hauser, and Wheeler were looking closely at the map. "If someone from Simpson Village wants to play baseball, he has to walk a couple of miles. And where is the closest basketball court?" Jim asked.

Soon, Wheeler pulled out a ruler and measured distances from Fourth and Bradley to various recreational opportunities. "This is a great story," an excited Wheeler said. "I would like to do the research and write it up." Hauser affirmed by nodding his head.

Taking off his glasses, Reverend Jefferson turned to Jim and Hauser and said. "We would appreciate any story you all could write to support us. If we could time everything towards our meeting on Friday, that would be great.

"In addition, we are also going to invite Mayor Weir and Chief Buckner to the community meeting to see if we can lower the temperature a bit between the police and the citizens. I don't think the Stones are really a gang. At least they are not a hard-core gang with initiations and such like some of the nefarious ones. Oh, for sure, they are involved in some petty stuff, but I think they are just young men with nothing to do. Just imagine if some of them could be involved in building recreation facilities on that old lot.

"It would keep them busy, tire them out from working all day, and put a little money in their pockets. It would be great." Reverend Jefferson said.

"That's where we need the News Tribune," Hansen said. "If we can get a front-page editorial endorsing the meeting and encouraging Weir and Buckner to come, we can get off to a great start. I have talked to the other board members, and when I showed them how unequally our tax dollars were being spent on recreation, they were embarrassed. I told them it was time to make things right, and I know there will be no objection to what I am planning to do," Hansen said.

After the meeting with Hansen and Reverend Jefferson, Jim suggested to Hauser that it would be good experience for Josh to work with him on the story. Hauser agreed. Then Audrey Hill stormed into the room.

"What is this garbage? And why wasn't I informed about it?"

Jim had never seen Audrey so angry. She threw that day's paper onto the conference table. It was opened to the editorial page.

Support the Police!

Stories have appeared in this newspaper on the tragic shooting of Deputy Mayor Jack Wilson and the armed robbery of Wilson Sporting Goods. To date, no suspects have been named, but the award-winning Chief of the Lincoln Police Department, Billy Joe Buckner contends the crimes were committed by members of the Stones gang. The Stones are a notorious black gang, headed by the controversial Edgar Johnson.

Chief Buckner is in the best position to know the truth behind the robbery.

The Chief has reported the Stones have been causing trouble, agitating the community, and promoting disrespect for the police. The Chief reported the gang has been spreading lies and defamatory stories about police harassment and brutality.

Follow-up stories in this newspaper have challenged Chief's Buckner's analysis, but It is the opinion of the editorial board of the Lincoln News Tribune that we support the police and Chief Buckner. The Lincoln PD is acting in the best interests of the citizens of Lincoln. Buckner has the facts at his disposal, and he will make the right call. We urge all citizens to support our local police.

"HOW THE HELL DID THIS GET INTO THE PAPER," JIM asked, ready to tear the copy to shreds.

Audrey answered, "I asked the same question of Willy, and he told me he wrote the editorial after having lunch with Chief Buckner. I told him he had to clear all editorials with me, and he told me he didn't have to do that when my dad was alive. He always likes to play that card, that he and dad were the best of friends. They weren't. I reminded him that when he was named executive editor, he was directed to clear all local editorials with the publisher.

"But his excuse was that I was busy, and he couldn't reach me. He contended he wrote it prevent violent confrontations with the police. He said his intentions were noble; he wants to keep people safe. I will take care of this, but I am angry."

"Well, there is something we can do about it," Jim said, and he briefed her on the meeting the three had just completed with Hansen and Reverend Jefferson.

"Yes, we will support it. Brad, please write a page one editorial for tomorrow's paper. Run it by me, but I am one hundred percent endorsing it. Jim, you write up the story on the planned community meeting on Friday night. Josh, I want a story from you about the distances from different neighborhoods to recreation facilities. This will highlight how much farther some citizens must travel to do something those in other neighborhoods have nearby. Brad make sure these stories are on page one."

22

The Lincoln News Tribune
Page One
Tuesday, August 10, 1965

Where Do the Kids Play Ball?

By Jim Monaghan
News Tribune News Editor

If you are a youngster in the northeast section of
Lincoln, where do you learn to play ball? If you want
to go swimming, where is the closest swimming pool?
If your family wants to go on a picnic, where is the
closest park? If you want to go for a walk, is your only
option crumbling sidewalks adjacent to busy streets? If
you just want to have fun, where do you go?

The sad answer to those questions is this: There
are no baseball fields, swimming pools, picnic areas, or
trails in northeast Lincoln.

Donald Hansen, long time Lincoln businessman,

owner of Hansen Manufacturing, and new president of the Lincoln Park Board told the News Tribune he wasn't going to tolerate such disparity any longer. And he said, his board agrees. He is spearheading a drive to build public recreation facilities in the northeast section of town.

The public is invited to a meeting Friday evening at seven p.m. at the Fellowship of the Disciples of Christ Church. Reverend Jeremiah Jefferson has agreed to co-chair the meeting designed to receive input from the local citizenry about their desires and needs. Hansen said the priority will be the vacant city block lot, owned by the Park District, located at the intersection of Fourth and Bradley.

Chief Billy Joe Buckner and Mayor Weir have been invited to the meeting as well. Reverend Jefferson hopes the appearance of Chief Buckner and Mayor Weir will help lower the tension that has been prevalent in the neighborhood.

W heeler's story highlighted the distances between Fourth and Bradley and the various Park District facilities. Hauser's editorial thoroughly endorsed the proposal and encouraged Mayor Weir and Chief Buckner to participate.

Mayor Weir cited prior commitments and declined to attend, but Chief Buckner said he would be delighted to be at the meeting.

Jim decided to spend the balance of the day nailing down the movements of Edgar and the Stones between the time he left them at Mercy Hospital and the armed robbery and shooting of Jack Wilson.

He called Hansen's manufacturing, and was told Edgar did not work on Tuesday afternoons. Curious, Jim went to the photo department looking for Haley, and found no one there.

As he turned to leave, he heard the door to the dark room open and was surprised to see Willy walking out. He had beads of sweat on his forehead and he halted abruptly when he saw Jim.

"What are you doing in the darkroom, Willy?" Jim asked. Then he saw Haley exit the darkroom behind Willy. Her blouse was partially untucked; her eyes were wide open and red; it was obvious she had been crying. Her lips were trembling, and her hands were shaking.

"Listen to me, you prick," Willy snarled, "I don't answer to you. I don't answer to Hauser. I am the executive editor of this newspaper and was working here when you were a snot-nosed kid. So, get out of my way."

"Something rotten is going on here," Jim said, "I intend to tell Audrey about it when she gets back from her meeting."

"What's with you and our young publisher? What kind of hold do you have on her? Are you having an affair with her? Wouldn't surprise me a bit and wouldn't surprise most of the people around here. A 24- year-old news editor, ridiculous," Willy snarled as he pushed Jim out of the way and waddled out of the photo department.

Stunned, Jim stood motionless thinking, *What an asshole. Audrey and me, that's laughable."*

Then he turned his attention to Haley, who was stuffing her blouse back into her skirt and wiping away tears with the back of her hand. "What's gone on here, Haley? Why was Willy back here and what was he doing? And why are you crying and why is your blouse out? My goodness, Haley, your hands are shaking."

"Forget it, Jim. Just forget it. What can I do for you?" she said straightening up and adopting a carefully neutral expression.

"No, Haley, when I came in your blouse was out and you had a panicky look on your face. Was that old bastard bothering you? If he was, we are going to Audrey just as soon as possible. You don't have to put up with that crap, or any kind of crap."

"I said forget it, Jim. Leave me alone," Haley said as she turned and walked back into the darkroom.

Jim was troubled, but he reluctantly went to his desk. He knew he had to nail down, exactly, where the Stones were on the morning of the robbery. He wondered what Willy was doing in the darkroom. He wanted to know Jack Wilson's latest condition. He needed Art Wilk's picture of the footprint in the blood next to Jack's body. And he asked himself, where was Edgar, and what was he doing?

23

It was late as Jim drove north on Fourth Street coming to a stop at Bradley Avenue. Surveying the barren city block lot on his right, he hoped things would change there soon. He imagined a lighted sports field and kids playing on warm summer evenings.

Jim pulled into a parking space behind the Johnson's unit.

Haley peeked around the half-opened door and exclaimed, "Jim, what are you doing here?"

"I am here to get some answers," Jim replied, and I am not taking no for an answer. Is Edgar home?"

"Open that door, Haley, and let Jimmy in. I made some iced tea - just right on this hot night. Come in, Jimmy, and sit down.

Maybelle, Haley, and Jim sat around the turquoise Formica and chrome kitchen table and sipped tea. "Well, where is he?"

"Edgar should be here any minute now," Maybelle answered. She untied and retied her yellow print apron, and she shook her finger at Jim, "But first, Jimmy, I want to know. Are you eatin' regular? You look a little thin. Jimmy, it is time you settled down. You need a wife and family and regular home cooked meals, not all those cheeseburgers you usually have for dinner,

"And are you goin' to marry that professor's daughter? We want to be invited to the weddin'."

"Whoa, slow down, Maybelle. Things are moving, but not that fast. And yes, I am eating regular. Maybe you are right, too many cheeseburgers. So, what did you have to eat tonight?"

"Baked chicken, mashed potatoes, and green beans. Let me get you a plate. Jimmy, I sure like your friend Jenny better than that Anna woman. She never liked us. I can always tell.

Your Miss Jenny seems right at home here. She helps me in the kitchen, always askin' questions about how I cook this and how I cook that. She's a nice girl.

One of my friends cleans that big house her parents live in. She tells me it takes her two days to clean it. Soon as she is done with one part, she has to go back and start over in another part of the house."

"I like her too, Jim," Haley said. "She stopped at the paper last week when you weren't there. We walked across the street and had a cup of coffee. She asked me about my high school classes and she brought an application to Hamilton. I am so excited. I told her there is no way I can afford to go to Hamilton, but she said I might be able to get a scholarship. She is wonderful Jim! So special."

Haley's face turned from friendly, as she finished talking about Jenny, to serious. "Jim Monaghan, if you are here to talk about the bullshit that happened…"

Before Haley could finish, Maybelle jumped up and

said, "Haley, this is a God-fearin' house, and we don't tolerate no swearin' or cusswords. Do you understand me, young lady?"

"Yes, mother," Haley said, looking away from Maybelle's angry gaze.

"What's everyone arguing about?" Edgar asked as he walked in the door toting an Ohio State gray and scarlet duffel bag. Edgar dropped the bag on the green linoleum floor, and it made a loud bang.

Jim laughed, "What do you have in that bag, Edgar, bricks?"

Edgar laughed and said, "Not bricks, Jim, not bricks."

Jim looked his friend directly. "Thank God you are here, Edgar. I need to talk to you. First, why aren't you working on Tuesdays, and where have you been?"

"Jim, I am not ready to talk to you about that. Maybe in a couple of weeks, but what I am doing is private, and it's between me and Mr. Hansen."

"Ok, fine, I will respect whatever you are doing, especially if Hansen is involved, but Edgar, I need you to tell me exactly what you and the Stones did after I left the hospital last Wednesday. It is very important you be totally truthful with me. Chief Buckner says the Stones are making up the stories about harassment.

"And he is saying Rufus getting hit by the police car was just an accident. In fact, he contends, Rufus was jaywalking."

Edgar frowned. "Jim, I have always been truthful with you. After you left, Sister Mary Mark asked me if I could move the Stones from the Emergency Room to the parking lot. She said they were getting in the way and bothering some of the patients and their families.

"So, I did. We talked about Rufus and we prayed.

Tommy wanted to attack some police, but we told him that was foolish, and all that would happen would be he would get shot. I wasn't sure what to do next, but I knew Reverend Jefferson could help, so I told the guys we should go to his church and wake him up.

"They all like the Reverend and I breathed a little easier when they agreed. It was 5:30 a.m., and I know the time exactly, because Simon's company's two ambulances arrived. We watched his drivers take two people into the emergency room. One of Simon's drivers told us there had been in an accident on the highway. I know the time, because I saw the clock on the wall outside of the hospital.

"That's exactly what Edgar told me that morning, Jimmy. He tellin' you the truth," Maybelle interrupted.

"We got to the church right before six in the morning. I knocked on the Reverend's door, and he came out in his bathrobe. I told him what happened and asked him if he could help calm the boys down. He managed to get us some Coca Colas and coffee and we sat in his sanctuary until 9:00 a.m. just talking. That's what we did.

"And one last thing. Jack Wilson is a friend of mine. He kept me stocked with balls, bats, and a new glove every year. He is a big supporter of baseball and always helps kids in the neighborhood. He is one of the good guys. The kids in our neighborhood would never hurt Jack."

"Edgar, you have just provided me with the proof I need. I don't know why I didn't ask you about this earlier. It would have made such a difference. But I have it now. I will confirm it with Reverend Jefferson. I always need two sources at least. I never believed the Stones were involved. I have no idea who robbed and shot Jack, but it is great I have the proof that the Stones were not involved.

Turning to Haley, Jim said, "Now Haley, you know we have to talk about what happened in the dark room."

24

"Jim, we are not talking about it."

"Damnit...."

"Jimmy Monaghan, you will not curse in my home. Do you understand that? I will not tolerate it, not from my children, and not from you," an angry Maybelle snapped.

"Tell him," Edgar said. "Haley, you don't have to put up with that crap. It's not right. Jim is a friend of Audrey Hill. She is Willy's boss, and I know between the two of them, they can get it to stop. And if they don't stop it, I will catch that little bastard on his way home and beat the shit out of him."

"Edgar! Edgar!" Maybelle shouted as she stood up from the table, hands on her hips and angry. "What's gotten into you three? What kind of talk is that in this house? You stop it right now! No more! Hear me, no more bad language."

For the first time, Edgar and Haley ignored their mother, staring at one another.

As Haley hesitantly started to talk, her chin began to quiver, and tears formed in her eyes.

"He's groping me, and it's getting worse. It started the soon after I went to work there. And, Jim, I love my job and we need the money. But, it's awful. When you came into the photo lab, Jim, he was just leaving. I was printing pictures, and he walked in. He knows the light exposes and ruins the prints, and that morning, it ruined the society department's special layout. I had to redo all the pictures.

"He just stormed in and grabbed me from the behind and he put his hands on my chest."

"That son-of-a-bitch" Maybelle yelled, slamming her fist on the kitchen table.

"Let her finish, Mom," Edgar said.

"When he grabbed me, he pushed against me and I could feel him. You know what I mean, Jim, I could feel him. I felt sick, but I couldn't do anything about it. I wanted to scream but couldn't. Then he pulled my blouse out and reached up and pulled my bra down.

"I turned around and he was sweating, like he usually does. I told him I didn't want him doing that again and to please leave me alone."

"He's a dead man," Edgar said, his was jaw clenched, and he pounded a tight fist into an open palm. The loud smack made everyone jump.

"Easy, Edgar," Jim said.

"You will do nothing, Edgar. Settle down everyone," Maybelle said. Her voice was calm, but her brown eyes flashed fury. "Get it all out Haley, tell us everything. How did it end?"

Haley, who was staring down at the table, lifted her head and said, "He turned to me and said, 'Listen you little nigger bitch. I'll do what I want, and you won't say a word.' Then he walked out. He has been doing stuff like that, ever since I went to work there."

Jim flinched with anger. Maybelle, usually sweet and collected, was shaking with anger. Her lips were set in a grim, determined line. She sat down heavily, and her breathing was labored.

There was silence around the table. Edgar repeatedly clenched and unclenched his fists. Haley covered her face with her shaking hands and was quietly crying. Maybelle jumped up again from the table. She paced the room, muttering curse words.

So taut was the tension, Jim feared Maybelle and Edgar were about to drive to Willy's house and attack him. He tried to settle everyone down.

"Look, I know you are upset and rightly so. But, you can't go off half-cocked and attack Willy. That would only get you all in trouble. I think there is a better way, and I want you to trust me to handle it. I will talk with Audrey in the morning. Haley, she will talk with you and this will get settled.

"Maybelle, let me promise you," Jim said. "This will stop, and Haley will never have to put up with this again. After I talk to Audrey, she will probably fire Willy."

As Jim was leaving, Haley pulled him aside. "Jim, a couple of things you should know. When this started, it wasn't as bad as it was when you came in the lab. It started out with him patting me on the butt and accidentally hitting my chest with his elbow. I called him on it and he said, "It's your fault for looking so good. If you don't like me, I can help with that—I will fire your cute little butt."

"He said, "Just go along and be a good team player, Haley and you may even get a raise--if you treat me right.""

"Bastard," Jim said.

"I need this job, Jim, and I can't afford to lose it. And, no, I've never gotten a raise. I know mom and Edgar are furious, but please be careful with this, Jim. He is the executive editor, and I can't afford to lose my job."

"I understand, Haley, and I will be careful, but no one should have to put up with that kind of crap. Let me assure you, when I tell Audrey, she will be outraged." Jim affirmed.

25

"I need to make three phone calls and I will have this story nailed. Hold the front page," Jim grinned at Brad Hauser. "It's going to blow the socks off this town, and it's going to put Chief Buckner in his place."

"Tell me what you have, Jim. I need to know the essence of your story now," Hauser replied.

Jim gave him an overview of Edgar's and the Stones' accounts of their whereabouts after Rufus was hospitalized, but said he needed to confirm with Reverend Jefferson, Sister Mary Mark, and Ken Simon.

"Then do it and start writing," Hauser said.

Jim's conversation with Reverend Jefferson confirmed Edgar's story. The Reverend added, "As the meeting went on that morning, even though the young men were angry and frustrated, no one left. We ended up talking about what we could do so the boys wouldn't have so much idle time.

"They were here until the Bible study ladies showed up at nine o'clock. There are at least fifteen ladies who will back me up," Reverend Jefferson concluded.

Sister Mary Mark and Ken Simon also confirmed the story.

As Jim pecked away at his typewriter, Hauser called him to the conference room.

"I don't have time for this," Jim complained, but Hauser, with Art Wilks standing beside him, motioned him into the conference room.

"Well, look who is here. The chief photographer who has been missing in action, Jim greeted the unusually stern-looking Wilks.

"It's time you just listen, Jim," Wilks snapped.

Wilks pulled a series of eight by ten photos out of a legal-sized manila folder. "I have never dealt with anything like this before. I have been taking photos all my life, and I don't think I've ever taken a more important picture. I think one of these pictures is key to finding out who shot Jack."

Wilks placed on the table a large photo of Jack Wilson, lying on the floor of his store. It was taken from about ten feet away. Even at that distance, Jim and Brad both noticed an imprint just beside the pool of blood beside Jack's face. Wilks set another picture in front of the duo and they both gasped.

"Is that what I think it is?" Jim asked.

"Yes," said Wilks.

Jim and Hauser grabbed the picture and looked closely at the area between Jack's legs. It was a boot print. Hauser grabbed a magnifying glass from a drawer in the supply closet, looked at the print and said. "For sure, that's a boot print and look to the right. Do you see a partial boot print in the blood spatter next to Jack's neck?

"No question about it being another boot print guys,

but wait until you see this one," Wilks said as he laid the third picture on the table.

Enlarged multiple times, the boot print was clearly legible. Also legible was a logo in the middle of the sole that read ***L.L. Bean Hunting.***

"That's a $200 boot, guys," Wilks said. "That's why it has taken me so long to get this to you. I wanted to get it right, and I mean right. I took my negatives over to my friends the Hamilton Journalism department where I used their state-of-the art equipment. Our enlarger here at the paper doesn't have this high resolution."

"Oh, my God," Jim muttered. Hauser's face showed a growing anger.

"I told them I had some sensitive stuff, so they left me in the dark room by myself. They think it's some divorce stuff that I sometimes shoot for the private dicks in town. But when I saw what I had here, I really worked hard at getting it right.

Wilks convinced Hauser the boot print picture would reproduce in the paper, so Hauser ordered a four column, five-inch plate for the first edition.

"Art, I know Willy asked you to make sure the police got copies of all the pictures you took at the crime scene. Did you give them a picture of the boot print?"

"Yes, I gave them a copy of everything, but the first picture, the one from about ten feet away, is the one they have on the boot. I haven't given them any of the ones I have blown up."

"Jim write your story and include Art's information about the boot print. Add that the police have a picture of the boot print. Let's get it done, so Audrey can read it when she gets here at nine.

26

The Lincoln News Tribune
Page One
Wednesday, August 11, 1965

Stones Didn't Do It

By Jim Monaghan
News Tribune News Editor

An exhaustive investigation by the Lincoln News
Tribune into the attempted murder of Deputy Mayor
Jack Wilson and armed robbery of Wilson's Sporting
Goods has produced unequivocal evidence that Edgar
Johnson and the Stones, an alleged gang from
Lincoln's northeast neighborhood, were not involved.

The Lincoln Police Department, through its Chief
Billy Joe Buckner, has stated consistently the Stones
and Johnson were the principal suspects. Chief
Buckner declared the Stones were responsible within
hours after the armed robbery and attempted murder.

Telephone calls to reach Chief Buckner and other Lincoln police spokesmen to react to the News Tribune's investigation have not been returned.

The News Tribune has confirmed, using three named sources, exactly where Johnson and the Stones were from three a.m. until nine a.m. the morning of the robbery. All the sources confirmed the Stones were nowhere near Wilson's Sporting Goods.

A photo, on this page, shows a hunting boot manufactured by L.L. Bean, imprinted in the blood beside Jack Wilson's body. Knowledgeable sources tell the News Tribune, the hunting boot retails for over $200, clearly out of the reach of the members of the Stones, who live in the public housing project called Simpson Village.

There are no secrets in the back shop of a newspaper. Unionized for years, they are partners with management, but the relationship has always been tenuous. Most of the people working the linotype machines had worked at the News Tribune for decades. A close-knit group, they battled, but respected Audrey's father. They weren't sure about Audrey and planned to push her in upcoming contract negotiations.

Most were friends with Willy, whom they considered cantankerous, but well liked, especially by Phil Summers, the foreman. The linotype operator who was creating the lead slugs which would be used to print Jim's story, was intrigued and brought it to the attention of Summers.

When Phil read Jim's story, he printed it on a tear sheet, along with a picture of the boot print, and brought it to Willy's office. Willy immediately raced to the city room.

"What the hell is this story? Why wasn't I told about

it? Then Willy looked at the clock. It was ten minutes until the first deadline. He grabbed Hauser's phone and called the back shop.

"Stop the presses! Stop the presses! We're going to be late. We are changing page one!" he screamed into the phone.

"We can't do that, Willy. We are going with Jim's story," Hauser declared.

Willy, turned to Jim, who peeked out from behind the file cabinets grinning.

"You! You! You're fired! I am just sick of you and all your speculation crap. This story is crap. Did you check it out with Chief Buckner?"

Shocked by the yelling and the confrontation, intern Josh Wheeler picked up the phone and dialed Audrey.

"I hate to bother you, Miss Hill, but Mr. Williams and Mr. Hauser are yelling at one another and Mr. Williams just fired Jim Monaghan."

Wheeler heard a click and moments later, Audrey Hill came running up the stairs. "What's going on?"

"This crap is not going into my newspaper, that's what's going on," Willy yelled, brandishing the tear sheet. His face was beet red and the veins in his neck bulged.

The usually raucous newsroom turned deadly silently as everyone stopped, fixated on the epic confrontation. The only noise was the clattering of the wire services teletype machines.

Audrey calmly walked over to Willy and said, "No, it's not your newspaper, Willy. It's mine. I personally signed off on this story. And it's going on page one, whether you like it or not. Now, go back to your office before you say something you will regret."

"This never would have happened if your father

were still alive," Willy fumed. And I am still the executive editor of this newspaper. I told the back shop to stop the presses. We are changing page one," he sputtered through clenched teeth.

Audrey took a step toward Willy. "Willy, I think it is time you took a vacation. And if you don't take a vacation, and I mean a long one, I am going to suspend you and tell security you are not to enter the building except to pick up your personal items. Now, which is it going to be?" Audrey asked.

Throwing the tear sheet at Audrey, Willy glared at Jim and Brad. Turning to Audrey, he shouted "Fuck you, Audrey." He walked towards the stairs, stomped down and out of the office.

Audrey, turned to Josh, and said, "You just got your internship extended."

27

Chief Buckner, Mayor Weir, and City Manager Arlen Davis were quick to respond to Jim's story exonerating the Stones and Edgar.

They called a news conference late Wednesday, but barred Jim and any representative from the News Tribune. Chief Buckner told the media, who never challenged him at the news conference, that the Lincoln Police Department had information that the News Tribune did not.

Chief Buckner and Davis called another news conference Thursday morning, where they referred to the riots in the Watts neighborhood of Los Angeles on the previous night. There, after a routine traffic stop and a field sobriety test, which the driver failed, a California Highway patrolman called for backup to impound the car.

A passenger in the stopped car walked to his home nearby and brought his mother to the scene. Words were exchanged, and a shoving match with the State Trooper ensued. Soon, crowds gathered, and additional police responded. Word spread that the young man, who was arrested, and who was black, had been roughed up along with a pregnant woman.

The tension escalated. Soon, shots were fired. On Thursday morning, the riots intensified with multiple confrontations between police and the locals. Reports of residents being shot were broadcast, further escalating the tension.

"If we have riots like this in Lincoln, you can blame the News Tribune and Jim Monaghan," Chief Buckner announced. "The gangs are committing all the violence in Los Angeles. Just like the Stones gang here in Lincoln. If there is a riot, it will come from the Stones.

We need citizen support as the police are battling the Stones who are spreading false information about police harassment. Especially wrong is their story about Rufus Burton being run over. He was breaking the law by jaywalking, and he was dressed all in black on that dark night.

Our officer simply didn't see him, and even though he braked, he could not stop in time. What Monaghan wrote in the News Tribune yesterday is all lies. Trust me, the police know what happened, and we will prove it soon."

Buckner said he had a very busy schedule, so he would accept only one question. A television reporter asked if Buckner was still going to the meeting on Friday night at Reverend Jefferson's church, Buckner said he would be there, and he would perhaps announce some news related to the Wilson investigation.

Jim wished he could have participated in the news conference, but he had Josh Wheeler go in his stead. No one knew Wheeler.

After the first deadline on Thursday, Jim was reading

the Post-Dispatch and catching up on the Cincinnati Reds. He had received many threatening phone calls since the story appeared, but they sounded mostly like cranks, so he wasn't worried.

He was especially fond of one phone call, from an elderly woman, who wouldn't give her name. "Bless you Mr. Monaghan. Nobody ever stands up for our boys, but you did. I am praying for you."

Jim was about to tell the switchboard to refer all his calls to the city desk, because it was almost time for lunch with Jenny, when his phone rang.

"My God, Jim, but you are one hell of a reporter. You certainly seem to find controversy. If this all pans out, I think you are going to win another award." Jim smiled as he recognized the voice of Charlie Sloan, Editor of the Columbus Post-Dispatch.

"No awards, Charlie, but thanks for the compliment."

"Jim, I am curious about this Edgar Johnson who figures prominently in your stories. What can you tell me about him?"

Jim described his friendship with Edgar, praising him for rising above his circumstances in the projects. He affirmed he was certain Edgar had nothing to do with the Stones, even though his brother was once their leader.

"Well, well, well, Jim, I may know something you don't. Does Edgar live at Number Eight Simpson Village?"

"How in the world do you know that?" Jim asked.

"Jim, I am an Ohio State graduate, both undergrad and master's degrees and I'm very active over there. I am chairman of the JFK Minority Scholarship program. We have an Edgar Johnson, Number Eight Simpson Village,

Lincoln, Ohio as one of our students, and let me tell you he is one of the top prospects in the program.

"He researched and wrote an outstanding report on how money is spent in the Lincoln Public Works department. In a few weeks, he will finish his freshman year and the professors tell me he is at the top of the class."

"Well, I'll be damned. I didn't know that," Jim responded. "I know he has been out of touch in the afternoons and some evenings, but I never thought about him being in college."

Sloan explained, "Last year I got a call from Donald Hansen, who is a big Buckeye supporter. He told me about Edgar, and I suggested the JFK program. It was a perfect fit.

"Jim, I know the meeting Friday has great potential, so I asked Hauser if we could use you as a stringer to cover the story for us. We will use your byline and credit the News Tribune. I would rather rely on your account, since you know the people there, and they know you, rather than send one of our own reporters."

Jim assured Sloan he would be glad to do it and promised that Art Wilks would make sure there would be photographers at the event and, if there were any good photos, he would send them along.

28

Jim was all abuzz with good news when he sat down with Jenny at O'Toole's. Jenny was in a great mood, too. She explained she had received a rare compliment from Judge McCallister on her presentation at his seminar. "Compliments from the Judge are as common as a snowstorm in July," Jenny said.

"Compliments. I compliment you all the time," Jim responded.

"Sorry, Jim, but you aren't the Judge," she responded

"I have missed seeing you this week. I have really been studying, but it was worth it for the compliment I received on my work."

Jim told Jenny about Edgar taking classes at Ohio State, some of the phone calls he had received, and how optimistic he was about the meeting on Friday night.

Holding the day's newspaper up, Jenny said, "The Chief of Police is saying if there is a riot in Lincoln, people can blame Jim Monaghan. That scares me, Jim. I know you don't think much of Buckner, but he is the chief of police. He says you are lying in your story about the Stones not robbing Wilson's sporting goods and shooting Jack Wilson."

"There is no question my story is accurate, Jenny. I have it sourced multiple ways. I talked to five of the ladies at the Bible Study, Reverend Jefferson, Ken Simon, and Sister Mary Mark. There is no way the Stones were involved."

"Jim, I think the world of you, but you are really naïve sometimes," Jenny argued sympathetically. "I remember the Judge told us in one of first classes, it makes little difference is true. What matters is what a jury believes. This is Lincoln and you are up against powerful people. You have a very tough jury. Jim, you are an idealist. I am practical."

Jim didn't respond, opting to signal Stavros for another drink.

"By the way Jim, Mother says Dad is upset about your story. She said he thought it would incite people and that investigations should be left to those in charge. The newspaper should report the news, not make it."

"Jenny, your father wouldn't approve of anything I wrote, even if I won the Pulitzer prize."

Jenny didn't respond, she just looked down at her lemonade. Jim sensed the environment was becoming tense, and he didn't want to argue with Jenny. He knew her father didn't like him or the News Tribune, so he decided to say no more. When the silence started to become uncomfortable, he switched subjects.

"Let's talk about your condo. Do you need any more furniture moved or pictures hung? I am going to be working very late Friday night, but I am taking the weekend off and would like to spend it with you. I sure enjoyed moving the furniture the last time I was over," Jim said mischievously

Rolling her eyes, but smiling, Jenny said, "I can't be with you Friday night. It's mother's 50th birthday and I have agreed to have dinner with my parents at the country club. I don't want to go, but it is her birthday and she is reaching out to me. There is one saving grace. Audrey is going to surprise mom with a special birthday cake.

"I would much rather have dinner at Maybelle's and then go to the meeting. I do love that woman, even though she almost breaks my ribs when she gives me a hug. But this weekend, I want a full report from you, Jim, not just what you write in the paper," Jenny winked.

"I will be glad when the meeting is over. I really have high hopes for what it can accomplish. I can't wait to spend the weekend with you," Jim said.

"There is nothing I would rather do," Jenny said, squeezing Jim's hand, as they picked at their lunch.

29

Jim stopped at the Lincoln Police Department at six a.m. to brief Lt. Malcolm on what he anticipated at the community meeting at Reverend Jefferson's church later that evening.

He said Reverend Jefferson expected the meeting would be well attended, and he even had Hansen arrange for loudspeakers to be placed outside the church, in case his sanctuary was not big enough to contain the crowd.

Jim went on to tell Malcolm that Reverend Jefferson had talked to Chief Buckner and the Chief had promised he would have a lot to say and hoped the meeting would cool temperatures in the community.

Malcolm shook his head. "Do you mean the Chief said he hoped his appearance would cool the temperature? That's such bullshit. He told me he wanted me to bring some guys in early from my shift. He said he wanted to have my men in the neighborhood as backup, but his special squad would have primary responsibility for his safety and for crowd control."

Jim asked, "Isn't that unusual?"

"Yes, of course it is. I have never been asked to come in for backup. For goodness sake, Lieutenant Goodman has a full shift working three to eleven. Jim, I think I would be more concerned about the Chief's crew than any of the residents.

"With what is happening in LA, I think he is just looking for an excuse to crack some heads. He keeps saying that if there is a riot, the Stones will be involved. The Chief told us he would not allow any Watt's-like riots in Lincoln. He said the police should have fired on the crowd who were rioting after a screwed-up arrest in LA. He said that would have stopped the rioters cold."

Jim replied, "Well, let's be positive and hope it is a step in settling things down. I do know the kids there need a place to play."

"Yeah, Jim, I read your story," Malcolm said with a wry smile.

As Jim drove to the newspaper office, he wondered how long his friend Malcolm would continue working for Chief Buckner. As he approached the stop sign at First and Main, he watched with surprise as Buckner, accompanied by Mayor Weir, drove through the intersection on First Street heading north.

Curious as to why they were together and what they could possibly be doing so early in the morning, Jim followed them at a distance. They went through town approaching Ronald Pugh's farm complex.

As they turned into Pugh's lane, Jim slowed enough to see them pull in beside Pugh's machine shed and was shocked to see Willy's Cadillac parked there, too. Knowing he would not be welcome, he drove north for a quarter of a mile, turned around and headed south towards Lincoln.

He again slowed going past Pugh's driveway, and he confirmed it was indeed Willy's Cadillac. As he picked up speed, Jim saw a blue Mercedes coming north. *Can't be, he thought,* but his worst fears were realized when Harrison Fowler made eye contact, as the cars passed one another. Shocked, Jim drove on for a half mile before pulling off the road onto an entrance to a corn field.

Realizing, he may have found the conspiracy group, he looked up and saw Alex Reid, and city manager Arlen Davis drive by. They didn't see him.

Jim remembered Delmer Batcher telling him and Sgt. Major Harlow they wouldn't believe who attended meetings at Pugh's machine shed. *Could this be the proof I have been searching for the past two years? Or is it just six guys having coffee? In his heart, he knew they were not just having coffee,* Jim thought.

Then it hit him. In two days, on August 15, it would be two years since the truck rammed his pickup into the utility pole, and Mary flew through the windshield and died.

"I haven't been thinking of Mary lately, and I am not going to make it to her grave on the anniversary of her death. I thought I would always do that. I am in love with Jenny Fowler and she understands all about Mary. Maybe, she would want to drive to Chicago this weekend. But how can I tell her I suspect that her father is part of the conspiracy behind the crime and corruption of the past few years?

Jim knew he had a heavy burden, and his first instinct was to go to O'Toole's and have a drink. But it was seven in the morning, so, he drove to Harlow's café, where he knew his friend, the Sgt. Major, would listen and give him advice. He called Hauser telling him he was going to be late but had nothing new to report.

As Jim drove to Harlow's, a different kind of meeting was taking place.

30

P ugh's machine shed was huge. It was down a lane
    paved with asphalt and lined with tall poplar trees.
The shed was about fifty yards from the entrance to his
farm. Nearly three stories high, with a large, windowed
cupola, and clad by gleaming white aluminum siding, the
building was imposing.

On the first floor, which was two stories tall, farm
equipment was parked on the spotless concrete floor. A
long, gleaming oak staircase led to the third floor which
was dominated by Pugh's office, with three conference-
like rooms off to the sides. One of the rooms was
protected by a solid steel door and was accessible only by
punching in the right code on the door lock.

The room itself had steel walls covered by oak
paneling. Inside were file cabinets opened only by keys
Pugh always kept in his possession. The cabinets flanked
a massive six-foot-tall and three-foot wide safe. It, too,
was opened only by a combination.

Pugh's office was expansive. The walls were oak-
paneled, and the floor was constructed of solid oak

planks. His personal desk was his pride and joy. He had it constructed as an exact replica of the Resolute Desk, found in the Oval Office of the President of the United States. In the middle of the room was a mahogany conference table which seated ten.

Ronald Pugh looked around the highly polished table at the six powerful men who had seated themselves in the black high-backed leather chairs. Sitting at the head of the table, in a chair that was larger than the others, Pugh's gaze lingered on each man.

Harrison Fowler, the newest member of the group, was tall, thin, and dapper in a tailored Brooks Brothers suit, starched white shirt with gold cufflinks and red bow tie. Mayor Scott Weir, even taller than Fowler, was dressed for work in his construction business. Khaki pants, work boots and a Lincoln Country Club golf shirt fit snugly on his athletic body. Weir's face had the rugged tan of a man who worked outdoors.

Willy was clad, as always, in a short sleeve shirt and clip-on tie. His wire-rimmed glasses were perched on top of his shining, nearly bald head. Short and paunchy, Willy was fidgeting with his car keys. Only Pugh knew why he was nervous.

Alex Reid had gained thirty pounds since his release from prison, and his paunch was straining the buttons on his white shirt. His navy-blue suit looked uncomfortably tight and the matching tie dug into his double chin. His deep scowl made him look older than his years.

City Manager Arlen Davis wore a muted brown plaid suit. At five-foot ten and two hundred pounds, he was surprisingly light on his feet, a fact he proudly attributed to his physical fitness workouts. He nervously twirled his horn-rimmed glasses, put them on, then removed and twirled them again and again. His thinning brown hair was closely cropped and only recently sprouted some gray.

Chief Buckner towered over all of them. His imposing girth was backed up by frequent loud outbursts. His friends said he had two voices, loud and loud.

All the men, leaders in their own worlds, deferred to Pugh as the head of this group, which Pugh had named America Incorporated.

Pugh leaned forward with his thin arms on the table. Pugh was five-feet-six and weighed less than 140 pounds. He was physically weak, an embarrassing attribute, which caused a rift with his father, a World War I veteran, when Pugh failed to pass the Army physical during the Korea. His gray, thinning hair was neatly combed. He wore, under a tailor-made blue blazer, a white shirt and a bolo tie with an engraved eagle on the clasp. His black cowboy boots had eagles stitched on the sides, but this morning, they were covered by tailored gray slacks.

Pugh sat facing north, with his back to his personal desk. The south side of the office featured floor-to-ceiling windows. Pugh regretted putting the windows there. His view was straight towards Lincoln, but between his office and downtown Lincoln, immediately adjacent to the south side of his property and only a half mile away, was Simpson Village.

He mitigated the view by planting large elm trees many years ago. The trees, while huge, were beginning to show signs of the dreaded Dutch elm disease. He knew he had to replace the trees, because he was certain he did not want to look out on Simpson Village.

Pugh was angry. He held Wednesday's edition of the News Tribune and threateningly asked Willy how such an article could appear in the newspaper. Willy's job was to control the news, and the story was unacceptable. Willy pleaded his case saying he couldn't control Monaghan because Monaghan and Audrey Hill had a special relationship.

Willy suggested they might be sleeping together, which drew a quick response from Hamilton Fowler. "Look, no one dislikes Monaghan more than me. But, for God's sake, and I am not proud of this, he is dating my daughter and there is not a damn thing I can do about it. But, for sure, he is not sleeping with Audrey Hill."

"Well, maybe he is sleeping with your daughter," Willy snarled.

"Be careful, Willy," Fowler countered.

"I don't care who Monaghan is sleeping with," an angry Pugh interrupted and looked directly at Willy. He told Willy he was disappointed, and if Willy couldn't control Monaghan and the newspaper, he had nothing to contribute.

Willy countered he had written a great editorial supporting Chief Buckner, but no one came to his defense. Pugh told Willy he heard he had been told to go on a long vacation. He excused Willy from the balance of the meeting because there were topics he didn't need to know.

Pugh liked to compartmentalize his meetings. He often used "need to know" to explain many of his decisions.

After Willy left, Pugh went on a diatribe complaining about Monaghan and the News Tribune. He told of making an offer through a New York attorney to buy the paper, but Bernard Hill, before he died, dismissed it and wouldn't even talk to the attorney about a potential sale.

Pugh reported Audrey would not return the attorney's calls.

It was obvious to everyone around the table, Pugh was livid. The men understood the depth of his anger. Everyone, but Fowler who thought the tantrum was a bit over the top.

31

Mayor Weir pointed out the News Tribune was fine until Monaghan started working there. Weir reminded the group that a little over two years ago, Monaghan started the copper casket investigation and that's when their trouble started. All around the table agreed. The mistake was made in not stopping the investigation and having Willy get rid of Monaghan then.

Weir pointed out that Monaghan was friends with the new Governor and was very close to Audrey Hill. Weir suggested Monaghan might be too important and too connected to be dealt with.

Chief Buckner laughed and told Weir no one was above his reach as Chief of Police. He suggested he could arrest anyone, and he just needed an excuse to go after Monaghan. Alex Reid chimed in, saying more needed to be done than just arrest Monaghan. He suggested while the Chief was arresting Monaghan, someone should arrest Edgar Johnson too.

"He's becoming a real pain in the ass with that gang

of his," Reid complained. "Why don't we get both of them out of town," Reid suggested.

Fowler felt a pang of discomfort when Reid talked about getting Monaghan and Edgar out of town.

Looking towards Fowler, Reid suggested Fowler would be happy because Monaghan was probably sleeping with his daughter.

Fowler reacted with anger at the second suggestion his daughter was sleeping with Monaghan. His face flushed, he turned to Pugh and said he was there to talk about investments. He didn't want to hear his daughter's name mentioned again. He reminded everyone he had kept a lid on the Shelby County Community Relations Committee, like they asked. He appreciated the investment returns he had received in the past few months, but enough talk about Jim Monaghan. He wanted to talk about investments.

Fowler's comments were met with silence. Finally, Pugh rose and asked Fowler to accompany him to an adjoining conference room. Pugh told Fowler there wasn't going to be any discussion of investments that day. Fowler told him that was fine and inquired when the next investment meeting would be. Pugh put his arm around Fowler and told him his time on the committee had come to an end. He told Fowler he just didn't fit in with the rest of the group, and he would receive a check early next week to clear out his investment account.

Fowler slowly descended the stairs, shaking his head and wondering what he had gotten himself into. Though he detested Monaghan and hated the relationship Jim had with his daughter, he was very uncomfortable about the talk of getting rid of Jim Monaghan and getting him out of town. But he dismissed it as guys just talking big. *How would they do something like that,* he thought. He was, however, troubled by no one objecting to Reid's comments about Jim Monaghan and Edgar Johnson.

After Fowler left, the discussion intensified. Pugh agreed with Reid that Edgar Johnson be added to the list of people who needed to leave town. Pugh reported he had people investigating Edgar and found him to be bright and articulate, even though he was Black.

He pointed out Reverend Jefferson was the leader in the community, but he was old, and the young people followed and respected Edgar. That community must not be allowed to rise and be a force. He cited the riots in Los Angeles and the potential for trouble where the Blacks lived. Edgar was a potential threat and must go, along with Monaghan.

Mayor Weir was becoming increasingly uncomfortable. Inquiring what Pugh meant by getting Monaghan and Edgar out of town, Pugh smiled. The others were silent.

Weir decided to leave, citing an appointment with one of his contractors. As he walked down the steps, he passed Slick, Pugh's number one employee. Weir was unsettled when Slick stared at him with menacing eyes.

Weir looked away as the men passed. An avid hunter, he noticed Slick's L.L. Bean hunting boots. Remembering Monaghan's story of the day before, he thought, *No, it can't be possible.*

Pugh looked at Reid, Davis and Buckner. He remarked he was glad the others had left. Now, that Slick had joined them, they could get down to real business. He reminded them leadership was a burden. He told them hard decisions had to be made to preserve the status quo and the four of them were privileged to wear the heavy mantle of leadership.

Reid told the group that every day he was in jail he

had thought of Monaghan. He hated Monaghan with every ounce of his being.

Slick said he thought there would be an opportunity that night at the meeting at Reverend Jefferson's church. He told them he had checked out the church and everything looked good. They all agreed Monaghan would be there and Edgar Johnson probably would, too.

Pugh provided Slick with pictures of Tyrell and Dewayne reminding everyone the Simpson Village duo were the source of a major cash flow. "Those Black fools have no idea where the marijuana comes from," Pugh said. "We don't want to do anything to upset that flow of money. So, memorize those faces, and make sure they aren't harmed, Slick."

"Not a problem, Boss."

As their plans finalized, Buckner laughingly told Pugh he shouldn't have made Willy leave. He suggested Willy did a good job of delivering Jim's truck to him two years before and maybe Willy could get Monaghan a good parking place at the meeting.

They all laughed.

32

J im sat in the back booth of Harlow's café. He stacked and restacked the individual packets of jelly and rearranged the salt and pepper shakers. His coffee sat cooling and his English muffin was untouched. Drumming his fingers on the table, Jim was relieved when Sgt. Major Hal Harlow served steaming plates of eggs, bacon, and hash browns to patrons at a nearby table, and joined him in the booth. Harlow sat down heavily, complaining about the pain in his back from old wartime injuries.

"Jim, you are borrowing trouble," Harlow pronounced after Jim recounted what he saw at Pugh's farm. "You don't know what those guys are talking about in Pugh's machine shed. It might be like a Rotary Club or an investment club. They are all rich, so maybe they are talking about what's the next business to invest in.

"Pugh is the money behind a lot of businesses in town. Perhaps he is just the front for those guys. You can't assume it is a conspiracy of evil and Jenny's father is part of it."

"Yes, but what if it is a conspiracy of evil?" Jim countered. "Buck and Clyde are Pugh's employees and so was Delmar Batcher. It can't be a coincidence. Remember Delmer telling us we wouldn't believe who goes to those meetings? I just can't believe they are talking investments.

"And you may have guessed, Sgt. Major, I am in love with Jenny. I think I want to marry her, but what if her father is part of the group that killed Irene, Steve, and Mary? I couldn't live with that. I could never face her father without wanting to bust his face in. I just think, if it is true, it will tear Jenny and me apart."

Harlow looked pensive. "Jim, you are worrying about things that may not be real. You need a diversion. Let's go over to Mercy and see how Jack is doing."

At Mercy Hospital, Jim and the Sgt. Major were greeted by Sister Mary Mark. "I think I know where you are heading, Jim, but let me save you some time. You can't visit Jack. He is still in intensive care, but the doctors are beginning to be optimistic. He lost a lot of blood before he got here, and he immediately went into a coma, but the doctors tell me his vitals are improving and they are hopeful he will come out of the coma soon.

"The best thing you can do for Jack is to say a prayer. We are taking good care of him. Check in with me tomorrow, and I will give you an update."

33

That evening, after a stop at O'Toole's for a burger and a couple of Bushmills, Jim parked directly in front of Reverend Jefferson's church. It was a typical August in central Ohio, hot and muggy. Jim had the top down on his convertible and had enjoyed the breeze as he drove, even though it was a hot breeze.

He was not surprised the church was packed half an hour before the community meeting was to begin. Interest in the topic of public recreation facilities was intense. Neighbors had questions and hopes. People jammed into the pews, and many stood along the back wall, fanning themselves with folded-up church bulletins. It was oppressively warm and muggy, made more so by the packed-in bodies.

Jim spied Donald Hansen talking with Reverend Jefferson near the front of the church, where three chairs were placed on a raised platform. As he walked towards them, he scanned the crowd and did not see Chief Buckner. *Maybe, he won't show up, or maybe he will make a grand entrance,* Jim mused.

Reverend Jefferson and Hansen greeted Jim warmly. "Quite a story on page one Wednesday," remarked Hansen. "I think it was one of your best. What the hell is going on in the police department? I'm really troubled about possible corruption in the department.

"Chief Buckner has been a concern of mine from the day Arlen Davis named him Chief. I thought there were several other candidates who would have been better. Many people, including me, were puzzled by Davis's hiring someone from the deep South with little experience as police Captain."

"I, too, am concerned about the Chief," Reverend Jefferson said. "But what I want to say to Jim, is thank you. Thank you for that story. It has relieved a lot of tension in our community. You know, Don, the police have been breaking in doors here in the village.

"They don't even knock. They just bust in and take the young men out, put them in handcuffs, and throw them on the ground or in the back of their squad cars. It's terrible.

"Then after an hour or so, they let them go. The boys say they are harassed, cussed, called nigger, and Lord knows what else.

"Thank you, Don, for hiring some of our boys, especially Edgar Johnson. I've watched Edgar grow up, and he has been able to keep himself out of trouble. He is a good young man. He is working hard and is going to make something of himself. If he can just get through the next year, maybe he can even move out of Simpson," Rev. Jefferson said.

"I know Edgar's a good man," Hansen agreed.

"Don, quite a secret you and Edgar have been keeping," Jim said.

"Proud of that young man," Don countered grinning.

"There's the Chief," Jim said. "We should go over and talk to him."

Chief Buckner strode into the Sanctuary of the church without stopping to say hello to anyone. He marched over to Hansen, Jefferson, and Jim and said,

"Let's get this damn meeting going. I have things to do."

Rev. Jefferson threw back his shoulders and replied. "Chief, this is my church, and this is where we worship Jesus Christ, the Son of God. I would appreciate it, no, I demand you do not use language like that in my Church."

"Whatever," the Chief said. "Where are we going to sit, and how long do you think this meeting is going to take?"

"We are going to be at the table in front. You see, Chief, it is elevated and there are three chairs there. You can pick out which chair you want to sit in," Hansen answered.

The Chief glared at Jim. "What's this shitass doing here? He ain't talking, is he? Cause, if he's going to talk tonight, I'm leaving."

Jim stood his ground. Hansen moved between them. "Jim isn't speaking tonight, Chief. You're just here as a reporter, right Jim?"

"That's right, Don, I'm just here as a reporter."

Rev. Jefferson, offended by the Chief's language, tried again. "Chief, I must insist you not use that type of language in my church."

"All, right, I will try," the Chief said. "But looking at Monaghan makes me sick. That was just a pack of lies you had in that newspaper Wednesday. Nothing but a pack of lies. It may surprise you, Monaghan, but the Lincoln Police Department does not share its investigation results with you.

"We work with the District Attorney, and we are close to an indictment. It's going to surprise you, so get ready to print a retraction of that crap you had on Wednesday."

"I didn't print any lies, Chief, and you know it. By the way, are you going to arrest someone before they are indicted or are you going to indict someone first?" Jim asked.

Buckner glared at Jim and took a step towards him when Hansen said, "Ok, it is seven-oh-five, and this room is packed. We need to start the meeting."

"Don, I want to open the meeting with the Pledge of Allegiance. Then, I need to say a prayer. I just received a phone call, and we all need to pray." Jefferson said.

"Then that's what we will do. Ok, Chief?" Hansen asked.

"Whatever," Buckner grunted. "As long as this doesn't turn into a prayer meeting. I get enough prayer on Sunday."

The three men took their chairs in the front of the room. Jim went to the right side, away from the main door but near the front.

As he sat down, Haley Johnson hurried up to him.

"Jim, I was in the dark room printing some pictures when Pete, the late shift photographer, answered the phone. I heard him say that he was going to the meeting tonight and then he asked, 'Are you sure? Jim and Hauser wanted me to cover the meeting'. Then I heard him say, 'Ok, Mr. Williams, I will cancel the assignment.'"

"I told him Mr. Williams was suspended or on

vacation or something and should not be cancelling the photo assignment. Pete said, 'Hey, he is one of the editors and if tells me the photo shoot is cancelled, then it's cancelled. I didn't want to go up there anyway.'

"Jim, I called Art, Brad Hauser, and Ms. Hill, but I couldn't reach any of them. So, I rushed over here to tell you."

"Why in the world would Willy cancel the photo assignment? That doesn't make sense," Jim said. Hearing Hansen start the meeting, he whispered, "Haley, you know how to use a camera. Go to my car—it's parked out front. In the glove compartment is a small 35 MM camera. You won't have a flash, but it should work inside this room. There's plenty of light."

Haley, smiling, ran to the car, got the camera, and was back in minutes.

As he listened to Hansen start the meeting, Jim wondered, *why would Willy do that? It didn't make any sense.*

34

Jenny pulled her car into the circular driveway of the Lincoln Country Club, gave her keys to the valet and walked in.

Her parents were seated at the number one table and to Jenny's pleasant surprise, she saw Audrey and her friends at the adjoining table. Greeting Audrey with a hug, she thought *what a wonderful addition to my life Audrey has become. I always wanted a sister, and now I have Audrey.*

Flashing a smile and giving her mother a kiss on the cheek, Jenny sat down and gave a cool, but polite, hello to her father. Despite the tension caused by her relationship with Jim and her moving into her own condo, she was determined to make the evening a success.

It was her mother's 50th birthday and her mom had been reaching out to her lately. Yesterday, her mother even asked about Jim and how he treated her.

After exchanging pleasantries and asking her mother what it felt like to be the big 50, she turned to her father and asked him what he thought about Jim's story exonerating Edgar Johnson and the Stones in Wednesday's paper.

Harrison was dismissive. He told Jenny she was late, they had already ordered cocktails, and that her martini would be there in a minute. Jenny told him she didn't drink martinis and would prefer, if anything, a glass of wine. Fowler told her she needed to learn to drink martinis because that was the drink of choice of the best people. He told her he wasn't impressed with Jim's story.

He cited Willy's editorial earlier and said when it comes to crime, always believe the police. He told her that newspapers don't solve crimes, the police do.

Jenny, restraining her frustration, told her father that Reverend Jefferson, the Bible study ladies, Sister Mary Mark, and Ken Simon all backed up Jim's story. Harrison retorted, noting the main source was Reverend Jefferson. He indicated Blacks stick together and everyone should wait on the police investigation.

Jenny was incredulous, but it was her mother's birthday, and she was determined to be pleasant and to make the evening a success. So, she held her tongue.

35

R everend Jefferson started the meeting with the Pledge of Allegiance. He introduced Chief Buckner, to a smattering of boos, and Donald Hansen, who received a standing ovation.

Reverend Jefferson quieted the crowd and scolded. "The Chief is our guest tonight. He didn't have to be here, but he is here. I am personally grateful to him and I would expect all would be respectful this evening.

"But, now I would like everyone to be quiet. I received a phone call just before the meeting, and we all need to bow our heads and pray. Rufus Burton, a young man from our community who was involved in an auto accident earlier, has died."

The room erupted in shouts of anguish and anger. Tears streamed down many faces. Buckner, who picked at a blemish on his nose during Reverend Johnson's announcement, glared. Jim sat back in his chair, stunned. *I wonder why Reverend Jefferson announced it this evening. It's really going to raise the temperature of this meeting.*

As the muttering quieted down, Hansen rose and

called the meeting to order. He told of his plans to make significant changes in the operation of the Lincoln Park Board.

"First thing we are going to work on is the barren lot across the street. It is owned by the Park District. I want your ideas for what we should build there."

The crowd knew Hansen and respected him for hiring young people from the community and for his dedication and fairness as an American Legion baseball coach. He was one of the popular businessmen in Lincoln.

After a few people offered suggestions, a young man, hands clenched on the pew in front of him, stood.

"Chief, Rufus is dead, and your cops ran over him. What you got to say to that?"

The buzz of voices intensified, and several echoed the young man's questions, "Yeah, what you got to say to that?"

The Chief stood. "Rufus Burton was in the middle of the street. One of my officers got a call, turned on his lights and siren, and took off. Rufus just stood there, and it was an accident." Then he sat down, glowering.

"That's bullshit," another young man shouted. "I was there, and your guy didn't turn on his lights or his siren. He just ran over Rufus."

The Chief didn't move, and the only indication that he'd heard the complaint was the flush creeping up his neck.

Jim felt the tension escalate. The crowd had turned hostile and fired questions and accusations. No one was talking about parks and recreational facilities.

Jim looked around and noticed there were only three white people in the room: Donald Hansen, the Chief, and himself. *There surely won't be any problems with the Chief here, or will there?*

Donald Hansen knew he was losing control of the meeting, despite Rev. Jefferson's opening prayer, which called for calm, dialogue, and hope.

Hansen tried, again, to bring the meeting to order, "We can start with the square block across the street from the church," Hansen said. It's on the books as a city park, but we all know it is filled with weeds and trash. On Monday morning, I'm getting a crew over here to clean it up.

"Then if we can get an agreement tonight, we can start the design phase next week. As I see it, we can fit at least two baseball diamonds in the northwest and southeast sections of the park and we can build basketball courts and tennis courts in the other corners of the park." Hansen announced.

The crowd had quieted to listen to Hansen.

"With all due respect, Mr. Hansen," an elderly man leaned on his cane and spoke up, "what we going to do with tennis courts? We don't know how to play tennis, and aren't you supposed to be in all white when you play? Well, I am black. How am I going to be in all white?" The crowd tittered nervously.

36

"I have a question for the Chief," a middle-aged woman, rising tentatively, said. "I have four boys. The oldest is eighteen and the youngest is twelve. They were playing cards Tuesday night in my front room. They weren't bothering anyone.

"Then your policemen bust my front door open. Chief," she said, tears forming in her deep brown eyes and her voice quivering.

"They busted through my front door. They didn't knock. They just busted in my front door. There were six of them and they grabbed my boys, put them in handcuffs, and took them outside. Even my twelve-year-old. I tried to follow, but one of your officers said to me, 'Listen, bitch, if you don't want to get arrested, keep your ass inside this house.'" The grumbling noise in the crowd increased noticeably.

"They kept my boys in the back of those police cars for about a half an hour, and then my boys came in and said the police threatened to arrest them if they didn't cooperate. The police wanted to know where Edgar

Johnson was and had my boys seen him. My boys were scared, and the youngest has been having nightmares. How can that be right, Chief?" the mother asked.

"Don't know nothing about that," the Chief said.

"Answer her question! Answer her question," a number of people yelled.

The yelling continued while Hansen and Rev. Jefferson pleaded for calm.

The Chief sat stone-faced, his cheeks and neck red and his lips taut.

Other residents complained about his officers breaking down doors, pulling young people out, handcuffing them, and putting them in the back of police cars. Still, the Chief sat mute.

"Chief, you have not answered any of the questions. Please answer this one. Are you breaking down doors in any other section of town except ours? Please answer," another elderly man pleaded.

Buckner clipped a reply, "We had a major crime, an armed robbery and attempted murder of the deputy mayor. It's the police department's job to investigate. And we investigate where we think the perpetrators are. If that's in this section of town, so be it."

"But are you looking anyplace else?" the man persisted.

The Chief, again, sat silent.

Another mother rose and, waved the Wednesday edition of the News Tribune. "Mr. Monaghan is here, and he wrote a story in this newspaper right here. It says Edgar and a bunch of the so-called Stones were here in this Church with Rev. Jefferson when that awful crime was taking place. What you got to say to that, Chief?"

At that moment, Maybelle Johnson caught Jim's eye and gave him a thumbs-up.

"I don't read anything Monaghan writes," the Chief said. "It's usually a bunch of bullshit. And he ain't talking at this meeting, or I am going to leave."

"Then leave," some of the residents shouted. "We want to hear from Monaghan!"

Rev. Jefferson called for order. "My dear brothers and sisters in Christ, we came here tonight with so much hope for our community. Mr. Hansen has told us he wants to build baseball diamonds and basketball courts in the park across the street. This is wonderful news, people.

"This is wonderful news! We did not come here to talk about the police and what they are doing or not doing. Let's not let this meeting degenerate into a police discussion. We can do that another time," he pleaded.

"Then, why is the Chief here," someone yelled. "Yeah, why is he here, and why won't he answer our questions?"

As the clock turned to seven-forty-five, and the meeting spun out of control, the door opened, and an ominous silence drifted across the room.

Led by Tommy, twenty members of the Stones marched in. Some of the young men had handguns stuck in their waistbands and a couple had bandoliers draped around their shoulders. Dressed in black tee shirts, blue jeans, and sneakers, they stared menacingly at the chief.

At that precise moment, Slick Beck positioned himself in one of the tall Elm trees on the south end of the Pugh Property. He pulled his M16 from his shoulder and lined up his telescopic sight, down Fourth Avenue, aiming at the front windshield of Jim Monaghan's car. He adjusted his radio headset and checked to make sure the communications were clear.

Hansen tried again, "Everyone settle down. Let's talk about baseball diamonds and basketball courts."

"Mr. Hansen, we ain't ever gonna get them courts and diamonds. Nobody ever does anything for us up here. It's all crap," someone yelled.

Suddenly, led by Tommy, the Stones started slowly chanting, "One, two, three, four, we won't take it anymore."

Trying to regain control, Hansen raised his voice, "No! I am going to build the courts and the baseball diamonds. You all know me. I've coached many of your kids in American Legion ball. You know my word is good."

Rev. Jefferson again took the microphone and shouted, "Folks, I have known Donald Hansen for years, and he's a friend of mine. He is a man of his word. Now, let's all settle down and get this meeting back to where we started. We can make some progress."

Rev. Jefferson was booed.

Hansen took the microphone from Rev. Jefferson. Both men looked knowingly at one another and Hansen said, "This meeting is over."

37

8 P.M

T he crowd, led by the Stones, filed out of the church. As Jim was finishing up his notes, a dejected Rev. Jefferson slumped down in the pew next to him.

"We tried, Jim, we tried. I just didn't realize there was this much hostility towards the police. It's sad, because we need the police in our community. There are so many good men on the police force. I am just sick the way this meeting went. The Chief is going to think we all hate the police, and that's simply not true."

Jim nodded, "I will include your words about the police in my story for tomorrow morning's paper. I'm not sure what happens next. There must be some leadership from your community, Reverend, and from City Hall.

"But the Chief, the Manager, and the Mayor are close friends. So, I am not sure what will happen next or what the News Tribune can do. I do know Audrey is one tough customer, and she is on the side of what is right.

Meet with her, I know she will continue to support the community.

"What about Harrison Fowler?" the Reverend asked. "He wasn't here tonight, was he? I'm not sure where Fowler is on these police issues. As chairman of the Community Relations Commission, he has done nothing —not even spoken up about the abuses. I have tried calling him, but he never returns my calls."

Jim looked away from Jefferson and noticed just about everyone was gone. Only a few people were hanging back. Hansen and the Chief had already left.

Jim smiled as Haley and Maybelle walked over. "Well, how's the newest News Tribune photographer, Haley? Did you get some good shots?"

"Yes, I think I did. This was so exciting—being a photographer! I loved it. Thanks for giving me the opportunity, Jim," and she reached down and hugged him.

Maybelle beamed. "Jim, if you can get any of her pictures in the paper, could you get me some copies? I want to send them to the cousins in Chicago. Imagine that, my daughter a professional photographer."

"For sure, I will get that done. Haley, I will take the camera to the photo lab, so Art can get the negatives and see what we can get in the paper tomorrow. I'm going to the office now to write the story, and then I will Western Union it to the Columbus Post-Dispatch. Their editor wanted a story about tonight's meeting for their Saturday morning edition."

Jim told Reverend Jefferson it would be a good idea for him and Audrey to have a long lunch to discuss what could be done to improve the environment around the neighborhood.

Jim suggested the next day, but Reverend Jefferson

declined saying, he needed to work on his Sunday sermon. Considering what had happened tonight, he said he had to be very careful with his words. He suggested they get together the next week.

"Let's plan on it," Jim said. As he walked towards the door, he noticed the room was empty except for him and Jefferson. The Reverend went the opposite direction to get a utility broom to clean up the room. Jim walked out the door and into a substantial crowd still milling around the front of the church.

Tommy and the Stones were surrounding his car.

Where the hell is Edgar? Jim wondered. *And where are the police?*

At that moment, Ronald Pugh climbed into the cupola high atop his machine shed, peered through his Steiner Police high-powered binoculars, adjusted his radio head set and confirmed with Slick it was working.

38

8:10 P.M

Chief Buckner hurried out of the church, jumped into his car, and turned his flashers on. He pulled away, then dashed them off and drove quickly to join the six officers of his special unit at the southeast corner of the barren field at Fifth and Piatt, catty-corner through the vacant lot, from the church. He jumped out of his squad car with his handheld radio next to his ear. He donned his bulletproof vest, grabbed his carbine rifle, and joined his officers, also armed with rifles, and advanced toward the church.

"Get your guns locked and loaded. I suspect there is going to be real trouble here in just a few minutes. I didn't see Edgar, but I know he's here, so be ready," the Chief ordered. "And remember, if you see a nigger with a gun, shoot 'em."

His radio buzzed. "Chief! Chief, this is Lt. Malcolm. Your guys are loaded for war. What the hell is going on? What are you expecting?"

"Malcolm, is that you? What the hell are you doing

here? You're supposed to be backup. Get your ass out of here. If we need you, we will call you. You and your guys stay back. This is a special assignment squad and you're not part of it, so get off the radio and get out of here."

Buckner turned to his squad, "Men, if you hear Malcolm on the radio, ignore him. I am in command. Listen only to my command. People are coming out of the church. Move toward the church, men," the Chief ordered.

Most of the officers, who were part of the Chief's special squad, had originally been assigned to the eleven-to-seven shift and knew Malcolm. They respected him. A couple of them were troubled by the exchange between Malcolm and the Chief. But it wasn't the first confrontation, many thought, and probably wouldn't be the last.

They continued forward. The chief had promised them bonuses and promotions. In the back of their minds, however, Malcolm's concern gave them some pause. In their early days on the force, Malcolm had gotten many of them out of tough spots. The Chief's setup, especially the order for using rifles, had many of them second guessing him, and they were glad Lt. Malcolm had shown up. But they continued forward as ordered, locked and loaded.

8:12 P.M.

FROM THE CUPOLA, OF HIS MACHINE SHED, RON PUGH looked down on Simpson Village. He pointed his high-powered telescope to the intersection of Fourth and Bradley and trained his view on Jim's car. Switching to his binoculars, he spied Slick in the elm tree, adjacent to Simpson Village. Switching back to his *telescope, he watched Jim walk towards his car, and was thrilled to see the car surrounded by Stones.* **Oh, this is perfect***, he chortled to himself.*

With a growing sense of fear, Jim approached his convertible, regretting that he had left the top down. He strode briskly to his car, brushed past Tommy, and opened the driver's side door. As he opened it, Tommy kicked the door shut.

"Where you going, Whitey? You in our neighborhood, and we tell you when you can come and when you can go. Right now, you ain't goin' nowhere. What you think about that, you White mother?" Tommy taunted.

Seeing the hate in Tommy's eyes, Jim spoke softly in reply. "Tommy, you know me. I'm just a reporter. I'm nobody. Your fight is not with me. Now, if you will excuse me, I have a story to write."

"Excuse me? That what you saying to me? Excuse me? Well, I don't excuse you. You going to answer some questions, White boy. Rufus is dead, man. You dealing with me."

"Tommy, I'm leaving," Jim said forcefully, but Tommy responded by grabbing Jim's shirt, pinning him against the side of his car, "You ain't goin nowhere."

The crowd outside the church quieted to a whisper. Maybelle and Haley, who were walking to their home, stopped in the middle of the intersection of Fourth and Bradley and watched the confrontation.

"Don't you think about going over there, little girl," Maybelle cautioned her daughter.

Haley responded, "I am not a little girl, Mama. I'm going to help Jim."

Maybelle grabbed and held her and said, "No you're

not. I see your brother walking over there. He will get it settled down."

From his leafy perch in the tree 200 yards from Jim's car, Slick Beck checked his sights and his magazine, cleared his safety, took deep slow breaths, and waited.

Pugh, in his cupola, viewed the verbal battle between Jim and Tommy and was disappointed he couldn't hear anything. Maybe the Stones will take care of that son-of-a-bitch Monaghan, Pugh thought.

Jim broke away from Tommy, opened his car door and jumped in.

He turned on his ignition, but the car failed to start, as it did occasionally.

With the young Stones surrounding the car hurling insult after insult, Jim tried not to panic. *Start Car! Start!* He kept trying, but the car would not turn over. *Where are the police? Where's Reverend Jefferson? Where's Edgar?* Jim's fear increased as he fumbled with the ignition.

A wall of angry young men, some with handguns, surrounded Jim and glared at him. Jim could understand their frustration and their hostility, and he knew their anger was not directed specifically at him. But he was there. He was vulnerable. And he was an easy target for their hopelessness.

Frantically, Jim wondered, *Where the hell are the cops? They're usually all over this neighborhood.*

Freddy, one of the Stones, yelled, "Hey, White ass, why can't your car start? You scared White boy? We gonna kick your ass, you White mother! Your momma's a whore. You a bastard." Two of the Stones pulled their handguns from their pants and aimed them at Jim.

It was not the first time, Jim, had faced guns. He'd had a gun to his head in Calvary Cemetery, and Lloyd

Collier had aimed a gun at him at the Members Country Club.

This time, Jim thought, *I am in real trouble. Where the hell are the police? Where is Edgar? Where is Reverend Jefferson?* The only thing Jim could do was pray.

39

8:13 P.M

R efusing to leave the scene, Lt. Malcolm ignored the Chief's orders and walked with three officers from his regular shift down Fourth Street towards the church. They had their .38 caliber pistols unhooked from their holsters. "Be calm men. Be calm," Malcolm cautioned. Then he radioed the Chief.

"Chief, that's Jim Monaghan in that convertible. I know the car and that's Jim. The Stones have him surrounded. Order the men in and get him out of there. He looks like he is in trouble."

"I told you to get off and stay off the radio, Malcolm. Men, ignore what Malcolm said. Continue walking slowly and be locked and ready. Besides, Monaghan is with his people. He'll be okay," the Chief sneered sarcastically.

8:14 P.M.

OUT OF THE CORNER OF HIS EYE, JIM SAW EDGAR

Johnson running across the intersection. Wearing a hooded sweatshirt, Edgar's head was completely covered. He vaulted over the hood of Jim's car and landed next to Tommy. Jim's sigh of relief was audible.

"Tommy, what the hell are you doing? Break this up, and break it up now," Edgar ordered.

"You ain't the leader of the Stones," Tommy countered. "I'm the leader, and what I say goes. Rufus is dead, man. Those White cops killed him. We Stones, we gonna light up this town like our brothers in Watts. We gonna start with this White mother.

"So, get your ass back to your house, Edgar. Your momma's over there. Go see your momma." Some of the Stones surrounding the car laughed, while others looked nervously at one another.

Edgar, who towered over Tommy but was not as thick, punched him in the mouth. Tommy went down on one knee but jumped back up. Two of the young Stones grabbed Edgar, holding him for Tommy, who pummeled him.

Edgar, stunned, fell between the curb and Jim's car. Kicking Edgar, Tommy said," Now let me tell you again, Edgar. I'm the leader of this group! I've had it with you and this White bastard"

The Stones started rocking Jim's car as he desperately ground his faulty ignition.

"I think it's time we offed this mother," Tommy shouted. "Freddy, off this white son of a bitch."

Freddy, slightly built and only sixteen, was one of the younger Stones. He pulled out his .357-magnum handgun, looked at Tommy, and asked, "You sure, man? You want me to shoot this bastard? They're a lot of people around here. They will see me shooting," Freddy pleaded.

"You want to be a real Stone? Be a man and shoot the mother," Tommy commanded.

8:15 P.M

THE CHIEF AND HIS SIX SPECIAL PATROLMEN WALKED briskly through the barren field, sidestepping trash, guns ready, watching the crowd of Stones surrounding Jim's car. Because of the crowd around the car and the people still in front of the church, it was difficult to see clearly, but the officers heard the shouting as they approached the sidewalk adjacent to Fourth Street.

Slick Beck kept muttering, "They have to clear out. I'm sure that's Monaghan. That's his car and I have seen him up close at the Country Club and in the driveway of the farm. I know that's him." Then he looked at the photo he had of Edgar, and he was certain. "That nigger on the ground is Edgar. Oh, happy day!" he muttered into the radio microphone attached to his headset.

Pugh, in his cupola, radioed back, "Agreed. Man, this is perfect. Get ready, Slick. If you happen to hit a few of the blackies, don't worry about it. There is always collateral damage in these situations."

Freddy, more scared of Tommy than of being caught, shakily held his gun and aimed it at Jim.

"Freddy don't do it," Jim begged. And he started to pray.

"Shoot him!" Tommy ordered. He was joined by other Stones, who chanted, "Shoot him! Shoot him!"

Freddy, standing in front of Jim's car, put both hands on the heavy gun, closed his eyes and shot.

As he pulled the trigger, the heavy barrel of the gun dipped, and the bullet pierced the front hood going through the front trunk of the rear-engine Fiat and splattered on the ground underneath the car.

One of the officers, hearing the gunshot, radioed the Chief. "Chief, was that a gunshot? Should we move in?"

"I don't think it was a gunshot, I think it was a car backfiring," the Chief said. "Just keep approaching the scene but go slowly. Be ready. I don't like what I'm seeing."

Hearing the gunshot, Haley, pulled away from her mother, ran across the street, pulled apart two of the Stones, who were blocking the passenger door, jumped in the car and crawled into Jim's lap. The diminutive Haley had both knees outside Jim's legs and was facing him.

"Haley, get out of here!" Jim pleaded. "This is dangerous! Get out of here! You don't want to be involved with me."

"Shut up, Jim," Haley said. She turned to Tommy, her voice rising with every syllable, "Tommy, you and your thugs get out of here. Jim Monaghan is a good man and he is a friend of my family. My momma cooks Sunday dinner for him all the time. He is honest, and he wouldn't hurt anyone.

"I don't know who the hell you are mad at, Tommy. You are always mad, but this is the wrong person to be mad at. Rufus liked Jim. He protected him from you that night last summer. You leave him alone."

Edgar pulled himself up from the curb and said, "Ok, Ok, Everyone, this is over. No one has been hurt. Jim isn't going to press charges against Freddy, are you Jim?"

Jim shook his head.

With Haley in his lap, Jim reached around her, grasped the key in the ignition, and tried turning it again.

Magically, the car finally started.

"Edgar, I'm leaving and I'm driving out of here. If these guys don't get out of my way, I'm going to run over them, but trust me, I am getting out of here now."

Opening his driver's side door, Jim urged, "Haley get out of the car."

"You can drop me off in front of my house, Jim. I'm not leaving until you are out of here," Haley said.

"Ok. It's over," Edgar conceded. "Guys, get out of his way." But Tommy shoved Edgar out of the way.

"Screw you, Edgar! I'm the boss. I said shoot this bastard. If Freddy can't do it, someone else do it." Four older stones pulled their handguns out as Jim slipped his car into first gear and started to slowly pull forward. "Shoot him!" Tommy's shout ended with Edgar's powerful punch.

"Leave, Jim! Leave now!" Edgar shouted. Seeing Tommy on his knees, the Stones put their guns down and parted in front of Jim's car. Jim slowly engaged his clutch and started to ease away.

"Bullshit, it's over!" Tommy yelled as he jumped up from the curb. He pulled his .357 magnum from the back of his pants and aimed it at Jim's head. As he started to shoot, Edgar grabbed his arm and pulled it down. The shot rang out flattening the front tire of Jim's car.

40

8:16 P.M

P ugh, *watching the Stones move back from Jim's car with lowered guns shouted, "Now, Slick, Now!"*

Slick Beck, perched in the crook of two branches, saw the Stones part in front of Jim's car. He sighted Jim perfectly, took a deep breath, and prepared to take his shot.

Haley watching her brother struggle with Tommy hugged Jim, screaming, "Get out of here, Jim! Get out of here!" Jim's car died again.

Slick pulled the trigger just as Haley hugged Jim. The shot pierced her back. "Shit," Beck said, and he squeezed off another shot hitting Haley in the back of the head.

Haley fell out of Jim's arms ending up half in Jim's lap and half outside the car. With Haley's blood and parts of her head splattered over his face, Jim screamed. "No! No! No!"

Edgar, stunned, reached over to his sister when two more shots rang out, hitting Jim twice in the chest. He slumped on top of Haley. Jim looked up into Edgar's eyes and, fighting for breath, gasped, "They are after you, too. Go to the farm," before he slipped into unconsciousness.

Edgar ran into the church and out the back door.

8:17 P.M.

"Shots fired! Shots fired!" the Chief yelled into his radio. "Advance. They have guns. Take out anyone who has a gun. Take out anyone who has a gun." Buckner commanded.

Buckner and his special force quickly advanced, while Lt. Malcolm and his three officers sprinted down Fourth Street, towards the crowd around Jim's car, but they were still a long distance away. Lt. Malcolm yelled into his radio,

"Hold your fire, men, until you see people with rifles. Those last shots sounded like a rifle. Those kids don't have rifles. Hold your fire unless you are in harm's way." The officers with Malcolm and Buckner and his crew started to sprint.

"Ignore Malcolm. Shoot anyone with a gun," the Chief angrily spat into his radio.

Buckner and his six officers stopped at the edge of the field, directly across Fourth Street from Jim's convertible. The Stones were frozen in place gasping at the blood pouring from Jim's chest and the back of Haley's head, a mass of hair, blood, and skin.

Buckner yelled! "See the Stones! They have guns and bandoliers. Shoot them! Buckner and his officers opened fire with their rifles. They fired indiscriminately.

Tommy raised his 357 and shot at the oncoming officers.

Like bowling pins, Stones fell to the ground, as did several bystanders who were watching in horror.

Lt. Malcolm shouted into his radio, "Stop! Stop! Stop shooting!" But Buckner's squad kept firing.

It was over in under two minutes.

Buckner's contingent converged, guns drawn, on Jim's car and the front of the church. Bodies were strewn on the Church front lawn, the sidewalks, and the street. Blood pooled in the gutter. And it was deathly quiet.

The Stones who were not shot and who had not run away, knelt on the ground with their hands up. Residents cried, screamed, and tried to help their fallen neighbors. Soon, ambulance and fire engine sirens echoed up and down Fourth Street and Bradley Avenue as aid vehicles raced to the scene.

Maybelle Johnson had run across the street when the shooting started. Fear-stricken, she slowed when she approached Jim's car. Seeing Haley, she screamed, "My baby, my baby!"

She pulled her daughter into her arms. Maybelle knew her daughter was dead. She cried out again and again. Soon, she was surrounded by friends trying to comfort her.

Rev. Jefferson ran out of the church, saw the carnage, and fell to his knees.

"No, God, no. Please God, don't let anyone die."

Chief Buckner peered into Jim's car. Seeing Jim laying half outside his car with blood oozing from his chest, the Chief said, "Well that's a shame."

Lt. Malcolm was seconds behind Buckner and heard the Chief. "That's a shame? That's a shame? That's what you have to say? For Christ's sake, Chief, this is…this is hell! I can't describe it!

"And all you can say is 'That's a shame.' For God's sake, that's Jim Monaghan lying there. What kind of man are you?" Malcolm yelled. "Look around. There are dead and wounded people everywhere. What were you thinking ordering the men in with their rifles? What were you thinking? This was a massacre!"

"Be careful, Malcolm. You're on thin ice. If you don't shut your mouth, I'll suspend you without pay."

"For what? "

"For insubordination, that's what."

"This all could have been prevented, Chief. You know that. How could you give an order to shoot before you even knew what was happening? Your guys never should have been carrying rifles. It damn near seems like you wanted this to happen!" Malcolm exclaimed.

"That's it, Malcolm, you're suspended. If you don't get your ass out of here, I will have you arrested for obstructing an investigation. Now shut your mouth and get the hell out of here."

Malcolm walked around the car, helped Maybelle with Haley, and held Jim in his arms. "Hold on, Jim, I'll get to the bottom of this. But damn it, I'm going to need your help. Now you pull through. Do you hear me, Jim? You hang on. Come on, Ken, get here! Get here now!"

Four ambulances pulled up. They represented two different companies, but all deferred to Ken Simon's leadership and direction. Soon the Lincoln Fire Department pulled in with four trucks, including their medical unit.

Simon and his staff quickly determined who was dead, and who was injured. Keeping the dead where they had fallen, Simon ordered triage for those who were injured. There were eight.

The policemen raced to the scene and helped the ambulance crew care for the injured. Many officers were crying and one or two were vomiting at the carnage.

When he saw his friend Jim, lying in a pool of blood,

Simon, who thought he had seen everything, found himself gasping. He pulled a towel out of his pocket and pressed it on the bullet holes in Jim's chest trying to stop the bleeding. "Get me big gauze pads and get a gurney now!" Simon screamed. "We need to get him to the hospital!"

8:23 P.M.

Slick Beck stayed in his perch and watched with satisfaction the scene at Fourth and Bradley. Switching from his scope, he brought up his high power 15 x 56 Leica binoculars and watched the results of the police attack. Like shooting fish in a barrel, he thought. He climbed down from the tree, regretting the fact that he didn't get a shot at Edgar, but there would be other chances.

Pugh, in his cupola, watched the entire scene switching from his telescope to his binoculars. As he climbed down the steps, he thought, Perfect. Now, those mongrels will know who's in charge.

41

After shooting photos at a Hamilton University softball game, Art Wilks monitored the police radio in his car as he drove towards the office. He left his car for a few minutes to pick up a burger and chocolate milk shake at his favorite Steak and Shake restaurant.

Seems like a quiet night on the crime front. Not much news for tomorrow morning's paper, he thought as he got back in the car.

Then he heard the Chief's voice on the radio. "We need more back up at Fourth and Bradley. We need more ambulances. And alert the morgue. We got a lot of dead ones here."

Startled, Wilks drove as fast as he could towards the church where he knew the big meeting was going on. *I hope Pete is there and he got some pictures. Jesus, I hope he's okay. What about Jim? I wonder if he went to the meeting. Of course, he did, I hope he is okay, too,* Wilks thought.

Breaking all speed records, Wilks pulled in behind a police cruiser, hopped out of his car, and started shooting photos. He saw Jim's car and almost dropped his camera.

Next to the car, he saw Maybelle cradling Haley in her arms and sobbing. "She's dead, oh Lord, she's dead. My baby is dead."

Jim, covered with blood, was sprawled next to his bullet-riddled car.

Simon and his team had applied pressure gauze pads on his chest and shoulder. They were trying to get him stable for the trip to the hospital. Lt. Malcolm's face was ashen. His tear-filled eyes met Wilks, and he slowly shook his head.

Simon was uncharacteristically frantic, shouting orders to his men. As they placed Jim on a gurney, Wilks grabbed Simon and asked, "How bad is he?"

Simon grimly answered, "Bad, Art, very bad. Those are huge bullet holes, and if they yawed, he's not going to make it."

Wilks ran past Rev. Jefferson who was still on his knees praying. Jefferson had convinced other residents to join him in prayer. Wilks turned and said,

"Where's your phone? Where's your phone?"

Jefferson pointed to the church door and said, "In my office."

Wilks dashed in, grabbed the phone, and called Brad Hauser at home.

"Brad, get ahold of yourself, because I have very bad news. Haley is dead and there are a bunch of others who were at the meeting who are dead or injured. Jim has been shot, and Simon says it's not good."

Hauser hung up the phone, told his wife he would be late, and raced to the paper. The first deadline for Saturday morning's paper was in less than three hours.

Wilks called Audrey at home. Getting no answer, he called the Lincoln Country Club. The receptionist confirmed Audrey was there and said she would bring her to the phone.

"My, my Art, this must be important for you to call me on Friday night. What's going on that you need to talk to your publisher?"

"Get ahold of yourself, Audrey. I have terrible news. Something happened at the community meeting at the church in Simpson Village tonight. You know the meeting Jim wrote about and you printed a page one editorial on? It all went bad."

"What do you mean it went bad?"

"Audrey, it's like a war zone here. There are bodies everywhere. Haley and a lot of people are dead. It's mostly the kids who are in the Stones, but there are others as well. I don't yet know who is dead and who's alive. But it's worse, Audrey, much worse."

"Dear God, tell me, Art."

"It's Jim, Audrey. He was shot, and Ken Simon told me it's very bad. He's rushing him to Mercy Hospital. Audrey, it's tragic!"

All Wilks heard on the phone was a cry of anguish and a click.

Audrey's cry echoed through the dining room and all eyes were focused on Audrey.

Ashen, with tears in her eyes, she strode purposefully to the Fowler's table and stood next to Jenny's chair. "Jenny, be strong, Honey, be very strong."

Jenny, shocked, stood and reached out her arms to Audrey, but Audrey stopped her. She put her hands-on Jenny's shoulders.

"There has been a shooting, Honey, and Jim has

been shot. They say it's bad and they have taken him to Mercy Hospital."

Jenny gasped, her knees wobbled, and she almost collapsed. Audrey hugged her and said, "Honey, I'm going to the hospital right now. Do you want to go with me?"

Harrison Fowler said, "No, she's not going to the hospital. Sit down, Jenny, and finish your cake. For God's sake, it's your mother's birthday. Audrey, I'm surprised at you. I am sure he will be okay. These things get exaggerated, you know."

"I'm going with you, Audrey." Jenny turned to her father. His callous comment, the months of criticism of Jim, and his pontifications exploded Jenny's composure. "I hate you, Dad."

As Audrey and Jenny ran out of the dining room, Mayor Weir, walked over to Fowler's table and asked, "What's going on, Harrison?"

"Oh, women, they get upset about anything. Apparently, there was a problem at that dumb meeting tonight. You know the one where Hansen was going to promise to build some sporting stuff. Well, apparently some things happened, and Jim Monaghan was shot. I mean, I don't know what the fuss is about. He'll be fine, I'm sure."

Weir turned pale and grabbed the back of the chair Jenny had just vacated, as his knees weakened. Not responding to Fowler, he stabilized himself, went back to his table and called the waiter over. "Please get me a double shot of whiskey, and get it quickly," he ordered.

"Darling," his wife said, "what's wrong with you? We are having white wine tonight to go with the fish. Drinking whiskey will affect your taste buds. Are you sure you want whiskey?"

Weir didn't respond. He thought, *No, No, it can't be. Monaghan couldn't be shot. Wait, maybe one of the Stones shot him.* But a feeling deep inside him told him, the Stones didn't shoot Jim Monaghan.

42

K en Simon rushed his friend the three miles to
Mercy Hospital. While he drove, his two
assistants knelt in the back of the ambulance, keeping
pressure on the two gaping bullet holes in Jim's chest.

"He's bleeding from his back, Ken," his chief
assistant called out. "I think the bullets went through him
or they yawed, and they are all over his insides. Let's
hope they went straight through.

Simon, fighting tears, stepped harder on the gas
pedal and grabbed the radio. "Mercy ER, this is Simon,
I'm bringing in a multiple gunshot victim, male, age
twenty-four. He's in bad shape. Call everyone in. We
have more injured coming in right behind me. Call
Doctors Ross and Cunningham and tell them Jim
Monaghan is the gunshot victim I am bringing in. I'll be
there in two minutes."

The reaction in the ER was instantaneous. It had
been a quiet evening for a Friday night, but the staff
mobilized quickly. Janice Bratton, supervising nurse of
the three-to-eleven shift called the Hospital Nursing

Supervisor. It was the supervisor's job to coordinate all activities in the case of an emergency.

The supervisor's greatest fear was to hear Code Gray. It meant all available personnel should report immediately to the Emergency Room, where multiple patients were being transported. On Friday night, the hospital supervisor was Kara Morgan.

"Kara, we have an all-out emergency, Code Gray. We are going to need everyone we can get. Please mobilize the other departments. Call the night shift in early and tell them to get in here right away. "Janice barked. "And Kara, call Sister Mary Mark and tell her Jim Monaghan has been shot and will be in the ER in just a few minutes."

"Will do," Kara confirmed, and she immediately contacted nurses from the other departments. She directed them to leave a skeleton staff in their wards and to send the balance of the nursing staff to the Emergency Room, where they should scrub, don ER scrubs, and be ready for anything.

Janice alerted her staff to the influx of emergency patients and said staff from the other departments would be coming down to help. She then called Doctors Ross and Cunningham.

"You won't reach Cunningham at home," a smiling Dr. Cunningham said. "I'm here. I just finished up a surgery. What's going on, and why is everyone scurrying about?"

The wail of an ambulance siren punctuated the air, and two nurses and two ER doctors rushed to the ambulance entrance, where Jim Monaghan was being rushed in on a gurney.

Ken Simon updated the ER doctors. "We hung a saline drip, and we used gauze pads to keep pressure on the wounds, but he is bleeding from the back, too, and we haven't done anything with that. We just discovered it on the way in," Simon said.

"What are his vitals?" the ER doctor asked.

"Not good," Simon said.

"Damnit, Ken, what are his vitals?" the ER doctor yelled as Jim was transferred from the ambulance gurney to the ER rolling table and moved into the number one ER patient bay.

Simon yelled out, "On the way in, his pressure was sixty-five over thirty-seven and his heart rate was 170—way high. Respiration rate thirty-five to forty–not horrible.

"I know what vitals mean, Ken. Now do you have any more information that might help us, you know size of the bullet or anything."

Turning away from Simon, the ER Doctor shouted. "We don't know his blood type, so get some O negative stat," the doctor called out. "Make sure it is a bucket pressure bag. It's obvious he's lost a lot of red."

Other doctors hurried into Bay One and started to help. Two nurses using scissors cut off all of Jim's clothes. They put them in a bag and threw the bag in a corner.

"Hey, don't lose those clothes, they could be evidence," Simon interjected. The medical team ignored Ken, so he grabbed the bag and gave it to his team. He told them to put it in his ambulance.

More sirens blared, and Ken's hand-held radio barked. "Simon, we have more injured to transport. Get back here as soon as you can!"

The ER doctor frustrated with the distractions, told Simon, "Ken, get the hell out of here. Let us do our job."

Wearing fresh scrubs, Dr. Cunningham hurried into Bay One. "How is he, folks?" he asked.

The newest ER doctor replied, "He had bad vitals, but they have stabilized a bit in the last couple of minutes. But these bullet holes are concerning. They are in the upper chest cavity, left side. They missed the heart, but I see specks near the lung and there is a lot of bleeding.

"Using that new machine, we did a quick x-ray and we don't see any bullets, but we see a lot of bits all over the place. That machine is new, and I don't know how good it is. God, I hope it wasn't one of those bullets that explodes when it hits something."

"It's called a yaw, young man," Cunningham said. "If it did yaw, we have serious problems. If the bullets went straight through and didn't hit any of the major organs, he will be lucky. But we don't guess at this.

"We are going to have to go in and look for ourselves. Get him stable as quickly as you can and get him to the OR. Let's use the new OR upstairs. You know, the same one we used for Jack Wilson. And let's get him stable STAT."

Cunningham went out of the bay and asked Janice if she had reached Dr. Ross.

"Not yet. We're not having much luck getting our other on-duty staff down here either, so I called the nursing dorm and asked for some third-year students to get here as soon as they can. They'll be able to help out, and it will be a great education for them."

"Keep trying Ross. I'm going to need him. Monaghan may have bullet debris throughout his chest cavity." As he turned, Cunningham saw three more gurneys being rolled in from the newly arrived ambulances. All the patients were covered with blood.

The Mercy Hospital emergency triage program took charge. Living up to Mercy's stellar reputation, teams of doctors and nurses were ready for each patient. Determining the condition of each patient was a priority. Each person was checked for vitals, location of bullet holes, and degree of consciousness. Those with gunshots to the legs and arms were put on hold, while those with wounds in the chest cavity or the head were immediately treated.

43

Simon arrived back at Fourth and Bradley and was surprised at the number of policemen who were standing around. *God, there must be thirty cops,* he thought. They had put up a perimeter around the church and closed Fourth Avenue and Bradley Street for two blocks in all directions.

Simon and his team found two people swaddled with homemade bandages on their injured arms. "Where are the other injured?" Simon asked.

Rev. Jefferson answered, "You took Jim, and three others went by ambulance. Two more were in bad shape. One of my church members has a pick-up truck, so they took them to Mercy Hospital in the back of the truck."

Good Lord, thought Simon, *I have never seen anything like this.* He examined Jim's car and said to Rev. Jefferson, "Look at Jim's car. There must be fifty bullet holes in it. Man, it's totaled."

"I know, and there are seven dead people in front of my church. There, next to Jim's car, is little Haley. She is in her mother's arms and Maybelle won't let her go.

Maybelle is inconsolable, and I understand why. Haley was a wonderful, beautiful, and good girl. And we have a mother, dead, lying on the street.

"It's Sylvia. She's only 32 years old. She has three little children, oldest is eight. She cleans houses for the rich people over at Country Club Estates. There is Sophie. She is everyone's grandmother. She was the best cook in my church. When we had a potluck, everyone would want her casseroles.

"Over there are two of the finest men in Lincoln. Both served in Korea. Imagine living through Korea and then dying outside my church. Henry worked at Mr. Hansen's plant. Clarence was everyone's handyman. He could fix anything. Anytime I had a problem, I would call Clarence, and he would say, 'Don't worry Reverend, I will get my toolbox and be right over.'

"Both men were grandfathers, loved by their kids and grandkids. What a waste! What a waste," Reverend Jefferson said, his voice quivering. "All these good folks have been coming to my church for years. They were God-fearing people. They were good people. I pray they are in heaven resting in the arms of our Heavenly Father.

"And look over there in the street. We have two young men with their bodies ripped apart by bullets.

"They were good boys. Sure, they had some problems. But to die that way? My God, My God!" Reverend Jefferson cried as he fell to his knees sobbing.

Two more ambulances, both competitors, pulled up. Simon's assistants told the drivers the people they were treating did not appear to be seriously injured but should be transported to the hospital for further evaluation. Simon told his team to let the other ambulances take them. He wanted to stay and help console the families of the dead.

As the ambulances sped away with the last two injured people, Simon glanced across the street at Simpson Village.

A crowd was gathering. About 100 and growing. They watched as the police roamed around the crime scene. Every media outlet in town had people on the scene. Both radio and television outlets in town were broadcasting live.

Chief Buckner was giving live interviews. Simon heard the Chief say, "We ain't having no Watts here in Lincoln."

Buckner broke away from the media, retrieved a bullhorn from one of the police cars and addressed the crowd forming in the middle of the intersection. The crowd had amassed, spilling over onto the barren city block.

"Okay, there's nothing to see here. Disperse. Disperse now. Go back to your homes. I don't want to arrest any of you, but if you don't break up this crowd, you are going to force me to," the chief ordered.

"We ain't doing nuthin' wrong," one of the residents called out.

The Chief quickly replied, "I said disperse now. I mean it, people. Get back to your homes." The crowd didn't move.

As the chief glared at the crowd, an elderly man hobbled up to him. "I don't mean no disrespect, Chief, and I ain't no troublemaker, but there is something you should know," he said.

"What's that?" Buckner asked brusquely.

"Well, I was standing beside Number Four, that one right there." He pointed across the street to his residence, which was located exactly at the intersection of Fourth and Bradley. "When that shot rang out, I ducked, because it was coming from behind me, like from that big elm there on the north edge of the Village. Then, three more shots, bang, bang, bang! They all came from that tree," the old man declared.

Chief Buckner, in an unusual move, put his arm around the old man's shoulder and said. "You're an old man, and I know, in chaotic situations, like this it is easy to be confused. Now, I appreciate you telling me this. But I know how easy it is to be confused."

"I ain't confused, Chief. I was in the War. I know what a rifle sounds like, and it was a rifle shot from that big tree over there on Pugh's farm."

The chief squeezed the man's shoulder tighter and said. "Listen, old man, you have done your duty. You have told me, and I will investigate. But the way this works, you don't tell anyone else or I will have you arrested for obstruction and you will go to jail. You understand me, old man?"

The old man, now intimidated, said, "Yes sir," and shuffled back to the crowd.

As the Chief turned back to the gathered media, he stopped when he heard one voice, then a couple, then hundreds sang out:

44

"Amazing Grace, how sweet the sound. That saved a wretch like me. I once was lost, but now, I'm found. Was blind, but now I see."

Rev. Jefferson with tear-filled eyes, rose from his knees and joined the crowd. Simon, moved by the scene, also walked over, as did his assistants.

They all sang softly.

Buckner went back to the news media and continued with the radio and television interviews. He rambled on about the need to nip the potential riot in the bud.

"We knew the residents here would be upset over the death of Rufus Burton. When I saw the Stones come into the meeting with their guns, I knew I had to act. I had my team ready. When the shooting started, I knew it was the beginning of a riot, so I stopped it.

" If we hadn't acted, it would be just like Watts, out there in California. Watts started slowly and now look at it. That ain't gonna happen in Lincoln. The police have control here."

As the Chief talked about quelling a riot, the notes

of *Amazing Grace* floated in the background mingled with crying and the screams of anguish as family members knelt over their dead loved ones. Soon hearses from funeral homes arrived to take the bodies away.

One of the police officers told the grieving families the bodies had to be taken to the county morgue, because autopsies had to be performed on all the dead.

Maybelle refused to take her arms from around Haley. The funeral home representatives and the policemen talked softly to her telling her, they had to take Haley away. She refused. An officer walked over to where the crowd had gathered and asked Reverend Jefferson for help.

"What's the hurry? Let her hug her baby," Reverend Jefferson said.

Reporters asked about Jim Monaghan and who shot him. Buckner said it was obvious the Stones did it "They were surrounding his car. "There would have been more innocent people killed or injured, if we hadn't acted. We took the Stones out and the shooting stopped."

One of the reporters noted only two Stones appeared to have been killed, but five people, who weren't Stones, were being taken to the morgue. Was the Chief saying the Stones shot five of their neighbors?

"Well, we know for sure, they shot that young black girl and the reporter, and my men only shot the Stones, so yes, they shot their neighbors."

The reporter argued that it didn't make sense that the Stones would shoot their neighbors and not the police.

One of the reporters asked, "Chief, if the police are coming from the field, across the street from the south, firing their guns, why would the Stones shoot in the opposite direction and hit their neighbors? Are you sure none of your men shot those regular citizens?"

"Not a chance. My men only shot at those with guns, and that was the Stones. The Stones must have shot the others."

The reporters pursued Buckner as he walked away. Finally, he snarled, "I'm not answering any more questions. You are interfering in a crime scene. Get out of here or I will have you arrested for obstruction."

Buckner looked over at the crowd, and to his dismay, he saw Lt. Malcolm and a few police officers singing with the crowd. The Chief glared at them, walked across the field to his car, turned on his flashers and drove back through the field into the intersection of Fourth and Bradley. Looking to his right, he saw the gathered crowd, *Assholes*, he thought.

He turned to his left and saw the carnage in front of the church and smiled. Humming softly, he stepped on his accelerator and sped away with his back to the singing crowd and those gathered in front of the church kneeling and crying over the dead.

After Buckner left, Lt. Malcolm instructed his officers to collect the handguns left on the ground by the Peace Stones. Later, one of his officers pulled Malcolm aside.

"Lieutenant, only two of these guns are warm. One was next to where Tommy was shot and another one was in the front of Monaghan's car. The gun in front of the car had only one bullet missing. It was fired once. The gun we found near Tommy had three bullets left in its chamber. Only two guns were fired. I don't think the Stones fired their guns at all. Their guns are cold. All the bullet casings we found were from rifles and, Lieutenant, the casings are from bullets we use in our rifles."

Malcolm told the officer to include the information

in his after-action report. As Malcolm left, he thought, *My God, all these people were shot by the police. But those bullet holes in Jim, were big, and had to come from a rifle. The Chief's people were coming behind Jim, from the park, and Jim was shot from someone in the front of his car. How could that have happened? Who shot him?*

45

Managed chaos reigned in the Mercy Hospital Emergency Room.

Eight gunshot victims, four seriously injured and four with non-life-threatening wounds were being treated.

Dr. Cunningham worked feverishly on Jim, prepping him for surgery. Cunningham was frustrated, as other victims were brought in and parts of his team working on Jim left to help the newly arrived victims.

Cunningham was surprised, when he looked up, to see a Franciscan Sister of Mercy in a completely white habit, maintaining pressure on one of Jim's wounds.

"Well, Sister, I didn't expect to see you here," Dr. Cunningham said.

"Well, Doctor, did you forget I'm a registered nurse?" Sister Mary Mark replied with a sad smile. "We're short staffed and I'm helping out. We should get some more folks here in about half an hour. I can still help, you know."

"His breathing is labored. I think we have a collapsed lung. I'm going to put a tube in, so watch yourself,"

Cunningham warned. He inserted the tube, temporarily lost control of it, and blood spewed all over Jim, Cunningham, Sister Mary Mark, and two other nurses.

"There, it's draining and that's good, but let's get another bucket of O negative and make sure it's a pressure bag," Cunningham ordered.

With the influx of nurses from other departments and the nursing students coming to assist, the immediate crisis passed as all patients were being attended.

"Let's just hope nothing else happens in the next hour, and we will be okay," Janice Bratton said.

As she walked towards the entrance to the emergency room, she heard a car screech to a stop.

"Hey, you can't park there, lady," the security guard shouted as two women jumped out of the car.

"Then please move it for me," said Audrey, tossing him the keys as she and Jenny raced into the building.

Spotting Janice, Audrey asked, "Where is Jim Monaghan, and how is he doing?"

"He's in Bay One. They are prepping him for surgery. He's in rough shape, but we have the best working on him. Dr. Cunningham is with him now, and Dr. Ross is on his way. He even has a special nurse with him, Sister Mary Mark. But you can't see him now. You will have to wait," Janice urged.

Jenny, hearing Jim was in Bay One, frantically looked around the ER. She walked briskly to Bay One, pulled the curtain back and stopped, aghast. Jim, a doctor, nurses, and a nun all in white were all splattered with blood. Jim's blood. Jenny blanched.

Then her eyes fell to Jim, lying naked on the hospital gurney with blood all over his chest, IV needles in both arms, an oxygen mask on his face, and a myriad of tubes and wires attached to his body. Jenny started to cry.

Audrey wrapped a protective arm around her and said, "Don't worry, Jenny. Jim is in good hands."

A nurse told them to leave, but Jenny and Audrey refused. Sister Mary Mark looked sternly at Audrey, "Audrey you and that young lady must leave. We are trying to save Jim's life, and you are in the way. Now please back out."

Jenny and Audrey moved back a few steps, out of the way, but were still able to observe.

The heart rate monitor tracking Jim's heart rate was beeping slowly. Looking at the readout, Audrey thought, *his heart rate can't be thirty. I must get Jenny out of here now.* Then the monitor beeped and flat lined. Audrey knew immediately, as did Dr. Cunningham and Sister Mary Mark, that Jim's heart had stopped beating. Cunningham started pounding Jim's chest, and other doctors came rushing in.

"What's going on?" Jenny screamed. "What's going on?"

"Audrey, get her out of here!" yelled Sister Mary Mark.

46

An uneasy quiet settled over the deserted intersection at Fourth and Bradley.

The door to the sanctuary of the Disciples of Christ Church was locked, and the windows were dark. Reverend Jefferson was alone in his sanctuary, on his knees, crying and praying.

At Simpson Village, families struggled with their grief. Unable to explain the inexplicable, they cried, some prayed. The memory of the dead, and injured, and the carnage of a few hours earlier stifled any thoughts of immediate revenge.

The bullet-riddled car of Jim Monaghan, his beloved Fiat Spider convertible, was the primary evidence of what had happened hours before. Over fifty bullet holes pierced the body of the car and two shot out tires flattened in silent reminder.

An occasional police car cruised the neighborhood. One officer, stopping at the intersection of Fourth and Bradley, looked at Jim's car and just shook his head before driving on.

Meanwhile at the hospital, chaos ensued and intensified in Bay One of the ER.

Audrey tried to pull Jenny further away, but she dug in, and they didn't move. Within seconds, a doctor rushed into the room pushing a crash cart with a defibrillator on top. The doctor brought the cart to the table and pulled out the paddles attached to the defibrillator.

He placed them on Jim's chest and yelled "Clear!" and everyone moved back from the table. "Now!" he shouted, and an electrical charge went through the paddles and into Jim. His body lifted off the table and then fell back.

"No, no, no!" Jenny screamed and began to sob.

Audrey, the doctors and the nurses stared at the heart rate monitor, which was still emitting a single high-pitched noise and was showing a flat line.

Again, the doctor placed the paddles on Jim's chest and zapped him once again. Still no change on the monitor. Again, the paddles were used. Each time, Jim's body involuntarily leapt from the table. Each time, Jenny convulsed, because she was certain Jim was dying.

After the third use of the paddles, the monitor quit emitting a solid noise and started ever so slowly to beep, and a very slight movement on the heart rate monitor screen occurred. Then it grew, and when it reached forty-five, Dr. Cunningham said, "Okay, I think we have him back. Let's move him to the OR."

As the nurses took Jim up to the OR, Dr. Cunningham approached Audrey and Jenny.

"Young lady, I am going to take really good care of him. My partner, Dr. Ross, will be here any minute, and we will do everything possible to get Mr. Monaghan back at his typewriter."

"Thank you," Jenny sobbed.

Cunningham asked Sister, "Who was that young woman with Audrey? She looks like Harrison Fowler's daughter. I think I know her from the Country Club."

"Don't worry about her. You have plenty to do," Sister answered.

47

Audrey and Jenny perched on straight-backed tan vinyl chairs in the OR Waiting Room, hoping for one of the doctors to give them an update on Jim.

Audrey had called Hugh, Jim's brother, who was on his way to the hospital.

They were occasionally visited by Sister Mary Mark, who had returned to her modest residence across the street from the hospital and put on a clean habit. Janice Bratton stopped by and introduced herself to Jenny, who recalled Jim talking about Janice. She knew Jim had dated Janice a couple of times. Red-eyed, both young women hugged. "Jim told me you were a good friend," Jenny said.

Janice smiled and said, "I'm going to the chapel for a while, and I'll be praying for him."

The operating room was not calm. Cunningham and Ross, on opposite sides of the surgery table, were assisted by four nurses and an anesthesiologist. Keeping a close watch on his vital signs, Cunningham and Ross prepared to open Jim's chest.

Using a chest-opening scalpel, they cut a straight line down Jim's chest from just below the neck to just above his navel. Pulling aside the skin and using a chest saw, they cut open the sternum and exposed the chest cavity. They used a retractor to separate his ribs. Examining Jim's heart, lungs and the tops of other internal organs, they agreed the bullet fragments had not damaged the lower organs, but some were present in his upper chest.

With forceps, they carefully plucked bullet fragment after bullet fragment from inside his chest cavity. Often, when they picked a fragment out of a vessel, the vein erupted into a bleeder. Using hemostats, they clamped the bleeders and used sponges to soak up the excess blood.

"Make sure we count the sponges and the hemostats. We don't want to leave any of them inside," Dr. Ross cautioned. The anesthesiologist kept Ross and Cunningham current on Jim's vital signs.

Back in the waiting room, Audrey tried to be upbeat telling Jenny she was sure Jim would pull through. He had the best medical care and he was a strong young man. He had a lot going for him.

Jenny was quiet, occasionally nodding to Audrey's comments. Not sure she herself believed what she was saying, Audrey stared at the entrance to the operating room where her employee and friend was fighting for his life. She closed her eyes and prayed.

The three huddled together in the harsh lighting of the waiting room, nervously watching the OR door, willing either Dr. Cunningham or Dr. Ross to appear. They were joined by Jim's brother, Hugh, who had driven the 30 miles from the family farm in record time.

Efforts to get any of the women to go to the cafeteria for coffee, go home and rest, or even to catch a quick catnap were met with a quick no and a disapproving stare.

Finally, a few minutes after midnight, Jenny, Audrey, Hugh, and Sr. Mary Mark rose stiffly when the OR door opened, and Dr. Cunningham walked out. Still in his operating scrubs, stained with blood, his face mask hanging around his neck, he went up to Jenny, who jumped out of her chair.

"You need to sit down, young lady. We haven't met, but it's obvious you care about Jim, and you have to be strong," Cunningham said.

"I'll stand," Jenny said.

"Go ahead, Doctor, tell us what his condition is," Sister Mary Mark said.

"First, Jim is alive, but he is very weak. He lost a lot of blood. As fast as we could pump it into him, he would lose it. We could not find where he was bleeding internally for quite a while. Finally, Dr. Ross found a vessel that had been nicked by a bullet fragment. When we got that stitched up, he started to retain blood. "

Jenny teetered. She was certain Dr. Cunningham was going to tell her Jim was going to die. Sister Mary Mark and Audrey took hold of her arms and helped her to a chair.

Dr. Cunningham squatted down in front of Jenny and said, "I know it sounds bad, but we will know more in twenty-four hours. Dr. Ross and I are going to get a little sleep, and then we'll go back to work on Jim, if he is stable, in the morning.

"We are both going to sleep here at the hospital, and if the nurses in the Intensive Care Unit need us, we're just in the next room. The staff in ICU are the best and they're going to take good care of him.

"He is young and healthy, and I suspect he has a

strong will to live, so let's be optimistic. We will know more in a few hours, and if he continues to be stable and his vitals remain good, we may be able to operate earlier. We need to remove the rest of the bullet fragments.

"Now, young lady, I'm telling you, go home and get some rest," Cunningham advised. He stood up, leaned over, and gave Jenny a brief hug.

As he walked away, he motioned to Sister Mary Mark. She followed him back into the OR and Cunningham told her, "I didn't want to say anything to that young lady, but I think you ought to call Msgr. Morris. He will know what to do. I know Monaghan is a Catholic, and it's time."

Sister Mary Mark nodded and went to the phone. She had made the same phone call two years ago, when life support was taken off Mary Ryan. Sister prayed Jim would pull through. She told Msgr. Morris to come in the back way and to avoid the ICU waiting room. Morris, pastor of St. Patrick's and chaplain of Mercy Hospital, had completed this task numerous times. He knew exactly what to do.

Knowing he couldn't be in the intensive care unit long, Msgr. Morris put a purple stole around his neck, took out his holy oils and made the sign of the cross in oil on Jim's forehead. He, with Sister Mary Mark, who joined him in prayer, uttered the words, "Through this holy unction, may the Lord pardon thee whatever sins or faults thou has committed." Sister Mary Mark and Msgr. Morris stepped away from Jim, said a silent prayer, and left the ICU.

Hugh was distraught himself, but he tried to distract Jenny by telling her about Jim growing up. He wasn't sure she heard a word he said. Audrey left them alone only for the few minutes it took to call Brad Hauser.

After talking with Audrey, Hauser had the last needed piece of information for his story and sent the copy, with the headlines attached, to the back shop.

The whole back shop was waiting for the story, and when the copy came back, they set it in type. Despite union rules regulating the number of hours they could work, the men stayed beyond their regular shift.

Within an hour, the first edition of Saturday morning's News Tribune rolled off the press. The men in the back shop and the printing press room grabbed the first papers off the press and read about Jim Monaghan and Haley Johnson. The hardened men, who had worked in the newspaper business for decades, had tears in their eyes when they finished reading. All put the papers under their arms, and rather than their usual stop at a tavern, they all went directly home.

48

Lincoln News Tribune
Page One Saturday August 14, 1965

Death, Carnage at Fourth and Bradley
Seven Dead, Eight Wounded at Park District
Meeting
Haley Johnson, News Tribune Employee, Killed
Jim Monaghan, News Tribune News Editor in
Grave Condition
By Brad Hauser *Managing Editor News Tribune*

Seven people were killed and eight seriously injured
when mayhem broke out at approximately 8:05 p.m.
Friday night outside the Fellowship of the Disciples of
Christ Church, at the intersection of Fourth and
Bradley in northeast Lincoln.

Haley Johnson, 19, a member of the News
Tribune's Photo Department, was killed along with
two other women and four men, two of whom were
members of the Stones, an alleged gang.

Jim Monaghan, the News Tribune's Award-Winning News Editor was shot twice and is in intensive care at Mercy Hospital. Hospital officials report his condition is grave.

Details of exactly what happened are sketchy at best, but as of one a.m. Saturday, this is what we know.

About 200 citizens of the northeast side of Lincoln attended a meeting called by Donald Hansen, president of the Lincoln Parks and Recreation Board to discuss more parks and recreation facilities for that area. Also attending were Police Chief Billy Joe Buckner and Rev Jeremiah Jefferson, pastor of the Fellowship of the Disciples of Christ Church. Interested members of the community were invited to provide input and opinions.

The meeting was tense, with tempers flaring about the number of police actions that have occurred since Deputy Mayor Jack Wilson was shot during an armed robbery on Wednesday, August Fourth.

At 7:45 p.m., Approximately 15 to 20 members of the Peace Stones entered the meeting. They remained quiet for a while, but then started chanting disapproval of police actions. The Stones were armed with pistols and some wore bandoliers. After a few minutes, Hansen asked for calm, as did Rev. Jefferson. But the shouting continued, and the tempers and tension escalated.

At that point, Hansen declared the meeting over. Hansen, Buckner, and others headed for the door.

According to witnesses, Jim Monaghan was one of the last to leave the church. As most of the attendees left the building, Monaghan was observed talking with Rev. Jefferson.

Around 8 p.m. Monaghan was seen walking out of the church and getting into his car, a convertible. The top was down, and his car was surrounded by the Stones.

Reportedly, for 10 minutes, Monaghan was shouted at, called names, and cursed. It was reported, but not confirmed, that among those surrounding Monaghan's car was Edgar Johnson, the alleged leader of the Stones. Whether or not Johnson was there is in dispute, due to conflicting eyewitnesses.

It was reported, but not confirmed, that during this confrontation, shots were fired into Monaghan's car.

Eyewitnesses report that Haley Johnson, Edgar's sister and Monaghan's colleague at the News Tribune, jumped into Monaghan's car and put herself in front of him.

A shot rang out striking Haley Johnson in the back. Three more shots were heard. Ms. Johnson was struck again in the back of the head, and Mr. Monaghan was shot twice in the chest.

Witnesses reported that almost immediately a police presence emerged, and a flurry of gunshots rained down on the crowd. Members of the Stones, mostly teenage boys, as well as innocent bystanders were cut down with powerful automatic weapons.

As of late Friday night, no suspects in the shooting have been named. Witnesses contend the police fired into the crowd. Lincoln Police Chief Buckner denied the charge, stating his officers only fired at the Stones, who he said were armed. Buckner blamed the Stones for the shootings of Haley Johnson, Monaghan, and the citizens, who were standing outside the church.

Buckner did confirm two of the Stones were shot by his officers.

Ken Simon, owner and operator of Simon Ambulance Service told the News Tribune, "I have never seen such blood and so many dead bodies, and I served in Korea."

Chief Buckner was interviewed by radio station WDFD and said, "My men acted appropriately, and I can tell you, we ain't having no Watts-like riots in Lincoln."

None of the other victims' names have been released.

At 12:15 a.m. Saturday, Audrey Hill, publisher of the News Tribune, called this reporter from Mercy Hospital and reported Monaghan was out of surgery where doctors worked nearly five hours trying to save his life.

A fter sending the copy to the back-shop Hauser waited for the paper to roll off the press. While Hauser waited, Charlie Sloan, editor of the Columbus Post-Dispatch, called.

"Where the hell is Monaghan?" an exasperated Sloan asked. "We saw a blurb on the wire about a shooting at that meeting Jim was going to cover for us. I am holding space on the front page for Jim's story, but so far, we have seen nothing on the Western Union.

"I saw the TV coverage and it looks awful. What's going on? I am already damn near an hour late with our first edition."

"Charlie, I am having my guys Western Union it to

you now, or I will have one of them call your copy desk and dictate, whichever will be quicker for you."

"Let's dictate it. That will be quicker," Sloan said. "But where's Monaghan. Is he drinking again?"

"No, he is not drinking, Charlie. I'm sorry to tell you what happened. I know you and Jim are friends."

Sloan was quiet while Hauser told the story of the events of the meeting. Hauser could hear Sloan gasp when he told him Jim had been shot twice and was in Intensive Care, where his condition was grave.

"My God, and I thought he was drinking again. I am so ashamed of myself," Sloan lamented. "Was Edgar Johnson there? Is he all right?"

Hauser told Sloan there was no solid information on Edgar, and he didn't have confirmed names of the victims other than Haley and Jim. Sloan told Hauser he was sending a couple of reporters to Lincoln and would appreciate it they could headquarter out of the News Tribune's office. Hauser quickly agreed.

49

It had been nearly twenty-four hours since the shootings.

Audrey and Jenny had taken turns getting catnaps in an empty hospital bed a short walk from the ICU waiting room. Friends had brought changes of clothes, and the cafeteria staff, like other staffers in the hospital, touched by the two women keeping vigil, had brought food.

Jim's brother slept in a chair in the waiting room when he wasn't drinking black coffee.

Judge McCallister, Sgt. Major Harlow, Bill Hauser, Donald Hansen, Art Wilks, Ken Simon, Lt. Malcolm, and others stopped by to offer support.

Conspicuous by their absence were Harrison and Martha Fowler.

Audrey made sure no one stayed long. Jenny was distraught, and the influx of visitors added to her distress.

The only exception she made was for Maybelle Johnson, Rev. Jeremiah Jefferson, and Sgt. Major

Harlow. Though consumed with grief for her Haley, Maybelle wanted to check on her Jimmy. Audrey knew Jim and the Sgt. Major were as close as brothers, so she made an exception for him, too.

Shortly after 6 p.m., Doctors Ross and Cunningham came out of the ICU, pulled up two chairs, and told Jenny, Audrey, and Hugh they had good news.

"Jim has shown tremendous improvement during the day. His vital signs are strong, and we feel he is in good enough shape for us to go in and clean out the rest of the damage. We will probably be in the OR for at least three hours, so don't expect to hear from us for a while. But we are optimistic. He is a very strong young man."

Struggling with her emotions, Jenny simply nodded.

9 P.M.

Lt. Malcolm hung up the telephone in his study and glanced at his wife, who was standing in the doorway. "I heard you cursing. What's wrong?" she asked.

"I've been suspended without pay. That was the Chief. He told me not to come in tonight or until further notice because I was insubordinate last night."

"Well, you better get your act together, because you have a bunch of policemen in our living room, and they all want to talk to you," she instructed, not unlike his old drill instructor.

Lt. Malcolm walked out of his study and into the living room where he six officers from his shift, plus two members of the Chief's special force.

They told Malcolm they were embarrassed and ashamed about what had happened the previous night, and they didn't want to work the eleven-to-seven shift that night.

They asked Malcolm if he thought the Chief had planned the attack from the beginning, because he had told his special squad, in their private meeting before going to their assigned spots, "If you see a nigger with a gun, shoot him."

Malcolm spoke calmly. He told them he couldn't believe the Chief had planned an attack. In his own mind, he thought it was possible, but he wasn't sure. What he was sure about, was that the Chief overreacted and probably didn't regret it. Malcolm was especially perplexed by the Chief's reaction to Jim Monaghan being shot.

It was like the Chief was almost pleased. But he didn't share his thoughts with his subordinates. He explained he was suspended and couldn't be with them, but they should report for duty and do themselves and him proud.

Reluctantly, they left.

Back in his study, Malcolm stared at the phone. He thought of Jim Monaghan and the others shot the night before. Seven dead, eight injured, many seriously and fighting for their lives. He thought of the Chief and recalled other incidents where rules were trampled.

He picked up the phone and called the Commandant of the Ohio State Police.

50

Jenny sat on the side of Jim's hospital bed, holding his hand and smiling. "You know, you don't look bad for a guy who nearly died last week."

Jim looked askance. He knew Jenny had been trying to be upbeat ever since he'd regained consciousness early Monday morning. He knew she had hardly left the hospital since he was brought in. But his depression was deep.

He knew he'd nearly died, and he kept thinking of Haley. He couldn't imagine how Maybelle was holding up and whether Edgar had made it to the farm. Reverend Jefferson had stopped by numerous times, prayed with Jim, and told him Maybelle wanted to spend time with him, but with Haley's funeral, she was just not able to make it to the hospital.

Jenny was talking like a sunshine pump. She excitedly told him Governor Anderson had called several times and wanted to know when he could visit. Jim thought of Anderson, *such an unlikely friendship. Me, friends with the Governor of Ohio.*

"Jenny, you have been spending a lot of time with me in the hospital, and Lord knows I appreciate it, but what about law school? You aren't getting behind, are you? I don't want the Judge getting upset with you and with me. He stopped by the other day, when you weren't here. I asked him about you and your studies, and he told me not to worry about you. He said he just wants me to get better. But I know he is a stickler."

"Last Friday was my last day of classes for the summer," Jenny assured Jim. I need to take three exams, but my professors said I could take them when I am ready. Everyone knows you were shot, and we are an item, so they told me, when you are out of the hospital, I will study and take the exams. I am in good shape. I aced all my quizzes and tests, so I know I am going to pass."

"Passing isn't good enough, Jenny. You need to be at the top of your class," Jim cautioned.

"Well, we will talk about that later. You are still weak and need to rest," Jenny said, smoothing Jim's blanket.

Jim closed his eyes and dozed. As Jenny was getting ready to leave, the door opened, and Lt. Malcolm entered.

"How's Jim doing?" Malcolm asked.

"He's doing great," Jenny said. "But he's resting, now."

"No, I'm not. I always have time for the Lincoln Police Department, at least some of them," Jim offered.

Malcolm was dressed in civilian clothes. It was the first time Jim had ever seen Malcolm not in uniform. Tall and muscular, Jim noticed he had lost the extra pounds he had been putting on while spending too much time riding in a squad car and filling out paperwork. The prominent scar Malcolm incurred while wrestling a drunk driver and his bottle of gin, was bright red this morning. That was usually a sign of stress.

"Well, I'm not with the Lincoln Police Department, Jim," Malcolm said. I am on unpaid administrative leave for my insubordination to the Chief last week at the scene of your shooting."

"Please fill me in," Jim requested. "No one has given me the specifics of exactly what happened. The last thing I remember is Haley getting shot, then, it is a blur."

Malcom told Jim, in detail, his memory of the night, starting with Chief Buckner telling him that he and some of his officers were to come in early for their shift. He was adamant, Malcolm said, that his crew was to serve in a back-up role only. He told of trying to slow Buckner and his people down, but he was overruled by the Chief.

Then, after the siege was over, he described his angry conversation with Buckner ending with the insubordination charge.

"I never thought he was that serious, because he has a hot temper. But he called me last Saturday and he put me on leave until further notice."

Malcolm went on to say Buckner was heading up the investigation himself. "He is telling everyone the Stones were responsible for everyone getting shot. All his officers did was shoot the Stones who had guns.

"But after he left the scene that night, I had my guys retrieve all the Stone's guns, and we examined them at the site. Only two guns were warm. The other guns were cold and had all their cartridges. They hadn't been fired.

"There is no question, everyone who got shot was shot by the police, except for you and Haley."

"How can you know that?" Jim and Jenny asked together.

"Because of the angle from which you were shot. The Chief and his guys were coming across the barren field behind you, and you and Haley were shot from the opposite direction. So, it wasn't the police who shot you, and it wasn't the Stones either.

"I talked with Dr. Cunningham and he got me some of the fragments from your chest and we found some large fragments of bullets in your car. They must have gone right through you and Haley. And Jim, they are from a high-powered rifle."

Stunned, Jim asked if all of Malcolm's information was part of Buckner's investigation.

Malcolm said, he didn't know for sure. All he knew, from the guys at the cop-shop was Buckner was looking for Edgar. Malcolm said Buckner is telling people, if he can find Edgar, he can solve the investigation.

Overcome by exhaustion, Jim's internal lament was *Damn. When will this shit ever end?* His eyes drifted closed.

Jenny told Malcolm Jim had had enough, and she would call him when Jim was able to talk more.

Jenny leaned over, kissed Jim on the cheek, and she and Malcolm, left the room.

The hospital staff woke Jim up in the evening and tried to get him to eat. He picked at the Jell-O. The nurse checked his blood pressure and vitals and Jim fell back onto his pillow, exhausted

Jim woke and looked at the clock on the wall. It was 12:25 a.m. The room was dark, but he felt a presence. He looked to his left and thought he saw a slightly built man, dressed all in black, sitting in the chair beside the bed.

Knowing no one could possibly be there, he thought he was hallucinating. Closing his eyes, he fell into a deep sleep.

51

J im woke up refreshed and was able to eat a portion of his breakfast of bacon, eggs, and a crispy English muffin, just the way he preferred it. Dr. Cunningham examined Jim and told him his progress was excellent and said he might be released in a few days. Jim told Dr. Cunningham about hallucinating the night before.

"Last night, I woke up and I swear I saw a guy, dressed in black, sitting beside my bed. But before I could say hello, I went back to sleep. Is the medicine making me hallucinate?" Jim asked.

"I doubt it. None of your medicine is mind altering. I suspect, you were just dreaming. I wouldn't worry about it. The important thing is you went back to sleep. Sleep is your friend now." Cunningham consoled, as he left.

Great news from Dr. Cunningham. I wasn't hallucinating. I could be getting out of here in a few days. Jim couldn't wait for Jenny to visit at noon so he could share his potential release date.

After breakfast, Jim spent the next hour reading the

News Tribune and the Columbus Post-Dispatch, catching up on the exploits of the Cincinnati Reds. He was disappointed he could find no stories on the shootings the week before.

The door to his room opened and a tentative woman's voice asked, "Do you mind if I come in?" Jim, delighted to have any company, but unsure who the voice belonged to, said, "Sure."

He was shocked to see Martha Harrison, dressed in a black summer dress highlighted by a string of pearls around her neck. She was carrying a dozen roses, arranged with other greens, in a vase. She placed the flowers on the counter next to the window.

I must be hallucinating again. Last night, I saw someone all in black and now Jenny's mother. Yikes, Jim thought.

"I am sure you are shocked to see me, but I thought I would take a chance that you would allow me to visit with you. I know Jenny won't be here until noon, and I just felt I had to come and see you."

Jim didn't know what to say. This is the woman who had criticized him for months. She had left him standing on the front porch in the freezing rain and other inclement weather. But he also knew she had made efforts in the past weeks to stay in touch with her daughter, even though she was upset with Jenny for moving out.

"Please sit down, Mrs. Harrison, and thank you for the flowers," Jim motioned to the chair beside his bed.

"I am so sorry you were shot, and I am so thankful you are getting better," Martha started tentatively. I can only imagine what you think of me and Harrison. We have not been good to you. In fact, we have been terrible. But I know what Jenny thinks of you, and I know your relationship is evolving. So, I thought it was time I got to know you. I want you to know, I was planning to tell Jenny that Friday night, but then this tragedy occurred. I am so sorry, but I am here now."

Jenny's mother sat erect in the chair next to Jim's bed. She was slim and tanned. Jim knew she was an avid tennis player. Jim was surprised when she smiled. It seemed genuine and warm. Speaking confidently, Martha told Jim neither Jenny nor Harrison knew she was there, but she was going to tell them. Jim enjoyed her Boston accent, still evident despite living twenty years in the Midwest.

Her strength reminded Jim of Jenny.

"I do appreciate your seeing me and not throwing me out of the room," Martha confided.

"Mrs. Harrison, I would never throw you out of the room, even if I could get out of this hospital bed. But I am still Jim Monaghan, newspaper reporter, Catholic, from Dale, Ohio. My parents were farmers. I am the same person."

Martha lowered her head and spoke softly. She told Jim she was ashamed of the things she'd said to Jenny for so many reasons, but one of them was hypocrisy.

She went on, her voice getting stronger, telling Jim about her family's history. She told of her ancestors coming over on the Mayflower, fighting in the American Revolution, and being in the Boston area for decades. She told of the clubs they belonged to and how silly a lot of it was.

"Jenny knows a little about my favorite Uncle Patrick. He died many years before she was born. She has heard me talk about him, but I never went into details about him. I foolishly thought she didn't need to know anything about him other than he was my uncle. Jim, his last name was Fitzgibbons. What Jenny doesn't know is my favorite uncle's name was Patrick Fitzgibbons."

"You have an uncle named Fitzgibbons?" Jim's eyebrows shot up.

"Yes. He married one of my mother's sisters. He was a rogue. He didn't have any formal education, but he was brilliant. He built one of the biggest businesses in Boston and when some members of the family had a need, Uncle Pat was always there for them.

"Even though he married into my Presbyterian family, he steadfastly went to Mass every Sunday and was good friends with the Cardinal. I even went with him a few times to Mass, much to my mother's displeasure. I wept bitterly when he died. He and his wife never had any children. In fact, I was named after my Aunt Martha."

Jim and Martha settled into a comfortable conversation, Jim telling her about his parents and his father and mother being from Ireland. He told of his brother Hugh and the family farm. He talked about raising pigs, steers, chickens, corn, and soy beans.

Jim was particularly touched when Martha asked about Mary Ryan.

"I read every word you wrote about that horrible casket switching scandal and that poor young girl dying. It must have been terrible for you and her parents. I know that Reid fellow from the Club, but never liked him. He was always telling people how much money he had, so disgusting. I was surprised he was allowed back into the club after he got out of jail. But of course, I didn't have a vote.

"I simply cannot imagine how you held up when that young lady died in that accident. It must have been terrible."

At 11:45 a.m., Martha noticed the clock on the wall, jumped up, and said, "I must go. Tell Jenny, that I stopped by, if you are comfortable. If you are not, that's ok. I will tell her."

And with that, Martha Harrison, leaned over, kissed Jim on the cheek and left the room.

Jim closed his eyes and thought, *that had to be a dream.*

52

Promptly at noon, Jenny bounced in dressed in a Hamilton University Tennis Team blue warm up suit, her hair pulled back in a ponytail.

"Playing tennis today?" Jim asked.

"No, I intend to spend a lot of time with you today, so I thought I would be comfortable."

"Well, that's good. I have a lot to say, and if it's possible, Jenny, could you just listen to me, until I am finished?"

"I won't interrupt, unless it is appropriate," Jenny winked.

Taking Jenny's hand, Jim began by telling her how much he loved her. He said he could envision a life together, despite their different backgrounds. He knew they would face problems, but he was convinced love could conquer them.

Jim tightened his hold on Jenny's and confessed he was shaken by Lt. Malcom's narrative of the shooting. He realized there was no question someone was trying to shoot him, to murder him. The gun at his neck in

Calvary Cemetery was one thing and Lloyd Collier aiming the gun at him was serious, but nothing compared to being shot. This time he was almost killed.

"I was thinking, as much as I would hate to do it, it might be best to leave Lincoln. It is a corrupt place. The Washington Post has offered me a job, and I can always get a job at the Columbus Post-Dispatch. You could transfer to Ohio State or to Georgetown, and we could be together.

"I am certain Pugh and his people are behind all of this," Jim continued. "I just don't know if I could forgive myself if I didn't pursue those bastards. I know they killed, Irene, Steve, Mary, and now Haley. I know Audrey is depending on me to stay at the newspaper, and I owe her so much. She was here yesterday and told me after I am out of the hospital, the paper would send me on a month-long vacation, and they would pay for it.

Jenny's eyes widened and she asked, "Where are we going?"

Missing Jenny's comment, Jim went on, "I told her I had no idea where I would want to go, and she suggested Ireland. So, I might do that, but only if it is okay with you."

Jenny had tears in her eyes as she listened to Jim. She crawled onto the bed and hugged him. "Jim, you know I love you. And whatever you decide to do, I am with you."

For several moments, they held one another, and Jim, in a hospital bed with two bullet holes in his chest, IVs in his arm, attached to a heart monitor, thought, *How could I be so lucky?*

Jenny sat up in the bed and said, "Jim, I know you are going to ask me a serious question one of these days, and I hope sooner rather than later, but there is something you need to know."

Jenny was interrupted by a nurse who flew into the room.

"Jim, sorry to interrupt, but we have wonderful news. Your friend, Jack Wilson, who is two rooms down from you, just came out of his coma. Dr. Ross is with him and he is doing great. Isn't that wonderful news?"

Jim and Jenny cheered, and Jim told the nurse to tell Jack, when it was appropriate that Jim was down the hall and they needed to talk. The nurse assured him, she would.

"Now, Jenny what's so important?"

"Jim, you have been asking me, time and time again, how I bought the condo. Well, there is only one way to tell you this. I am rich. I am rich now. Not when my parents die, and I inherit whatever they have. I am rich now. Can you be comfortable being with a girl, who is rich?"

"What do you mean rich? Did someone give you money for the condo? And if so, who?" Jim said, beyond curious.

"I had a great uncle. He was my mother's favorite uncle. He was married to one of my grandmother's sisters. I don't know much about him other than he was very successful back in Boston. But he and his wife never had children, so he set up a trust fund for any of mother's children.

"And I am the only one. I don't even know his last name. The trust was named the Patrick and Martha Trust. When I graduated from Hamilton last spring, I received the first installment. It was five million dollars! When I turn thirty, I receive the balance, which I understand is enormous. It's managed by one of my mother's cousins back in Boston who owns a bank."

Jim just looked at Jenny with a smile beginning to form.

"Don't smile at me, Jim, this is serious. I don't yet know how much is in the trust, but it's a lot. So, you see why I am concerned? If we are together, we will never have any money problems, but can you live with my having so much?"

Jim broke out in a big smile and asked Jenny, "How did Patrick Fitzgibbons make all his money?"

"What? This is impossible. His last name can't be Fitzgibbons, can it?" Jenny exclaimed. "What do you know?"

"Why don't you go over to the counter by the window and look at those beautiful roses."

Jenny hurriedly walked over to the roses, grabbed the card and exclaimed. "My God!"

The card read, "Jim, I hope you feel better soon, Martha Fowler."

"You mean mother was here? When?" Jenny asked.

"She left just before you got here. She came around ten, and we had a nice chat. She apologized for being so mean to me. She didn't say anything about a trust fund, but she did talk about her favorite uncle, Patrick, and we both had a good laugh about him being Irish.

"My goodness, Jim, that's the best news. Everything is going to be great. Now, if we can just get dad to come around." Jenny sat carefully on the bed, and gently hugged and kissed Jim. She couldn't see Jim's deep frown.

How do I tell Jenny, her father was at Pugh's machine shed Friday morning?

53

Jenny and Jim were locked in an embrace, when a nurse poked her head around the privacy curtain.

"Hate to interrupt you love birds, but I need to check your vitals before I let your very impressive company come in. And by the way, Jack Wilson is acting like he just woke up from a deep sleep."

After checking Jim, she started for the door. "Your vitals are great, Jim. We are all so excited on the floor. You are doing great and it looks like Jack is going to be ok. Jenny, you might want to get off the bed, you have serious company."

She opened the door and in walked Governor Lucas Anderson, Shelby County District Attorney George Rogers, Ohio's Attorney General Peter Johnson, Lt. Malcolm, and two men Jim didn't know.

"Well, how's the patient?" the affable Anderson asked as he led the group into the room.

"Well, I was doing pretty well until I saw all of you. Am I in trouble? Who are the guys, I don't know?" Jim asked.

"Jim, this is Charles Adderley. He is the United States Attorney for our district. He worked with Bobby Kennedy on the civil rights actions in the south. I have asked him to join our team," Anderson explained. "And this is Dan Byron, the Commandant of the Ohio State Police.

"What team are you talking about?" Jim asked.

All turned to Lt. Malcolm.

Malcolm explained that after the Chief put him on unpaid administrative leave for the foreseeable future, he called Commandant Byron. He also initiated meetings with the Commandant, George Rogers, and Charles Adderley.

Knowing Jim's relationship with the Governor, Malcolm requested a meeting with him.

"I told the Governor I thought there were problems in Lincoln that crossed many lines. I told him it was impossible for the Lincoln police department or the Shelby County Sheriff to do a proper investigation. I had done a lot of research and knew there were possible violations of the civil rights acts, so the Feds had to be involved."

Malcolm nodded at Anderson, "Your friend the Governor is a man of action, Jim. He had me wait while he called Mr. Adderley, the Commandant, and the State AG. They were in his office in less than an hour. They spent the balance of the afternoon listening to me tell everything I knew for a fact as well as my suppositions. The key to the investigation is the fact that the Stones' guns were cold; and the trajectory of the bullets indicates Buckner's squad shot everyone except you and Haley. I told you earlier, it was impossible for them to shoot you, so there is a murderer out there somewhere.

Jim squeezed Jenny's hand as he looked around the

room. The somber demeanor of the men betrayed the gravity of their visit.

"We have formed an unofficial committee that crosses city, county, state, and federal lines. We promised to work together to get to the bottom of just what the hell is going on. And, Jim, I am the chief investigator" Malcolm concluded.

Stunned, Jim felt Jenny's fingers squeezing his hand. He asked, "How are you going to do that, Lieutenant? Won't the chief stop you?"

The Commandant stepped forward and said, "It's not Lt. Malcolm anymore, it's Special Agent Malcolm of the Ohio State patrol."

"Jim," Adderley said, "I don't know you, but Special Agent Malcolm has told me you have done a great deal of the investigation, going all the way back to the start of the copper casket research. We are going to want all your files, even your guesses. And I want to talk to Reverend Jeremiah Jefferson and Edgar Johnson. I would like you to call Reverend Jefferson and tell him he should talk with me.

"I briefly met Reverend Jefferson several years ago. Bobby Kennedy sent me to Birmingham when all the trouble occurred there. The Reverend was in jail with Dr. King, and we were introduced, but he wouldn't remember me. I work for Attorney General Nick Katzenbach, now. He's not Bobby, but he's just as interested in civil rights. I know I will have his support. When we get your information, I will get it to the FBI. I have already talked to the Special Agent in Charge in Columbus. He told me he has talked to Washington and they are on board. They are thinking of a task force to help us with the investigation.

"And, as I understand it, no one knows where Edgar

is. If you could help us get in touch with him, I would appreciate it.

Stunned, but with total confidence in the group, Jim replied, "You can probably find Edgar working on my family's farm just outside Dale, And if he isn't there, check with Donald Hansen or with Charlie Sloan of the Columbus Post-Dispatch."

Mouths dropped open when Jim mentioned Edgar's possible whereabouts.

"How the hell is Charlie Sloan of the Post-Dispatch involved with Edgar Johnson?" a shocked and befuddled Governor asked.

Jim smiled, "Sometimes things are not as they appear. Edgar is a special young man and nothing, absolutely nothing, Chief Buckner says about him is true."

"I told you all Jim knew what was going on," Malcolm grinned.

Everyone left, but Governor Anderson.

"Jim, Ann and I were distraught when we read about you nearly being killed. You know how much we think of you. Even our girls were praying for you. I have talked with Audrey, and she insists you are going on a vacation when you get out of the hospital.

"I have an offer for you. I know how much you are impressed with the Augusta National Golf Course. Here, I bought you a Masters' windbreaker," he said, handing Jim a package. Augusta has private cottages right on the course. My father-law wants to host you there for a while, and he has promised to have the golf pro give you some lessons."

"Lucas, that's beyond generous. I don't know what I am going to do, but that's a wonderful option," Jim said. "And Lucas, how can I ever thank you for putting this group together? Maybe, just maybe, we will finally find justice."

Jim told Jenny he was exhausted at the end of an incredible day. He asked her to make sure she told her mother he was grateful she'd stopped by.

54

It was almost midnight when Jim woke. He rang for the nurse, who promptly came.

"If it's all right with you, I am going to walk down to Jack's room and just sit there for a while."

"Probably do you some good. You slept most of the afternoon and evening, so a little walk should be just fine," the nurse said.

Three nurses hovered over Jack Wilson's bed, and Jim feared the worst.

"Jack, your vital signs are strong," one of the nurses said, and Jim immediately relaxed. "And you have company," the nurse remarked, as she and the other nurses quietly left.

"So, they shot you, too, huh Jim? What the hell is going on? You got any ideas?" Jack's voice was raspy from the breathing tube that had recently been removed.

"I have some ideas," Jim said, "but let's not talk about them now. How are you feeling, and do you remember anything that happened to you?"

Jack Wilson recounted his morning, walking around

the store, making sure everything was in its place, cleaned and polished. He remembered waving at Sgt. Major Harlow.

"I hate drinking Nescafe, but I am pretty inept except for boiling water. I was really looking forward to my assistant coming in, so I could go over to the Sgt. Major's and get a good cup of coffee. Besides, with the new bond issue, we are trying to pass, I wanted to get his feedback as to what the folks are saying."

Jack went on to say he never heard a thing until a muffled voice warned him not to make a sound. He said he turned around, got a look at the guy, but then was hit in the face with the barrel of what he thought was a sawed-off shotgun. Then, he said, he was thrown to the ground, but got another look at the masked guy just before he opened fire.

"Any idea, who shot you, Jack?" Jim asked.

"I know it sounds crazy, but the guy seemed familiar. His voice was muffled by a ski mask he had pulled over his mouth, but he had a southern twang. I recognized the camo outfit he had on, because I am pretty sure I carry that brand. I may have even sold them to him.

"As they were leaving, I asked him, 'Don't I know you?' It obviously pissed him off, because that's when he shot me. If I had to guess, I would tell you he was the same size and had the same accent as Slick Beck, Ron Pugh's number one man.

"I'm tired, Jim. Let's talk tomorrow and let's plan on getting those bastards."

Jim made his way back to his room shaking his head. *With the Governor's group, especially with Malcolm involved, and Jack's recollections, I think we might, just might, get to the bottom. But I don't dare be optimistic. I have been before and then nothing happened.*

As Jim walked into his dimly lit hospital room, he halted abruptly at the door. A man, all in black, except for a white minister's collar around his neck sat in a chair across from his bed. The man appeared to be same one Jim saw the previous night. *But I was dreaming then. Or was I?*

The man slowly and painfully rose. He was slightly bent-over and looked old. His face was thin except for loose, droopy jowls. His gray hair was cut short, almost a burr. Jim had a fleeting sense of recognition, but he dismissed it.

"I think you are in the wrong room, pal. This is my room," Jim said with authority.

"No, Mr. Monaghan, I am not in the wrong room. I was here last night, but you were sleeping, and I didn't want to bother you. I have come to ask your forgiveness. I have harmed you and many others. I am trying to make amends for the evil I have done."

In the semi-darkness, Jim saw the man approach him with open arms. Believing the man had escaped from the psychiatric ward, Jim backed up towards the door and said. "Pal, you have me confused with someone else. I have never seen you before in my life. Now, please leave. I am calling out to the nurse's station and they will escort you back to the psych ward upstairs."

"Yes, you have seen me before, Mr. Monaghan. I am Rev. Raymond Smallwood.

55

J im was so shocked he stumbled, and he was grateful when the man, who identified himself, as Rev. Smallwood, took his arm and helped into bed. Jim turned on the dim light behind his bed and looked at the man.

The Reverend Smallwood Jim stared at did not resemble the man Jim and Mary Ryan saw standing at his pulpit at the First Baptist Church, railing against JFK, Martin Luther King, Jr., and the Civil Rights movement.

Jim remembered Smallwood then, dressed in a too-tight black liturgical robe, white silk gold-embroidered stole, and with a heavy, shiny gold cross hanging from a gold chain around his neck. His beady brown eyes darted around his congregation.

Short, but over 250 pounds, Smallwood's slicked-down brown hair contrasted with the soft folds of his florid face. Nevertheless, with his deep voice and commanding presence, Smallwood was imposing from the pulpit.

The man Jim was staring at now, was thin, almost gaunt. He was wearing a long-sleeved black shirt that hung on his frame. His cotton pants were black, wrinkled, and too short. The cuffs of his pants just barely reached his sockless ankles and, Jim noticed, his shoes were not matched. This man hadn't shaved in a few days and he had two teeth missing. But, he wore a minister's collar.

"Mr. Monaghan, I need to talk to you. You are still in danger, no matter what anyone says. I, and others, bear responsibility for the accident in which your friend Mary died. I know these people and I know they won't rest until you are gone. You are a threat to them. I need to talk to you--to tell you how sorry I am for my role in what happened to your Mary, to Mrs. Dunn, and to Steve Hampton. I need to make amends to you any way I can."

Jim sat up in his bed, but in doing so, he accidentally pulled the string which rang the nurse's station.

Beulah, the night nurse supervisor on the floor, planted her hands on her wide hips, stared at Reverend Smallwood and demanded, "Who are you and what are you doing here past visiting hours? Jim, we make exceptions for Jenny, but no one else. Now, Mister or Reverend, you need to leave.

"No Beulah, he can't leave. He is my minister and we need to talk. Please let him stay," Jim pleaded.

"No, he is going, and he is going now. Jim, you missed your midnight medication. How do you expect to get better if you don't take your medicine? And you should be asleep. No, this man is out of here and you are going to sleep."

Reverend Smallwood, looking even more deflated than he had when Jim first saw him, said, "I will be back in the morning, Mr. Monaghan. I know you have no reason to trust me, but you can. You can trust me. Here is how you can get in touch with me. I live in Columbus now, and people at this telephone number will know how to reach me. But I will be back in the morning. I desperately need to talk to you."

Smallwood gave Jim a crumpled and soiled card emblazoned **Columbus Mission**. Jim recognized the address as being close to the state capital building.

Smallwood left, and Beulah went on about the nerve of some people. Jim took his medicine and, as Beulah left, he said, "I hope you haven't made a big mistake.

She turned to him and said, "You are my only concern. I am here to make sure you get better and having visitors at midnight won't get you better."

After Beulah left, Jim walked over to the window and down to the parking lot. He saw Reverend Smallwood get in an old junker of a car and drive off.

Quite a step down from the Mercedes he drove, when he was pastor of First Baptist, Jim thought. *Maybe, he has changed, and maybe he has something to say that will be truly enlightening.*

As Jim started to step away from the window, he abruptly stopped. Following Reverend Smallwood's car were two pickup trucks. They had eagle emblems on their driver's side doors.

Oh, shit, Jim thought, *not again.*

Closing his eyes, Jim thought, what a day. He said a prayer of thanksgiving for all the good things that happened, and a prayer of hope that Reverend Smallwood would show up in the morning.

56

Jim was awakened Sunday morning. by Dr. Ross, who gave him a thorough exam. "You're looking good, Jim. Your numbers are improving, and your wounds are healing very nicely. I think a few more days and you can be back at your typewriter. You must have had a restful day yesterday and gotten a good night's sleep last night, because you are looking great this morning."

Jim smiled, *if he only knew what I went through yesterday and last night. It was exhausting. And was Reverend Smallwood here last night, or did I dream the whole experience?*

Jim's mind was conflicted. The man looked like Reverend Smallwood, but how does a guy go from two hundred fifty pounds to one hundred forty or one hundred fifty? And even if it is Smallwood, what all does he want to say? Jim knew he was involved in the casket switching operation, but he confessed only to getting a cut on the sale of the copper caskets to the grieving families. *God, I hope he shows up,* Jim thought.

Lost in his thoughts, Jim didn't notice Jenny, in a pale

green blouse and tan Bermuda shorts, until she jumped in his bed, gave him a big hug and a lingering kiss.

"Wow, that's quite a hello," Jim smiled.

"I've made some decisions," Jenny said. "I saw Dr. Ross in the hallway and he said you would be getting out in a few days, but you would need some time to recuperate. You know, lots of rest.

"Well, I've decided, you can't do that at your messy apartment, so when you get out of the hospital, you are coming home to my condo. I can take care of you until you are completely healed," she said, then smiling she added, "and that might take a while."

"So, you've decided that all by yourself? Do I have a say, or are you making all the decisions?" Jim asked playfully.

"Well if you don't want to," Jenny said, frowning.

"No, that will be great. Hopefully, now that I have a relationship with your mother, she won't mind."

"Oh, I have already told her. She just said it probably isn't proper, but it's 1965 in Lincoln, not 1945 in Boston."

"Jenny, you aren't going to believe this, but I think Reverend Smallwood came to see me last night. It was after midnight, I was exhausted, and it was dark in my room. But he said he was Smallwood. He has lost over one hundred pounds and looks totally different.

"He said he would be back this morning because he wanted to make amends to me and confess. I need you to be here, so I have a witness."

Jenny reminded Jim she had never met Smallwood, and only knew of him from Jim's writings. She would like to stay, but she had a problem. Judge McCallister offered to go over her notes and prep her for her exams from her summer school classes.

"It's an offer I can't refuse, Jim. It's very generous of the judge and with his tutoring, I will do great on my exams."

"No question, Jenny, but call him and tell him Smallwood came to my hospital room last night and wants to make amends and confess. The Judge will understand. Please tell him I would really appreciate it if he could reschedule.

After calling the Judge and rescheduling, Jenny sat on the bed making small talk. The clock ticked past ten and Jim started to give up on Smallwood. Ringing the nurses' station, he told them he and Jenny were walking down to Jack Wilson's room. As they passed the nurses' station, he mentioned that if he had a visitor, especially a man dressed in black, like a preacher, they should come and get him right away.

Then, Jim told Jenny if Smallwood showed up, she should call Governor Anderson and tell him the investigation was about to break wide open, and he should dispatch Lt. Malcolm, now Special Agent Malcolm, to his hospital room right away.

Jack's smiling family surrounded his bed. The room was filled with flowers from well-wishers. Jack was sitting up, sipping tomato soup.

"Jim, I think they make hospital food this crappy, so you will be in a hurry to get out," Jack joked.

"You are really looking good, Jack. I think you know Jenny Fowler," Jim said introducing Jenny.

"Of course, I know Jenny. Captain of the NAIA championship Hamilton University Tennis team and the NAIA individual tennis champion. My store supplies Hamilton with all their tennis equipment. I've seen Jenny play dozens of times. She was one of the best in the entire history of Hamilton tennis. Beating Stanford in the finals was a great day."

Jenny smiled, cheeks flushing.

After exchanging pleasantries with Jack's family, Jim said. "We need to talk about the robbery and what we talked about last night. You remember Reverend Smallwood, don't you? He was in cahoots with Alex Reid on the casket switching scam.

"Well, he is supposed to come see me this morning and give me some information, but I would like to get as much information as you can tell me about your robbery."

Jack's wife stood, arms crossed and said firmly, "No, Jack is not saying anything about the robbery."

Jack looked askance at his wife. "What has gotten into you? This is Jim Monaghan, my friend. He was shot, I was shot. We are trying to figure out if the same people shot us."

Jack's wife's chin quivered. "Jack, I got a call last night. The man didn't identify himself. He told me to tell you to keep your mouth shut and not say anything to anyone about the robbery. I'm scared, Jack. We have three boys. I don't want them in danger."

Jack opened his arms and his wife sat on the bed and hugged him. Jim told them of the special task force started by Governor Anderson and charged with investigating corruption in Shelby County. He explained that Lt. Malcolm, now a Special Agent of the Ohio State Patrol, was the lead investigator.

Jack's wife was not convinced. She said too many people had died. "My goodness, Jim Monaghan, you were shot and nearly died. Now, people in town are talking about crime gangs in Lincoln. Most thought it was the Stones, who were the biggest threat, but now folks are saying, it is bigger and scarier than a group of Blacks from Simpson Village."

Jack listened intently and answered softly, "I wouldn't have believed any of this, but when Jim told me Lt. Malcolm knew, for a fact that Jim was shot by a high-powered rifle for a long distance away, and not by either the police or the Stones that changed everything. Plus, I know the Stones didn't rob me. Those were white guys. And I am going to call a news conference and make sure everyone knows Edgar Johnson had nothing to do with my robbery. I've known Edgar for years. I supported him in baseball, football, and everything he did on the sports field. He's a good kid.

"No, we are not going to be intimidated or lie down in front of these bastards. They are not going to ruin the town I grew up in and love," Wilson declared.

Wilson's wife weakly asked, "What about the telephone call?"

Jim interjected, "And we are not going to make the mistake we made with Delmar Batcher. Malcolm promised to provide security for you, Jack, and for your family. He vowed to make sure all of you are safe."

"Make sure you get protection for yourself, Jim," Wilson cautioned.

As Jack and his wife nodded their heads in agreement, one of the nurses told Jim he had a Reverend waiting for him in his room.

Jim told Jenny to use Jack's hospital room phone to call Governor Anderson's private number. Listening to Jenny talk to the Governor, who got on the line immediately, Wilson turned to Jim and said, "How in the hell do you have the Governor's private number and how could Jenny get him on the phone that quickly?"

"Jack, I have friends in high places. Not bad for a kid from Dale, huh?"

"Ok, hot shot" Jenny said, "the Governor said hello, and Malcolm is in Lincoln this morning and is on his way," Jenny said.

Jim smiled, took Jenny's arm and walked to his room; his anticipation level sky high. What could Reverend Smallwood say. Could he be the key to unlocking the mystery that had been baffling Jim for years?

57

J im and Jenny stopped at the nurses' station where
Jim told the head nurse, to tell Lt. Malcolm to stand
at the door, listen to the conversation, but not to
come in.

"I will leave the door ajar. Just have Malcolm stand
there and listen and, please, no interruptions for a
while," Jim pleaded.

Reverend Smallwood was sitting in the same chair as
the night before and rose as Jim and Jenny walked in.
Jim immediately noticed Smallwood's face was bruised,
but otherwise his appearance was the same. Same long-
sleeve shirt, cotton pants, no socks and mismatched
shoes.

Jim asked Smallwood what happened to his face and
did it have anything to do with the fact that Jim had seen
two pickup trucks follow him out of the parking lot the
night before.

"I saw the trucks. I see them often. But no, they just
followed me back to Columbus. There were a couple of
tough guys next to the mission. They got angry when

they found out I didn't have any money and they roughed me up. It happens. It's a tough neighborhood.

Jim sat on his bed while Jenny and Smallwood pulled up chairs.

"Nothing personal young lady, but I don't know you and I am not comfortable talking in front of you," Smallwood said.

"My name is Jenny. Jim and I are going to get married, and we don't have any secrets," Jenny said authoritatively.

Smallwood, who was looking at his shoes, did not see Jim's surprised reaction. He looked over at Jenny, who just smiled.

"I don't know where to begin, Mr. Monaghan," Smallwood said.

"Just start at the beginning and don't leave anything out, no matter how insignificant you might think it is."

Jenny opened her briefcase, took out two legal pads and pens, and gave one to Jim.

"Ok, Reverend Smallwood, let's start at the beginning. Please call me Jim, and her name is Jenny."

Smallwood kept staring at his shoes, his hands clasped, but shaking. His lips were moving, and Jim initially had no idea what he was doing. Finally, it dawned on him, Smallwood was praying.

Speaking softly, almost in a whisper, Smallwood began to tell his story.

He began by telling Jim and Jenny he grew up poor, in rural Alabama. He told of having an alcoholic father who beat him and a mother who didn't protect him or his brothers and sisters. The only place he found peace was at the Baptist Church. There he was protected from his parents and from the bullies at school, who made fun of him because he was fat and not athletic.

The minister at the church took him under his wing and suggested he enter the seminary when he graduated from high school. Smallwood jumped at the chance to leave his dysfunctional family and Alabama.

He was accepted at the Christian Theological Seminary in Indianapolis where he flourished. He was at the top of his class and the leaders of the seminary predicted great things for him. He felt he was truly called by God.

He was assigned as an assistant pastor in Indianapolis, where he met his wife. But he longed for a bigger church, and he wanted to be pastor. He wanted to be in charge.

He lusted after the careers of Oral Roberts and Jerry Falwell. He saw the money they were making, and he wanted to be at their level. His best asset at the theological seminary was his hellfire and brimstone preaching.

He told about one Sunday morning, when he really felt strong and railed against the blacks, the non-believers, and the liberals in Washington DC. After the service, a man, he later learned was Ronald Pugh's cousin, came up to him and asked if he would be interested in interviewing for the job of Pastor at the First Baptist Church in Lincoln.

"That was when I first met Ronald Pugh. My immediate reaction was negative. I felt he was a sinner. I found it interesting that he wasn't interested in what programs I might bring to the church, what I could do for the youth, the sick.

"He told me he had only one request. He never wanted to see a black face in the congregation. 'Blacks are responsible for all our problems,' he said. I was so hungry for my own church and the potential money he talked about, that I just followed my evil instincts. I took the job."

Smallwood recounted that soon after he moved his family to Lincoln, things got complicated outside of the Sunday services. He said, Sunday Services were a dream. The church was always filled. He had two assistant pastors and had many programs to serve the flock. His sermons continued the fire and brimstone against the blacks and the liberals, because Pugh told him that's what he wanted.

Within months of being in place, he had lunch with Pugh, who told him how pleased he was with Smallwood's sermons. He knew Pugh was rich and he shared with him his own desire for money and how he wanted to be on TV like Roberts and Falwell.

"I remember it like yesterday. He said to me 'You don't have to be on TV to make money. Work with me and you will have more money than you can spend.'"

Jim and Jenny were fascinated by Smallwood's story, but the notes they had taken so far were worthless in determining what was going on. Jim decided to push Smallwood for the criminality of Pugh's operation, when he was interrupted by the head nurse.

"Hate to interrupt, but it's time for your medicine, Mr. Monaghan."

Jim was incensed by the interruption, but as the nurse leaned over to give him his pill, she whispered, "Lt. Malcom is outside, and he said to keep him talking. That he will get to the good stuff."

The nurse left, and Smallwood continued.

He told of Pugh coming to him with Alex Reid in tow. They told him they needed help in selling expensive caskets and how, as a pastor, he could influence grieving families. Smallwood told of his regret in convincing families to spend money they didn't have, to bury their loved ones in caskets they couldn't afford. "I would tell them, the better casket, especially copper, would speed their loved ones into heaven," Smallwood said shaking his head.

"I never knew about the switching of caskets until later, but by then, I was in too deep and they wouldn't have listened to me anyway."

Jim chewed on the end of his pen.

"After less than a year working with Reid," Smallwood confessed, "I was invited to the early morning meetings at Pugh's machine shed. And that's when the serious money started coming in. Pugh and his cohorts would give me a check for a few hundred dollars and then thousands of dollars in cash.

"I would deposit the money in a special account at First National, where we had the Church's account. No one at the bank ever questioned the cash. I always made the deposits on Monday and I guess, they just assumed it was part of the Sunday collection."

Smallwood took a deep breath and went on.

"Then, I would write checks to the guys at the meeting, with Pugh always getting the biggest share. They created a phony charity and made themselves directors. I always put on the checks, 'Director's Compensation." Of course, I took my cut.

A tear glistened in Smallwood's eye. "I never questioned my actions. I drove a Mercedes. I belonged to the country club, and we lived in a great house. My wife never complained. But I knew in my heart, it was very wrong.

"But the story gets worse, Mr. Monaghan."

58

Smallwood stood up and paced around the room. He said he knew what he was doing was wrong and, finally, one day, he started to ask questions. Pugh, in a rare moment, took him up to the cupola high atop his machine shed. There, Smallwood, said, in between rows of corn were wide swaths of green. Pugh told him, he was growing money there and it was going to continue to make Smallwood rich. Pugh told him to keep the faith and be a good soldier.

"I finally figured it out; it was marijuana. One day, I was early for the weekly meeting and I found out there was a meeting before the meeting. I heard some of the guys talking about truck shipments to Chicago, New York, Miami, and Philadelphia. I knew then, it was a criminal enterprise.

"He called our group America Incorporated. He always started the meetings with a preamble. It varied, but usually it centered on how certain people were born to lead and the blacks were a threat to the status quo. I was a poor kid from Alabama, and it was heady stuff, being told I was a leader and belonging to the country club.

"It was intoxicating. So, I continued to go along, because I was getting rich and living a life I could only dream about when I was a kid. But it was all wrong, all illicit, all evil."

Jim glanced over at Jenny whose mouth was set in a grim line.

Smallwood looked at Jim and said, "When you started looking into the casket- switching operation, Pugh went nuts. He said you and Irene Dunn had to be stopped. He didn't know then about Steve Hampton. We did everything to slow you down, but when Steve got involved, we knew we had been caught.

"Jim, they killed Irene and Steve. They didn't intend to kill you. You were just a reporter and they just wanted to slow you down. No one knew your friend Mary would be in the truck that night. I am so sorry."

When Smallwood mentioned Mary, Jim's heart rate increased, and Jenny squeezed his hand.

Smallwood never noticed the interaction between Jim and Jenny and went on. "I told Pugh what we were doing wasn't right, and then everything changed. He became cold. I told him an innocent person was killed and all he did was shrug and say, 'Collateral damage." He is an evil man. He calls his office, the Eagles Nest. He thinks he is Hitler.

Jim gripped Jenny's hand tighter and clinched and unclenched his other fist. He knew what was coming.

"I can't prove it, but I am certain Pugh is the one responsible for you being shot last week. Of course, he didn't fire the gun himself, but he had his people do it. I suspect it was Slick Beck. He was a sniper in the Army.

Or it could have been Buck or Clyde, but they aren't as good sharpshooters as Beck.

"Beck is very professional. Everyone who works for Pugh is skilled with guns and are mean, evil men." Smallwood twisted his hands and shook his head.

"Reverend Smallwood, this is not the first time I have heard about Pugh and his involvement in Mary, Steve, and Irene's deaths. Delmar Batcher told me and Sgt. Major Harlow that Clyde and Buck were responsible. One pushed Irene down the steps and the other shot Steve. But Batcher never told the authorities. I appreciate you telling me, but you have to tell the authorities."

"Jim, I will tell anyone, I just don't know who to trust. Pugh owns a lot people in law enforcement here in Lincoln and Shelby County."

The door opened, and Lt. Malcolm walked in, "He doesn't own me. He doesn't own the District Attorney, the State Attorney General, the Governor, or the United States Attorney.

Smallwood turned to Malcolm, dropping his head into his hands and muttering, "Thank you Jesus, it is finally over."

59

Jim was angry and sad, but mostly relieved. Finally, after two years of agony, optimism, crushing defeats, false hopes, and depression, he felt relief. Everything was said, and a law enforcement officer heard it all.

"I will take Reverend Smallwood to Columbus and we can provide security and hear the rest of his testimony. There are others who need to hear it, and I want it recorded. And we are going to have a ton of questions for you, Reverend," Malcolm said.

"I will answer any questions, but first, if it's all right with you, officer, I want to finish telling Mr. Monaghan. He needs to hear it all," Smallwood countered.

"Please let him talk, Lieutenant," Jim said.

Malcolm nodded, "You have the floor, Reverend."

"Jim, I told you when you started to look at the casket switching, Pugh went nuts. He couldn't afford to have the tip of the iceberg bothered. He was afraid, if you got into that operation, you might look further. That's why you had to be slowed down. Without Irene and Steve, you couldn't find anything else out about Reid.

"And that would keep you out of his other operations. Those operations were what he wanted to protect. The casket switching was the tip of the iceberg, but it was the key to other more profitable operations.

Smallwood explained that Pugh's operations include drug dealers, loan sharks, and prostitutes in Columbus, Cleveland, Cincinnati, and even in Lincoln. Smallwood said Pugh was involved with crime syndicates in Philadelphia, Chicago, Miami, and New York.

"You know those moving vans, with 'Moving Specialists" painted on the sides?

They haven't moved anyone's furniture in years. Inside those trucks are some wooden boxes of furniture, but mostly the cargo is illegal drugs. His people pick drugs up at the Gulf of Mexico and haul them to Miami, New York, Philly, Chicago, and of course, here in Lincoln and the rest of Ohio. It's been going on for

years. He invests in businesses in Lincoln, but always has one of his people

running them. They are all money laundering operations.

And his marijuana business is thriving. He uses those 18-wheelers to distribute it in Chicago, Ohio, and up and down the east coast. But Ohio is a small-time operation compared to the other cities. He pays his people well and no one talks. I understand he makes a ton of money out of it. Reid is a wizard with numbers. He launders the money into accounts all over the country and even in Switzerland.

"What will surprise you the most is one of his most lucrative marijuana operations is right here in Lincoln. There are two young men, who live in The Simpson

Villages. I believe their names are Dewayne and Tyrell. Pugh has one of his people sell the stuff to those two at his most inflated price. He brags that he has hardly any overhead and it's almost all profit."

"You understand now, Mr. Monaghan, why you had to be stopped."

"I do, Jim said, "and I appreciate your telling us all of this, but why now? Why are you coming forward now?"

Smallwood smiled and said, "I finally found Jesus."

He told of feeling abandoned when he was arrested. "They provided me with a lawyer, but all the effort was to save Reid. Among other things, he was Pugh's accountant."

At the Ohio State Reformatory in Mansfield, Smallwood and Reid were in the same cell and, at the time, both hated Blacks. Pugh put them in touch with some KKK guys and together they planned an attack on some of the Blacks.

"I didn't want to be part of it. I was beginning to feel remorse for what I had done. But the KKK guys, excuse me, Miss," Smallwood said looking at Jenny, "the KKK guy told me he heard the Blacks were going to sexually attack me the next time I was in the showers. So, I joined Reid and the KKK, hoping to convince the Blacks I was no one to mess with. I couldn't have been more wrong."

Reverend Smallwood told them his guys lost the fight. Even though the guards gave them batons to use, the Blacks overcame them, and Smallwood was brutally beaten.

"I was in the hospital for months, and I was taken care of by an older black man. Later, I found out he was Edgar Johnson's father. He kept me alive, making sure I got my medicine and did my rehab. There is no question, he saved my life. While there, I prayed every waking moment and I found Jesus again.

"I wept for days in sorrow for what I had done. When I was able to get out of the hospital, I asked the Warden if I could stay and help minister to the sick and the dying. I told him I didn't want to go back to the cell with Reid.

"The Warden, a devout Christian, took pity on me and assigned me to the hospital. My life changed."

Smallwood told the group, he was surprised when he was pardoned. A week before the pardon, an attorney from Wilbur T. Waters' office came to visit him in the prison. He was told a pardon was coming down the road, but there were stipulations.

He had to leave the area, never return to Lincoln, and never to speak to a policeman or to Jim Monaghan. If he did, there would be consequences.

On the day of the pardon, he was held back, while Pugh picked up Reid in front of the prison. No one was there to get Smallwood.

The prison gave him bus money to Columbus, where he walked to the Columbus Mission, and where has been ministering to the addicted and the homeless ever since. He proudly announced he has been sober since he went to prison.

"I drank a lot when I was living the big life with Pugh and Reid. We always had the best wine and whiskey and I acquired a taste for it. Sometimes, I was hung over when I stepped behind the pulpit on Sunday morning," Smallwood confided.

"Then why now?" Jim asked. "Why are you in my hospital room now? Why didn't you go to George Rogers when you were arrested? You could have cut a deal and never have gone to prison.

"Because Pugh told me, through one of the deputies at the jail, that I would be killed if I talked to anyone. The deputy told me they would kill me and my family. They told me just to listen to my attorney and take a plea for getting a cut of the commissions.

"But that's all in the past. My wife divorced me when I was fired from First Baptist and she has moved back to Indianapolis. She has remarried and has a restraining order against me. I can't come within a mile of her or the kids. I am dead to them. If I died, none of them would even come to the funeral."

"I am so sorry," Jenny said.

"I decided to come to you, Jim, when I read about you being shot, I prayed for your recovery, and I knew I had to do something. I knew Pugh was behind the shooting."

Malcolm, who had been feverishly taking notes looked up and said, "Jim, this is what you have been waiting for. Reverend, I am going to take you into protective custody. You don't have to worry about consequences. It's unfortunate, you don't have any documentation of your story. I'm sure Pugh and Reid will say it's just a bullshit story."

For the first time, Smallwood smiled. He opened his shirt and pulled out a large manila envelope. "It's all here. Notes from my meetings, copies of cancelled checks. When I had an inkling there was illicit activity, I started taking notes and keeping records. In here, among other things, you will find the cancelled checks I sent to Clyde, Buck, and Delmar for killing Irene, Steve, and ramming your truck.

"I also have a note about my phone call to Pugh to make sure he wanted the checks to be so generous. The checks were written out of one of the Church's charity accounts."

Smallwood gave the folder to Jim.

"Hang on. That's evidence, Jim. It belongs to me," Malcolm said.

"You can have the originals, but I want copies," Jim said. "I won't use them until you and the team say it's okay, but I want my own copies," Jim insisted.

As Malcolm left, he told Jim and Jenny he was going to assign an Ohio State Trooper to both Jim's and Jack Wilson's hospital rooms as well as Wilson's home.

"We won't make the same mistake we did with Delmar," Malcolm said.

Jenny walked to the window and reported two pickup trucks with eagle emblems on them were in the parking lot. Jim told Malcolm about the trucks following Smallwood the night before. After a short discussion, Jim suggested calling Ken Simon, putting Smallwood on a gurney with a sheet over his head and placing him in Simon's ambulance. After they left the hospital area, Malcolm could drive him to Columbus.

Smallwood was just about out the door, when Jim called out, "Reverend Smallwood, was Chief Buckner an attendee at those early morning meetings?"

"Yes, he was. I am not going to tell you about anyone else. I know I am going back to jail, but hopefully, if I cooperate, and give the prosecution the names, I can get assigned to the hospital at the prison, where I can do some good.

"But, Mr. Monaghan, when I tell the prosecutors, I will tell you too."

60

A fter Malcolm and Smallwood left, Jim and Jenny spent the afternoon talking about Smallwood's amazing story. They called Audrey Hill, Brad Hauser, and Judge McCallister and asked them to stop by the hospital. Midway through their conversation, Jim sat up in bed and said, "You told Reverend Smallwood we were going to get married. I know you have a lot of money, but aren't I the one who asks that question?

"Well, I know you are going to ask me. I just wanted to make the Reverend comfortable," Jenny smiled.

"Well, young lady, when I ask you, or I should say, **if** I ask you, I will buy the diamond engagement ring. We are not using your money."

"Oh, Jim, I don't think I want one. They are so ostentatious. At the sorority, the girls would come back at night and go around showing their rings off. I thought it was a bit much. I think we should have just plain gold bands."

"Jenny, I haven't asked you yet!"

"Well, how are you guys doing? Jim, you look great!"

a smiling Audrey chirped as she led Hauser and the Judge into the hospital room.

"You aren't going to believe what I have in this manila folder and what Reverend Smallwood told us this morning. And Lt. Malcolm heard it all."

"So, tell us, Jim. All the details, please," Hauser said as they all pulled up chairs.

The three were sober as Jim and Jenny took turns telling Smallwood's story. Jim added that Jack Wilson, who was recovering nicely, told him earlier that he thought it was Slick Beck, Pugh's number one employee, who shot him.

Jim pointed to the manila envelope. He told them Malcolm didn't want him to have it, but Smallwood insisted on giving it to Jim. Jenny had gone to Sister Mary Mark's office and made copies. Malcolm had taken the originals.

"I told Malcolm, we wouldn't do anything to upset the investigation, but we wanted the documents and we want to be first with the story."

Jim gave the envelope to Hauser, who complimented Jim on his instincts. He said he would stop by the newspaper office on his way home and store the documents in the publisher's safe.

"Even in your hospital bed with two bullet holes in your chest, you are still the reporter, aren't you Jim? Bernard would be so proud," Judge McCallister beamed.

No one was surprised Chief Buckner was involved with Pugh. Audrey had read her father's file on Buckner. It didn't show any criminal activity, but there was ample evidence, he was involved in the KKK in the south.

McCallister asked Jim and Jenny if Smallwood had given any indication who else attended the early morning meetings at Pugh's machine shed.

When the judge asked the question, Jim felt like a sledge hammer had hit him in the chest. He slumped in his chair and his hands came to his face.

Jenny rushed to his side and said, "What's wrong Jim, what's wrong. Somebody call for a nurse!"

"I'm okay, I just got exhausted. I need to rest. Could all of you leave? All of you except Audrey," Jim pleaded.

"No, I am going to stay with you Jim," Jenny said, "Where is the nurse?"

Jim made eye contact with Judge McCallister and said, "No, Jenny, I am going to be fine. I know you and the judge were supposed to meet earlier today and go over your notes for your summer school classes. Now would be a good time for that. I just need to rest and talk to Audrey about something personal."

Jenny looked at him suspiciously. But Judge McCallister read the situation and said, "Jenny, we really should spend some time going over the notes, so let's drive over to my office and we can get started."

Jenny stared at Jim. "Considering what we talked about today, I want you to know, I think you are holding something back from me, Jim. I respect the judge's time and I appreciate his help, so I am going to leave, but, Jim Monaghan, I am not comfortable."

Jenny stared at Jim, but eventually walked over and gave him a soft hug. She hugged Audrey and together with the judge and Hauser, Jenny left the hospital room.

Audrey was totally confused by Jim's sudden exhaustion followed by his walking purposefully to the door to tell the nurses they were not to be disturbed.

At the window Jim waved at Jenny, who blew him a kiss and he returned it.

When Jenny was out of sight, Jim started to cry. Audrey was befuddled. Not knowing exactly what to say, she said she understood how emotional the day must have been. After two years, it would be over soon. She asked if he was thinking about Mary. If he was, she understood, and Jenny would understand, too.

"No, no, that's not it. It's much worse," Jim whispered.

"Audrey you know I am in love with Jenny. I know Mary would understand and would be happy for me. Jenny and I talked today about getting married."

"Jim, I am so happy for you two. You are a great couple. So, what is bothering you?"

"Audrey, I know who goes to the meetings at Pugh's machine shed. I know the people who are involved in this conspiracy, this money laundering operation, this whole pile of shit."

"That's great, Jim, who goes to the meetings?"

"I know Chief Buckner, Mayor Weir, the City Manager, Reid, and get this, Willy. I saw his car parked outside Pugh's shed."

"Goodness Jim, I can't believe Mayor Weir is involved. His family has been around for years. He has a very successful home building business and is one of the most prominent families in town. And what would Willy be doing there?"

"Willy has been fighting me from the day I told him about Irene Dunn's phone call. I may never have told you this, but when Mary and I were having dinner that night, he showed up all smiles and said my truck had been delivered to the paper's parking lot, but it was in the sports department space and had to be moved.

Mary and I got in the truck and, within minutes, I was rammed, and Mary died. Quite a coincidence.

"But I don't give a shit about Weir or Willy. Audrey,

Jenny's father, Professor Harrison also drove into Pugh's driveway. Jenny's father is part of the group."

Audrey shook her head. "You don't know for sure, Jim. Please don't jump to conclusions."

"Audrey, I was right about the copper casket. I was right about Buck, Clyde, and Delmar Batcher; I was right about Lloyd Collier. I have the same feeling about this group.

"How do I tell Jenny? We talked about getting married. How do I tell her that her father is part of a group that tried to murder me? My God, I am sick. I think I want to puke."

"Jim, you need to handle this delicately. You can't jump to conclusions. You need to talk to Lt. Malcolm and proceed very carefully. Jenny is strong, Jim. She and I are as close as sisters. I know her well. I knew she was in love with you before you did. She told me months ago. Trust her, Jim. But don't say anything until you know for sure."

Audrey left, and Jim was alone in his hospital room. He rang the nurse's station and a nurse hurried in.

"Could I get a sleeping pill tonight? I need to knock myself out."

The nurse looked at him and told him, he had too many visitors and probably needed to sleep through the night. She gave him the pill.

Before the pill took effect, Jim cried and prayed. As he drifted off to sleep, he thought of his friend Sgt. Major Harlow. 'Don't borrow trouble, Jim.'

61

This place is beautiful and spacious, a long way from my dreary apartment, Jim mused as he walked around Jenny's condo. The condo had a large living room with sliding glass doors opening to the wrap-around balcony. The tidy kitchen had new appliances and a curved marble island, with four upholstered bar stools.

The dining room was empty as Jenny hadn't yet purchased a dining room set. The three bedrooms included a large master suite, a guest bedroom with an attached bath, and a smaller room Jenny had converted into an office. Jim smiled when he saw his framed picture, sitting prominently on her mahogany desk. Law books were neatly arranged on matching book shelves on each side of the desk. Artwork added color and style throughout the condo.

The walls were all painted creamy white. White carpet was in the bedrooms and gray marble tile in the kitchen, while the balance of the condo featured oak flooring.

Jim sat on a patio chair, put his feet up on the patio

table, looked out from Jenny's balcony at the new country club being built around the Lincoln reservoir, and sipped his Bushmills on ice.

He had been out of the hospital for almost four days and was feeling stronger each day. Jenny was at the law school taking one of her summer school exams. She was going to spend the balance of the afternoon with Judge McCallister, preparing for her last final.

Jim knew he had to address the tension that was building between him and Jenny. It started over a week ago in his hospital room, when he slumped in his chair remembering watching Jenny's father drive into Pugh's lane early that fatal Friday morning.

Jenny accused him of keeping something back from her and kept trying to get him to talk about it.

Even after moving in with Jenny, the tension continued. Though they had been intimate before, Jenny made sure Jim was ensconced in the guest bedroom. The only physical contact they'd experienced, since Jim came home from the hospital, was an occasional hug.

Before she left for her law school exam that morning, Jenny told him the air was going to be cleared one way or another before her mother came for dinner that night. "Something happened that day at the hospital. You haven't been the same since, Jim, and I want to know what caused that. I just don't believe you suddenly got tired," Jenny said sternly, face grim and hands on her hips.

Jim called Special Agent Malcom and asked to see Reverend Smallwood. Malcolm objected, telling Jim, they were still debriefing Smallwood. But Jim was forceful and told Malcolm, he was bringing Audrey Hill with him. And if he didn't cooperate, Jim was going to call the Governor.

Malcolm relented and surprised Jim by telling him Smallwood was being held in a suite at the Ramada Inn in Lincoln. They could visit, but Malcolm was going to be there. Jim agreed, called Audrey and asked her to pick him up, as he was not yet allowed to drive.

Smallwood looked immeasurably better. His face was less wan, and he didn't seem so stooped over. His new clothes fit, and Jim smiled as he noticed his black loafers matched.

"Delighted to see you, Jim. How do you like my accommodations? Unaccustomed as I have become to such luxury, I slept on the floor the first couple of nights, but I am getting used to sleeping in a real bed."

Malcolm briefed Jim and Audrey on the progress they were making. The only question he and the team had was which grand jury to bring Smallwood's testimony to. Both the United States Attorney and the Shelby County District Attorney wanted first crack at him, but they were concerned about getting an impartial grand jury in Lincoln. They were leaning towards a grand jury in Columbus.

"It would be more convenient in Columbus, because we could have him brief the federal and the county grand juries, without going back and forth from Lincoln," Malcolm reported.

"I am glad things are moving along, but I have a more pressing problem. It's personal and I need answers, straight ones, from you, Reverend Smallwood. You want to make amends to me, well this is your chance.

"Tell me what you know about Professor Harrison Fowler. What role did he play in Pugh's conspiracy? Did he have anything to do with the decision to ram my truck?" Jim asked, his heart pounding.

Jim wanted the answer but was afraid of what Smallwood would say.

Smallwood looked at Jim, then at Audrey and finally at Malcom.

"Who's Harrison Fowler?" Smallwood asked.

"Are you telling me you don't know a Harrison Fowler? That Harrison Fowler was never at any of your meetings in Pugh's machine shed.

"I've never heard of the man. He was never at any meeting I was at and I believe, no, I know, I was at all of them, or at least the important ones."

Jim sank in his chair, relieved.

"Mr. Malcolm, I haven't given you any of the names yet because I am holding out for a guarantee I will be assigned to the hospital at the prison, but seeing Miss Hill here, I feel an obligation to tell her, her man Willy, was always there.

Audrey's mouth formed a silent Oh.

Smallwood looked at Audrey. "Willy is a real weasel. He was always whining about Jim and your father. He said that he was responsible for the success of the newspaper, but your father never paid him what he was worth.

"Jim, he delivered your truck to you that fateful night. That was not an accident; it was planned. Pugh owns the repair shop where you were getting your truck tuned up. When it was there, they adjusted your brakes, so they wouldn't work like they should. They didn't want you to stop and have Pugh's truck miss you. They made sure they got it back to your newspaper in time for you to take it home. Willy told us you were going to this hotel, so they set it up for Clyde and Buck to ram you."

Audrey listened with her hand over her mouth.

"My God, Jim, why didn't my father or I figure out

that Willy's opposition to you was more than just professional jealousy. I am so sorry."

Jim reached over, squeezed her hand and said, "I don't care about Willy. I am just relieved Harrison wasn't part of the murderous conspiracy. But I still want to know why he was at the meeting on Friday morning, when, I assume, they finalized plans to shoot me. It's still not over, but at least he wasn't one of the original ones.

"But I for sure saw him drive into Pugh's driveway that morning. We made eye contact and he glared at me. I didn't think much of it, because I know he hates my guts. He has been against my going out with Jenny from the very beginning. It's hard to believe, he would be part of trying to kill me, but he was there at the meeting. And that evening, I was shot."

"Wait a minute, Jim. I want to know all about Harrison Fowler. What do you know?"

"Later, Lieutenant. I will call you later today or tomorrow, but right now, there is a young woman, I need to talk to."

Malcolm objected and stared at Jim. He held the stare causing Jim to think. *I must handle this right. Maybe I should just go alone, but this is going to be a shock to Jenny and Audrey is her best friend, so she should be there. Malcolm is a police officer and that could make her uncomfortable. But, this is the man who put everything on the line for me many times. I don't know how Jenny is going to react to my telling her about her dad. Maybe it would be best if Malcolm came with us.*

62

J udge McCallister's secretary said the judge was tutoring a student and didn't like to be disturbed. But Jim insisted. After keeping him, Audrey, and Malcolm waiting, for what Jim felt was an eternity, but was less than five minutes, the secretary escorted them into the judge's office.

Jenny and the judge were deep in discussion and didn't notice the three enter the room. Looking up, Jenny stared at Jim. "This better be important. I am having trouble with some of these concepts and my exam is tomorrow morning at nine."

The judge, noticing Special Agent Malcolm was with Jim and Audrey, knew it was important.

Jim and Audrey went to Jenny, and Jim put his arms around her.

He told Jenny how much he loved her and how he wanted to spend the rest of his life with her.

Audrey joined in the hug and told Jenny she was the sister she'd never had and no matter what, she would be there for her.

Jenny broke away, looked at Jim and said, "This has something to do with your reaction in the hospital room when the Judge asked you the question about who went to Pugh's meeting, doesn't it, Jim? Doesn't it?

"Yes, it does Jenny. Please sit down."

"I'll stand. Tell me. Tell me quick and don't leave anything out. Isn't that what you always say, Jim? Don't leave anything out."

Grabbing Jenny's hand, Jim told her that on the Friday morning of the shooting, he saw Buckner, Reid, the mayor and the city manager all go to Pugh's machine shed. He told her Willy's car was there and he knew Willy was part of the group.

"What does any of that have to do with us?" Jenny asked.

"Jenny, I saw your dad drive down Pugh's lane and park at the machine shed."

"Are you saying you think my dad is part of this conspiracy? This conspiracy you think plotted to kill you?" Jenny said, sinking into her chair.

"I don't know what to think, Jenny. I just know he was there Friday morning. He's your dad and can you understand why I have had such a hard time telling you."

Jenny looked at the faces of Audrey and the Judge, who were looking sympathetically at her, and at Malcolm, who had the face of a law enforcement officer, who just heard incriminating evidence.

Then she looked at Jim, who was kneeling in front of her and holding her hand. His face was contorted in anguish and tears were glistening in his eyes.

"My dad is a putz. He can be a pompous ass. But he is not a criminal, and he would not have anything to do with having you or anyone else shot. No, Jim, he doesn't like you and doesn't think you are good enough, but he is not a criminal.

"I refuse to believe that. I am going over to his office right now and confront him. And Jim, I want you to come with me. Let's go!" Jenny said standing and heading for the door.

"Wait a minute, I want to go too," said Audrey and Malcolm in unison.

"I think Malcolm should join us, Jenny," Jim said, "but Audrey, I don't think you should go."

Judge McCallister said, "I think just Jenny, Jim, and Everett should go. Having a law enforcement officer will give Harrison pause. But I agree with Jenny. I know him a little and I don't think he is a criminal. He certainly isn't in the same league with Buckner and the others."

63

"Come in," Professor Fowler barked. "I don't have much time. I am preparing for my seminar."

Jim, Jenny, and Malcolm walked in and found Fowler sitting with his feet up on his desk, reading a book.

Coming face to face with Fowler, Jim lost his temper. The months of being treated like a second-class citizen, the meanness, the criticism of him and his family, brought Jim to a boil. Thinking of Haley and his own close call with death, Jim stared menacingly at Fowler and shouted,

"What were you doing at Pugh's machine shed the Friday Haley Johnson was killed and I was shot? What did you guys plan that day?"

He pounded his fist on Fowler's desk and shouted, "I said, what the hell were you doing at Ron Pugh's barn the Friday morning I was shot."

Fowler pulled his feet off the desk and pushed his chair back into his credenza.

Jim's hand, moist with sweat, found a check attached as he raised his fist to pound Fowler's desk again. Jim looked at it and shouted, "What the hell is this? Blood money? You are taking money from that no-good son-of-a-bitch, Pugh. This check is from America Incorporated, Pugh's operation. What kind of a man are you?"

Jenny astonished at Jim's outburst, grabbed him by the arm and told him to settle down.

Fowler recovered from Jim's outburst and snarled, "Monaghan you've gone too far this time. How dare you come into my office shouting at me. I don't give a rat's ass about my wife visiting you in the hospital. It makes me sick knowing you sleep overnight at my daughter's condo. I don't like you and I never have. And your behavior now just proves my point. Jenny, I hope you are seeing this jackass for the uncouth bum he is.

"I am going to call the police and have them throw your ass out of here. Jenny, I wish you would come to your senses. This man is trash."

Grabbing the check from Jim's hands, he shouted back at Jim, "This is an investment check, you asshole. An investment check. What the hell are you talking about, blood money.

Jenny's hands were to her mouth, shocked at the exchange between her father and the man she loved.

Malcolm walked over to Fowler and said, "You don't need to call the police, Professor, I am an Ohio State Trooper." Malcolm showed Fowler his credentials.

"What is going on? Why is there a state trooper in my office?" Fowler said, slightly shocked.

Regaining her composure, Jenny said, "Everyone stop it! Stop it! I will handle this," Jenny yelled as she pulled Jim away from the front of Fowler's desk.

Standing and pointing his finger at Jim, Fowler replied, "I don't have to answer any of your questions,

Monaghan" Looking at Malcom, he said "Trooper, get this man out of my office."

Malcolm didn't move.

"Stop it, both of you. Stop it now!" Jenny pleaded. "We are here for some serious reasons. Now, everyone, calm down."

Jim regained some of his composure and backed away from Fowler's desk. Fowler remained standing, staring at Jim, his contempt for the younger man visible.

Jenny walked around his desk and hugged her father, but then she backed up.

"Dad, I love you. I am sorry for telling you I hate you. You are my dad. But you may be in serious trouble, but I don't believe it. I can't believe you could be involved in a conspiracy that wanted Jim dead."

"What are you talking about, wanting Jim dead?. I don't like him. He's not good enough for you, but for God's sake, what are you talking about, Jenny? I don't want him dead; I just want him out of your life."

Harrison and Jim stared at one another. "Is this another one of your conspiracy theories, Monaghan? You know how I feel about you, but for God's sake, how could even you or anyone think I had anything to do with the shooting?"

"Trooper, why are you here? Am I in trouble? Should I have a lawyer?"

"Professor, I am investigating the murders of Irene Dunn, Steve Hampton, Mary Ryan, Haley Johnson, and six others from Friday night at the church. And the attempted murder of Jim Monaghan. Let me ask you, do you think you need a lawyer?"

64

F owler slumped in his chair. He looked at Jim and said, "You hate me, don't you?"

"This has nothing to do with my personal relationship with you, Mr. Fowler. All I know is I saw you drive into Pugh's farm that Friday morning, and that night someone shot me, killed Haley and others," Jim icily answered.

"Dad, please answer the question. Do you have anything to do with Pugh and his group?" Jenny pleaded.

Fowler looked up at Jim. "I saw you watch me drive by and go to Pugh's that Friday morning. It is an investment club. They asked me to join it at the same time they asked me to become chairman of the Shelby County Commission.

"I have made a few bucks there, but it's not any of your business Monaghan. I have done nothing wrong," Fowler said coldly. "And I sure as hell don't answer to you for my actions."

Malcolm put his hands-on Fowler's desk, leaned over and said, "Professor, Jim Monaghan is not your enemy here. He is your friend. He has brought us together in an informal setting to find out what you know. Based on what I have learned from Jim and one other individual, I could put you in handcuffs and bring you to Columbus for questioning. Now, I am asking Jim to tell you what he knows and then, Professor, you might reconsider your attitude."

Fowler leaned back in his chair, stunned.

Jim summarized for the professor.

"We know for a fact that Ronald Pugh runs a criminal enterprise. He has a massive money laundering operation; he works with crime syndicates in Miami, Chicago, Philadelphia and New York. He runs drugs, prostitutes, loan sharking and other nefarious enterprises. He has a moving company that moves drugs all over the eastern seaboard.

"We know he and his gang are responsible for the deaths of Irene Dunn, Steve Hampton, and Mary Ryan. They were murdered. We know what I have just told you to be true. It's not a guess. It's not suppositions. We have a witness and the documents to prove it.

"We don't know for sure they shot me and killed Haley and others Friday night, but we are getting closer. We hoped you might be helpful. I don't want to believe Jenny's dad and Martha's husband could be a part of it, but the circumstances are not favorable for you. Because you are Jenny's dad, we are here, informally. Can you help us and help yourself?"

Fowler shook his head as if to clear it and exhaled a long sigh. He turned to Jenny, "Jenny, I had nothing to do with any of those ghastly events. I thought I was part of an investment club, and I was honored that Ron Pugh had invited me to join. Prominent men in town were also members, and I felt flattered. I also wanted to make money, so we didn't have to depend on your mother's wealth.

Fowler reached for his daughter's hand and drew her close. "Jenny, please believe me. I know nothing about any murders. I may not be a perfect person, but I would never be a part of anything that evil."

Turning to Malcolm, Fowler said, "Mr. Malcolm, I believe I can be helpful to you, and I will cooperate fully. He stood to address Jim.

"I swear I never participated in any discussion that even remotely referenced shooting you or anyone else. Trust me, I was there only for investment talk.

Fowler placed his hand on his forehead, dropped into his chair and said, "Oh my God." He placed his head in his hands and was silent. Jenny reached over and touch his shoulder.

"It's ok, Dad. Tell Trooper Malcolm what you know."

Looking up, tears in his eyes, Fowler turned to Jim and said, "Let me tell you this. Early in the meeting that Friday morning, Jim, your name came up and it was suggested it would be good if you were out of town.

"I told them I didn't want to talk about Jim Monaghan. I asked when we were going to talk about investments. Pugh told me they weren't going to talk about investments. He asked me to leave and not come back. Then he gave me a final check."

Jim, Jenny, and Malcolm exchanged glances while the Professor talked. Jenny grabbed Jim's hand and squeezed it tight.

"I had no idea what they mean by getting you out of town. For God's sake, the Chief of Police was there; so was the mayor and city manager. Surely, this cannot be true."

"It's true, Professor," Jim said.

"Mr. Malcolm, as I promised, I will cooperate with you any way I can, but I'd like to call Judge McCallister and get a recommendation for a lawyer. I know several lawyers, but I think it would be prudent to seek the judge's advice on who would be best for me under these circumstances. Now, am I under arrest?"

"No, you are not under arrest, Professor," Malcom assured. He told Fowler he would appreciate it if Fowler and his attorney could plan to come to Columbus in the next few days to meet with other members of the team. He asked Fowler to bring all records and notes regarding his discussions and meetings with Pugh, Buckner, Willy, Weir, and the city manager Davis. Malcolm stressed to Fowler to write down from his memory every detail from the meeting that referred to getting Jim out of town.

Fowler agreed.

Jenny wrapped her arms around her father and said she was proud of him. She went on to tell him her mother was bringing dinner to the condo that evening, and she wanted him to be there. "It's time, Dad," she said.

Harrison looked at Jim and asked if he would be comfortable with him being at dinner? Jim slowly nodded his head in agreement reached over and shook Harrison's hand.

As they were leaving, Fowler said, "One more thing. They wanted Edgar Johnson out of town, too."

Jim and Malcolm shared a knowing look of another

nail being hammered into the coffin of Pugh Incorporated.

Jenny and Jim walked out arm in arm.

"I need to stop at the Judge's office and see if I can get my final changed from tomorrow. I hope my classmates don't hear about all these changes. They will think I am the teacher's pet," Jenny said mischievously.

65

F or two weeks, the investigation intensified each day
as additional information was uncovered. Working
with the Franklin County District Attorney in Columbus,
County District Attorney George Rogers had empaneled
a Grand Jury. Two blocks away, United States Attorney
Charles Adderley empaneled a Federal Grand Jury.

Using Reverend Smallwood's testimony and records,
along with the bank records from the Alex Reid
litigation, the attorneys and the grand juries received
mounds of evidence. Much to Jim's relief, Harrison
Fowler was considered a minor player in the events
surrounding Pugh's operation. Malcolm put it best to
Jim, "Wrong place, wrong time."

Jim made an unexpected contribution when he
called Anita Winston, the roommate of Cindy Jenkins,
who was murdered by Governor Anderson's one-time
aide, Lloyd Collier. Cindy and Anita were high-end
prostitutes. Anita told Jim the girls on the street all
worked for pimps who were well organized. She gave Jim

the names of five of the girls who would be helpful in finding out who was behind the pimps.

Adderley was particularly interested in interviewing Reverend Jefferson and Edgar Johnson. He was shocked to hear of the police harassment, Haley's kidnapping and assault, the burning of Reverend Jefferson's church, and the garbage-tossing Edgar and his fellow residents endured. He was especially interested in the stories about young men and boys detained, questioned, roughed up, and intimidated by Chief Buckner's special patrol.

Adderley obtained copies of the suspended sentences of Buck and Clyde. After interviewing the original judge on the case, who told him he had been threatened if he didn't call in sick, Adderley told his colleagues he had never seen such blatant corruption.

He planned a series of indictments of Buckner, his special squad, and others, including Judge Lawlor, who were involved. Jim told him Buck and Clyde were the force behind the harassments, but he was certain it was ordered by Pugh.

Rogers and Adderley coordinated their efforts, and, on Friday, indictments were presented to the respective state and federal judges, who ordered arrests and issued warrants for searches and seizures of additional records and products.

Earlier in the week, the Ohio State Police flew a traffic plane over the Pugh Farm. Using a Super Eight Kodak movie camera, the photographer captured rivers of green throughout the brown ripened corn fields. In keeping with the cooperation between the authorities and the News Tribune, Art Wilks was beside the state photographer, taking still photographs.

After reviewing the evidence, the State Police inserted two undercover officers on the north end of

Pugh's property. Walking a half mile through the cornfields, they came across the plants and took samples to the State Labs which identified the product as illegal marijuana.

Multi-faceted law enforcement raids on multiple sites were set for Saturday morning.

Jim and Jenny met with Malcolm, Rogers, and Adderley for lunch on Friday. Knowing the grand juries had been meeting and suspecting a raid was planned, Jim asked, if there was a raid, could a certain police captain from Chicago be part of it.

Both Rogers and Adderley were sympathetic to Jim's request, but he was told no.

"It wouldn't be appropriate for him to be involved and besides, Jim, it's too late for him to get here. Things are moving too fast," Adderley said.

Jim had been kept in the dark about the grand jury testimony and the plans of the law enforcement agencies. D.A. Rogers told Jim, he wanted him to be at coffee at the new Holiday Inn at 5 a.m. the next morning.

Jenny picked up on the invitation before Jim did. "I want to come, too," she pleaded.

"No, Jenny, I am making an exception for Jim. He can bring the Sgt. Major, too, but, I'm sorry, I just can't make an exception for you," Rogers said.

"By the way, Jim," Rogers said. "I think we just got the last nail we needed to seal this case up tight. Sgt. Major Harlow came to see me yesterday and brought a friend with him.

"The gentleman, and you won't need to know his name, lives at Simpson Village. He is a member of the legion and had quite a story to tell. He told us he was standing outside his residence at the intersection of Fourth and Bradley. He was watching the Stones surround your car and wanted to do something, but he is old and was afraid. Now, remember, he was north of you, not twenty yards from your car.

"He was in the infantry in Korea and said he could identify guns by the sounds each type of gun made. He reported he heard a gunshot and he ducked and fell to one knee. He testified that the shots were coming from behind him. He turned to look north and heard three more shots and he swore they were coming from one of those large elm trees on the north side of Simpson Village, right on Pugh's property line.

Rogers' eyes narrowed as he continued, "He said he told Buckner, but the Chief brushed him off and told him if he told anyone about what he heard, he would be arrested. So, Jim, I think it is safe to say someone in a tree on Pugh's farm shot you."

"Damn," Jim said. "I was lucky. Poor Haley never had a chance."

Jenny appealed Rogers' decision that she be barred from joining the team in the morning, but Rogers was firm in telling her, she couldn't go along.

Jenny was still miffed by the time they reached her condo. They had to change clothes and go to the country club for dinner with Jenny's parents.

"You know, I'm not sure I like this new arrangement with your parents. I never had to dress up like this for dinner on Friday night," Jim quipped.

"Yeah, but an exciting dinner on Friday night for you Jim, was eating a cheeseburger at Harlow's. I am just grateful my parents are accepting you. Dad still has a long way to go, but he is grateful you brought Everett Malcolm to his office that day. It saved him a lot of embarrassment.

Going to the country club was pleasant for Jim, and

it had nothing to do with the food. Dressed in his best and only suit, he walked in with his head high. The first person he saw was Audrey. He hugged her and whispered, "Five a.m. tomorrow."

She whispered back telling him Adderley and Rogers had called her. Wilks would be with Jim, but other photographers and reporters were meeting at the paper at five and would be assigned then. She told him she originally wanted one of the television news crews to go with Jim, but Malcolm told her he didn't want any media other than Jim to be present because he thought there could be substantial resistance.

Malcolm said they expected the other arrests to be routine, but Pugh was a wild card. Knowing Jim was going to Pugh's, she decided not to argue with the law enforcement officials.

Dinner with the Fowlers was pleasant, also. Jim was impressed with Harrison asking questions about farming. He wanted to know about the process, from planting to marketing. Was it possible the bread he was eating came from wheat that was raised on Jim's farm? Jim told Fowler that the soy bean was the miracle crop. "Ninety-nine percent of the soybean is protein," Jim informed him.

"Impossible," Fowler said. "That's impossible, how can that be?"

Jenny and Martha smiled at the exchange, but both women knew there was still a substantial amount of tension, resentment, and distrust between the two men.

Both Jenny and Martha were concerned about the number of Bushmills Jim was consuming. At one point, Jenny leaned over and asked if he thought he was drinking too much. Jim answered, "They relax me."

As dessert came, Jim looked around the room. He

purposely kept his eyes away from any of the others in the dining room. But as he ate his butter pecan ice cream, he watched Mayor Weir and city manager Davis having dinner. Chief Buckner was at another table as was Judge Lawlor. Jim allowed his eyes to meet Alex Reid, who stared. Jim lowered his eyes and looked away.

As Jim and Jenny left the club, the two women exchanged warm embraces while Jim and Harrison shook hands.

As they got into their car, Jenny turned to Jim, gave him a hug and whispered in his ear, "Do you think it is time you moved out of the guest room?"

66

SATURDAY, SEPTEMBER 11, 1965

Five A.M.

Jim had never seen so many police cars. Federal Marshalls, Customs Agents, Federal ATF Agents, Ohio State Police, Shelby County Sheriff's and special deputized sheriffs from Franklin County assembled for a coordinated assault on seven locations in Lincoln.

The main contingent of State Troopers and FBI Agents, led by Special Agent Malcolm and the Special Agent in Charge of the Columbus office, would descend on the Pugh Farm at precisely six a.m.

They were to be accompanied by Jim, Sgt. Major Harlow, and Art Wilks, with stern orders from Malcolm to stay in the background. Jim had told Malcolm he expected Pugh to be in his machine shed, but Malcolm said he had enough troopers to swarm the residence and the machine shed.

Other contingents of Ohio State Troopers, FBI agents, Shelby, and Franklin County sheriff deputies would make their assaults on the homes of Mayor Weir, Manager Davis, Judge Lawlor, Alex Reid, and Zack "Willy" Williams.

Most of the men were asleep when the police knocked on their respective doors. Eventually someone at each residence opened the door. Everyone except Alex Reid. The police had to use a battering ram to open the door. Entering the home with their guns drawn, they yelled out for Reid to come down the steps with his hands up, but they heard only silence.

Reid's sister-in-law, who was visiting, ran down the stairs in her nightgown, tears streaming.

"He is in the children's bedroom and he is hiding behind my daughters!" she told the officers.

"How old are your children? Where is his wife?" the officers ask.

"They are eight-year-old twins," the mother sobbed. "My sister is pleading with him at the door."

The officers quietly went up the stairs. Reid's wife, on her knees, clutched her robe tightly with one hand and the doorknob with the other. The officers asked if Reid had a gun and she told them she didn't think there was a gun in the house, nor had Alex ever fired a gun.

The officers moved Reid's wife out of hallway and down the stairs and began a conversation with Reid. They told him he was in enough trouble and didn't want kidnapping to be added to the list of charges.

Reid told them to go to hell and the twin's sharp cries were immediately muffled. Just as the officer kicked open the door, the twins each bit down hard on Reid's fingers causing him to let go. They ran from him, while the trooper tackled their uncle. He was handcuffed and brought down the stairs and out of the house into a waiting squad car.

This time his wife didn't ask if he would be home in time for brunch at the club. Rather, she told her sister she hoped he would never come back.

It was a completely different story at Mayor Weir's house.

Weir hadn't slept in days. Despite the early hour, he was in his study drinking coffee, when the doorbell chimed. He knew trouble was coming. He kept replaying in his mind the conversation about getting Jim Monaghan out of town. And that same night, Monaghan was shot.

He knew the shooting of a newspaperman would bring a lot of heat. He remembered Slick's L.L. Bean boot and Monaghan's story about the footprint at Jack Wilson's store. He instinctively knew who was at the door and confirmed it when he looked out the window.

"I've been expecting you, officers." Sticking his arms out to be handcuffed, he said, "You won't have any trouble with me. Please tell the district attorney, I am ready to cooperate." The only redeeming fact for Weir was his wife was asleep upstairs and his children were away at college and didn't see him being taken away in handcuffs.

Judge Lawlor and Manager Davis were both asleep when the police knocked on their respective doors. Both men had household help, who answered the door. Davis naively thought the police were seeking his help on a city issue.

Shocked when told they were there to arrest him, he told them to call his attorney and started to close the door. The lead officer pushed it open, threw Davis on the floor, and handcuffed his wrists behind his back.

Judge Lawlor handled his arrest with as much dignity as a 20-year circuit judge could do. His wife kept asking the officers, "Don't you know he is a judge. You can't arrest a judge. What did the judge do? What did he do?" Lawlor made no comment. He didn't say good bye to his wife.

Willy Williams had one comment when he was arrested. Meeting the officers at the door he growled, "That damn Monaghan, I should have fired him two years ago."

Chief Buckner decided he would take charge when the officers came to his door. Led by a captain of the Ohio State Police, the officer contingent was the second largest group at any of the houses.

Buckner's wife answered the door and yelled to her husband, "Billy Joe, some of your officers are here." Buckner came to the front door in full uniform, including his hat. Strapping on his gun, he stopped short when he saw no Lincoln police officers, only Ohio State Troopers and sheriff's deputies.

"What the…, what's going on, Trooper?"

"Billy Joe Buckner, you are under arrest for conspiracy to commit murder, money laundering and a series of other charges. You have the right to remain…"

"I know the damn Miranda," Buckner said.

"You assholes will never make any of those charges stick. This is just bullshit. I bet Monaghan and News Tribune are out there. Well, tell him we will beat him again. Now, there is no need to arrest me.

"I will just be released on my own recognizance, so why don't you troopers go out to the interstate and arrest some speeders and let me and real law enforcement officers work on real crime here in Lincoln."

The Ohio State Police Captain had heard enough. "Stick out your hands, Chief, you are under arrest."

Buckner glared with venom at the officer, but slowly lifted his hands.

Concurrent with the home raids, U.S. Marshalls, FBI Agents, Custom officials, and A.T.F. officers, working with state police up and down the eastern seaboard, stopped and inspected all ***Moving Specialists*** eighteen wheelers. They confiscated hundreds of thousands of dollars of illegal drugs and arrested the drivers. At the company's headquarters in Lincoln, officials found a treasure trove of drugs and cash.

67

The largest contingent of officers, led by Everett
Malcolm, convened at the entrance to Pugh's
farm. Twenty FBI agents were spread out among the
officer contingent. In addition to regular Ohio State
troopers, a special force of specially trained assault
officers, was included.

If Pugh and his men decided to stand and fight,
these officers would lead the assault on the machine
shed. All the officers hit the edge of Pugh's driveway at
exactly six a.m. There were thirty squad cars in all, each
with two officers inside. Jim, Sgt. Major Harlow, and Art
Wilks were in the last car.

Five squad cars peeled off at Pugh's residence while
the others continued down the lane and surrounded
Pugh's machine shed.

At Pugh's home the troopers found Mrs. Pugh, who
said her husband was in his machine shed. They radioed
Malcolm, who confirmed his officers had secured the
perimeter of the machine shed.

Jim, Wilks, and Harlow were standing at a distance

behind the ring of officers. Wilks had a telephoto lens on his camera and like Jim, who had small binoculars, trained his sites on an open window on the second floor on the west side of the building.

Both Wilks and Jim noticed what they thought was movement behind the window and they told the officer next to them who radioed Malcom. With his telephoto lens focused on the window, Wilks yelled out, "Pugh is at the window."

Malcolm lifted a bull horn to his mouth ready to issue a call to Pugh to come out with his hands in the air when the long muzzle of a high-powered rifle poked out the partially open window.

"Gun! Gun! Gun!" Numerous officers yelled as bullets started zinging.

Bullets flew from Pugh's office window striking the ground and police vehicles, but no officer was hit. Jim, Sgt. Major Harlow, Wilks, and the other troopers were able to get cover behind the squad cars. Once under cover, under Malcolm's order, the officers returned fire.

After the first few volleys, every window in Pugh's office was shattered. Pugh had stopped firing and the officers stealthily approached the building. Jim, Wilks, and Harlow watched from a distance.

Malcolm led his officers to the front door of the machine shed. They banged on the door and were surprised to hear a voice say, "It's open and we aren't armed."

They found Clyde, Buck, and Slick, all standing legs apart and arms in the air.

"We don't want no trouble," Slick said, "He's upstairs. He's armed, but I suspect you know that."

Jim crept to the shed in time to see Clyde, Buck, and Slick face down and handcuffed. Jim stood over Clyde and Buck and said, "Well, boys, we meet again." Clyde and Buck said nothing. Jim stared down at Slick. Knowing, he was the one who probably shot him and killed Haley, he wanted to kick him in the face.

"Don't do anything, Mr. Monaghan. I know how you feel, but you can't touch him," one of the officers said. Harlow grabbed Jim's arms and pulled him away.

Malcolm, and his officers, stood to the side of the door to Pugh's office. Malcolm yelled, "It's over, Ron. Come out with your hands up. Let's end this before anyone else gets hurt."

Malcolm's plea was met with silence.

"Don't make me break this door down, Ron. We can handle this peacefully and no one else needs to get hurt. What do you say, Ron? Let's end this"

There was no answer.

The sound of a single shot from a high-powered handgun shattered the silence.

Malcolm and his officers smashed the door open and raced into Pugh's office.

Behind his replica of the Resolute desk, with blood pouring out from under his chin and the top of his head, Ron Pugh was dead.

Malcolm called to Jim, who raced up the steps. "Just look, Jim, don't touch anything," warned Malcolm. "This is how the whole sordid, sad story ends," Malcolm said.

Looking at Pugh, blood pouring out of his head and a 357-magnum hand gun off to the side of his right hand, Jim thought. *The tough guy, the bully, the mean son-of-a-bitch, in the end, couldn't face up to what he had done, so he took the coward's way out.*

Harlow put his arm around Jim, who told Malcolm he didn't want to spend any more time with Pugh, and together they walked out. Wilks had come up with Jim and Malcolm told him, in all their planning, they didn't think to bring a photographer. He asked if Wilks could take some pictures of the crime scene for the State Patrol's records.

Wilks agreed.

When Ken Simon's ambulance crew picked Pugh up and transported him to the county coroner's office, a slew of FBI agents swarmed through Pugh's office. They found a wealth of files in Pugh's desk. The steel door to one of the conference rooms proved a bigger challenge, but once inside and surveying the file cabinets and safe, the head FBI agent requested an industrial copy machine be delivered as soon as possible. He estimated it would take at least 48 hours to sort through the files.

Like his hero, Adolph Hitler, Pugh kept meticulous records.

"He has names, dates, accounts, payoffs. It's all here, Malcolm. It is a treasure chest of evidence. I can't wait for Adderley to see all of this," the agent said beaming.

68

J im's story on the arrests of six of Lincoln's leading
citizens and the suicide of Ronald Pugh was the
banner headline, page one story on Sunday
morning. In a sidebar highlighted story, Jim wrote a
summary of events leading up to Saturday's raids and
arrests.

Jim's summary started with a phone call from Irene
Dunn more than two years earlier.

He retold the story of Reid's arrest, trial, and his
sentencing and subsequent pardon. He told of Buck, and
Clyde, and Delmar Batcher and their bizarre story. Both
stories ran four full columns on the front page. With
Wilk's photos and others provided by other
photographers, who were at the arrests of the others, the
entire front page was devoted to the arrests and raids.

Page Three was filled as well. In the middle of Jim's
story, a box indicated it was the first of a five-part series.

Audrey had assigned eight reporters and six
photographers to the events of the fateful Saturday. With
Hauser, she evaluated all the stories and photographs.

While Sunday was always the largest paper of the week, she and Hauser decided, they needed a six-page special section to be included in Sunday's edition. On the front page of the special edition, she placed pictures of those killed by the alleged conspiracy.

A publisher first, she ordered thousands of extra papers to be printed and was told by ten a.m. on Sunday all the newsstands were empty and all the newspapers in the hotels, grocery stores and gas stations were sold out.

On page one of the special section, Jim wrote a short story about the man in black. He told of believing he was hallucinating in his hospital room one night when he thought he saw a man in black at his bedside. The man turned out to hold the keys to the investigation. Jim didn't name Reverend Smallwood and none of the defendants knew who it was.

Mayor Weir had suspicions but kept them to himself. Weir had already decided to put distance between himself and the others.

On Sunday morning, Jim sat on Jenny's balcony and, with a scotch on the rocks in hand, he read the special section. On the top left-hand side was Mary Ryan's picture. As he looked at Mary's picture, he turned and looked at Jenny.

"You know I loved her, don't you Jenny."

"Of course, I do, and I love you for it. You haven't called her parents yet. Don't you think you should?"

Jim nodded, went inside, and placed a call to Chicago. He reached Mary's mother and asked that she get her husband on the phone. Together they listened to Jim's story. They were delighted those responsible for Mary's death were finally behind bars. They told Jim they were delighted he was feeling better. They had sent flowers and best wishes to him in the hospital when they had read in the Chicago Tribune about the tragic events that Friday evening at Fourth and Bradley.

In his Irish brogue, Mary's father lamented a police chief was involved and regretted that Pugh had committed suicide. "I'm not surprised he shot himself. Tough guys like him are rarely courageous. Really a coward.'

Promising to keep in touch, they hung up. *I hope that news brought them some peace,* Jim thought.

As soon as Jim hung up the phone, it rang again.

"Not sure where you are Jim, but Audrey gave me this phone number," said Jim's friend, Charlie Sloan, editor of the Columbus Post-Dispatch.

"My friend, you are one hell of a reporter. I have the Sunday News Tribune and it has taken me a couple of hours to read your stories and those of your colleagues. What a fantastic job. Jim, I can't say for certain, but I think you are going to win another award."

"Thanks Charlie, but no award this time. This story is too personal. We can't get an award if we don't submit the story and I've already talked to Audrey and Brad, and we all agree, this one is private. I mean, for goodness sake, our executive editor is one of the people arrested. No, Charlie, I appreciate the compliments, but this one is private," Jim answered.

"Jim, I have been watching the wires. Your story has been picked up by the AP, the New York Times, the Washington Post, the Chicago Tribune, and the Los Angeles Times. Everyone in the business is going to know this is your story. And everyone knows who you are because of those two AP awards.

"You have done one hell of a job, my friend. You deserve the credit. But, let's get serious, Monaghan. When are you coming to work for the Post-Dispatch? I just have to get you on my team before you get picked up by the Times or the Post."

"Not now, Charlie. I am happy working for Brad and Audrey. But thank you."

Freshening up his scotch, Jim walked back to the balcony where he kissed Jenny and told her the Ryan family was fine, and Charlie Sloan offered him a job again. Jim was bothered by a lack of warmth from Jenny.

"What's wrong? I thought you would be happy this morning," Jim asked.

"Jim, it's ten in the morning and you are drinking your second scotch. Don't you think it's a little early for two scotches?"

Jim stared at Jenny, who stared back.

"At dinner with my parents, you had a ton of that damn Bushmills. I quit counting after three and you had a couple before we left. Jim, you drink too much. Even my father mentioned it to me as we were leaving, that he was concerned that you had drunk too much to drive."

"Your father would criticize me if I won the Pulitzer Prize and they struck oil on our family farm. I will never be good enough for you in his eyes, and he is just using the drinking to criticize me."

"Jim, we have so much going for us. Let's not let this drinking get out of hand."

"Jenny, I'm Irish and Irish people drink."

Jenny's expression was somber, and with her hands on her hips, she continued her stare.

Jim got up, went into the kitchen and threw his drink down the drain.

69

In Ohio law enforcement circles, September 12 through September 17 was referred to as the week that brother turned on brother.

Reid, Buckner, Weir, Davis, Williams, and Lawlor were locked up in individual cells in the Shelby County jail, three in a row with three across a short walkway. They could see one another and carry on conversations with one another.

They all requested the services of Wilbur T. Waters, famed defense attorney from Columbus, who had defended Reid in his previous trial and had defended Buck and Clyde as well. When he didn't respond, they got worried.

Some speculated he was working with Slick, Buck, and Clyde. The three, along with other minor players, were taken to the Franklin County Jail. There were too many people arrested for the Shelby County jail to house.

Buckner tried to put everyone at ease, telling his fellow defendants that they couldn't be arraigned until

Monday and Waters probably was busy but would be there before Monday morning.

But Monday morning came and no word from Waters. When the judge heard none of the defendants had counsel, he deferred the arraignment until Tuesday and told each one they didn't qualify for a public defender.

They needed a lawyer. Reid was able to get Waters on the phone. Waters told him, that in the earlier cases, he had been retained by Pugh and paid by Pugh. No Pugh, no money, no representation, Waters said.

Reid asked how much Waters would charge. He demanded a down payment of $50,000 and a hefty hourly charge on top of that for him and each of his associates. None of the defendants had $50,000. Pugh controlled all the money and they had no access to it, so they started to scramble.

Weir was the first. On Monday he told the clerk of the court, when he was scheduled to be arraigned, he wanted to talk to George Rogers.

Rogers met with Weir and listened for an hour. Weir asked for no special treatment, but he hoped Rogers would consider his attitude and his testimony.

His first dealings with Pugh began years before. His home building business had been hit by hard times. Cutting corners in the quality of materials, he ended up remodeling and repairing many houses his company had built. Some of the windows fell out of the houses, the ceilings and walls cracked and even the cheap tile he had put in the kitchens in his "elite" homes broke. Weir was almost bankrupt. Pugh loaned him money and he kept digging himself deeper in the hole with Pugh.

He told Rogers of seeing Slick's L.L. Bean boots and knew, in his heart, Slick was involved in Jack's robbery and shooting. He said he left the meeting when they started talking on that fateful Friday morning that Jim Monaghan had to be gotten out of town. He said he knew it was code talk, especially when they said they wanted Edgar out of town, too.

But he did nothing to stop them, and he had to pay a price. He told Rogers when Monaghan was shot, he wanted to come and talk to him, but was afraid of Pugh and was too cowardly to come forward.

He told Rogers the key players were Reid, Buckner, and Davis along with Pugh. He admitted Pugh pressured him to hire Davis as city manager, who then hired Buckner.

"I didn't know at the time, but they were all in the KKK down south. And Ron was the Grand Goblin of central Ohio, but I never knew any of that then. By the time I found out, I couldn't do anything about it."

Going back to his cell, his co-defendants wanted to know where he had been and who he had been talking to. Weir told them simply he was trying to get a lawyer.

All the defendants were trying to get lawyers and none of them wanted to share a lawyer with the others.

As Bernard wisely said the previous year, when the conspiracy was uncovered, "Those in it will turn on one another."

Late Monday evening, the turning had begun, and, with each passing day, it became a torrent. By Friday night, none of the defendants were speaking with one another and all asked that their cells be moved. DA Rogers refused.

The lawyers for the defendants, citing not enough time to prepare, asked for the arraignments to be postponed until Friday. In a move that showed the inexperience of Williams' attorney, he asked Willy to be released on his own recognizance. The judge and others in the courtroom laughed.

By Friday, all defendants were charged and arraigned with a variety of crimes from conspiracy to commit murder, to money laundering, theft and many others. None were granted bail. If found guilty on all the counts, most of the defendants would die incarcerated. Judge Lawlor told them, as they were complaining about the number of charges, they should relax. They hadn't heard from the United States Attorney yet, and he would have charges, too.

After Lawlor's comment, silence fell on the cell block. Each defendant started to think how he could testify against his fellow defendants, so he might benefit.

70

The last of Jim's five-part series on the crimes of the century in Lincoln and Shelby County appeared in Friday's News Tribune. Each day, Audrey ordered more papers published, and each day they completely sold out.

In addition to writing his series, as News Editor, Jim was covering the upheaval in the city of Lincoln. People were shocked, angry and demanding leadership. They had lost their Mayor, City Manager, and Police Chief. They were appalled at the corruption.

Deputy Mayor Jack Wilson had called Jim late Thursday evening and told him of a news conference he was calling for ten a.m. the next day. He hoped there would be enough time for Jim to get the story in the afternoon paper. Jim asked what the big news was, but Jack told him he still had a T to cross and an I to dot. But he would see Jim at ten in the morning.

As Jim walked into the city council chambers at nine forty-five, he was pleased to see Donald Hansen, Judge

McCallister, Reverend Jefferson, and Edgar Johnson sitting in the front row.

"Well, look who's here," Jim greeted his friends with open arms. "You guys have any idea what Jack has up his sleeve this morning?"

"Well, Mr. Investigative Reporter, maybe we know something you don't," a smiling Edgar chuckled.

Befuddled, Jim turned to see Jack Wilson walking towards him. "Have you got Art Wilks here, Jim? I want a lot of coverage for what I am going to do today. Sorry I couldn't give you a heads up, but I think you will be pleased."

Wilson walked to the podium and called the news conference to order. Jim was surprised that Audrey's television station was broadcasting live and there were two TV stations from Columbus and a reporter from the Post-Dispatch in addition to the usual Lincoln city hall reporters.

Jack called the news conference to order and spent some time lamenting the news of the past week. "The city is strong, and we will deal with this unprecedented crisis in a professional way. But, let me assure everyone, there are changes coming to the city of Lincoln, your city government, and your city police department."

"We are starting a search for a new police chief and a new city manager. We will find the best. In the interim, I have directed the personnel department of the city to immediately begin an aggressive search for Black and female candidates for our police and fire departments. It's about time. I expect a report back by the first of the year and I expect female and black recruits to be on the police and fire departments by the end of the first quarter."

Looking into the camera of the live television feed,

Jack said, "To those of you who don't know, Lincoln has a city manager form of government. We have seven at-large city council positions and from that group of seven, one is elected to serve as Mayor for a four-year term."

Jack went on to note the Lincoln city charter dictated when the Mayor was unavailable to serve, the deputy mayor, became Mayor until the next mayoral election, some three years in the future. Jack reported he had received Mayor Weir's resignation as mayor and city councilman. Wilson told the assembled he, as mayor, had the authority to appoint a replacement to fill the remaining three years of Weir's city council term.

Taking a deep breath and looking out over the crowd of reporters, Jack looked directly in the lens of the television camera. "In the new spirit of cooperation, I have talked with my fellow council members and we are all in agreement in naming Reverend Jeremiah Jefferson to fill Weir's vacancy.

There were gasps amongst the press corps. Reverend Jefferson was the first Black to hold city-wide office in Lincoln's history.

Jim's head snapped at the news. *Son of a gun, that's brilliant. I wonder what else Jack is going to shock the city with.*

When the muttering stopped, Jack went on. "Further, I've talked with Professor Harrison Fowler, and he has told me circumstances have caused him to tender his resignation as Chairman of the Shelby County Community Commission. In consultation with District Attorney George Rogers, we are appointing Judge McCallister to head up the commission and we look forward to working with him.

"Finally, the youth of Lincoln need a voice in our city government. I have asked Edgar Johnson to create a Youth Advisory Board. I expect Edgar to recruit both white and black young men and women to a ten-member committee to help me and Donald Hansen, of the Lincoln Park District, plan activities, parks, and facilities to help the youth in our town stay busy and be productive.

"I expect recreational and job training opportunities and I am counting on Edgar's leadership.

"Now, are there any questions?" The media peppered Wilson with questions, but comfortable in his new role as Mayor, he handled them with clear, concise answers.

Jim had none. He was just pleased. Getting some quotes from Reverend Jefferson, Edgar, Donald, and Jack, Jim raced back to the paper and wrote his story.

The headline on page one was:

Lincoln Turns A Page

71

WEDNESDAY, DECEMBER 22, 1965

A lex Reid, the last of the Pugh Conspiracy was to be sentenced Wednesday afternoon. He had been charged with conspiracy to commit murder, fraud, theft, drug running, and money laundering. D.A. Rogers had personally prosecuted the case against Reid, who was the only one of the six defendants who would not cooperate.

Despite the overwhelming evidence, including his own accounting ledgers, Reid told Rogers, the judge and the jury, he knew nothing. He was just a victim and was innocent of all charges. The jury did not believe him. He was found guilty on all counts.

When the judge gaveled his courtroom to order, he asked Reid if he had anything to say before sentencing. Reid maintained his innocence.

The Judge disagreed and sentenced Reid to life in prison without the possibility of parole. Then in an unusual move, and probably unprofessional, he said may Irene Dunn, Steve Hampton, Haley Johnson, and Mary Ryan rest in peace. Glaring at the judge, Reid was led away in shackles.

Chief Buckner and City Manager Arlen Davis also received life without parole. Willy Williams and Judge Lawler each received twenty-year sentences. Mayor Weir who provided the most damning information against the other defendants received only ten years.

Clyde, Buck, and Slick were charged with murder, conspiracy to commit murder, and assault and battery. They were found guilty and sentenced to life in prison. Other members of the various criminal enterprises pled guilty and received appropriate sentences. Justice officials joked they needed to build a new prison, just for Pugh's group. No one laughed.

As the members of Pugh's conspiracy were tried, convicted and sentenced, United States Attorney Charles Adderley called a news conference. Flanked by Attorney General Nicholas Katzenbach, he announced sweeping indictments of individuals in Chicago, Miami, New York, and Philadelphia on various counts of drug trafficking, money laundering and a host of other federal charges.

Men with names like Lenny the Chin, Charlie the Nose and other mob bosses up and down the coast were arrested in early morning raids.

"This is one of the largest roundups of organized crime figures in the history of law enforcement. I want to thank Jim Monaghan of the Lincoln News Tribune for his assistance in uncovering this conspiracy."

Adderley went on to say that federal charges against members of the Pugh Conspiracy in Lincoln would be announced later. "We are not in any hurry to prosecute those individuals, because we know where they are," he said smiling.

Jim never disclosed the name of the man in black and Reverend Smallwood never made an appearance in court. From his secret location, he gave insight to the prosecutors and provided background information to seal the cases against the six.

For his efforts, Adderley invited Smallwood to be in the federal witness protection program. He promised him a new name and a new life just about anywhere in the United States.

Smallwood surprised Adderley, but not Jim, when he opted to be a Minister at the United States Penitentiary in Leavenworth, Kansas. He only asked that he be provided living quarters in or near the prison. Jim and Smallwood had lunch before he left town. Jim told him he forgave him. He told Smallwood if it hadn't been for him, Pugh and his group would still be working the system and hurting people. Then Jim did something he thought he would never do, he hugged Smallwood and wished him well.

72

The relationship between Jim and Jenny's parents improved with every visit, but Jenny's father remained reserved. Despite this, Jim was impressed Harrison had resigned from the County's Community Relations Commission.

Harrison had asked what Jim thought he should do to be of service, Jim suggested he be an advisor to Edgar's committee. Jim was stunned when Harrison told him, he wasn't sure what he could add to the group, but would Jim set up a lunch with Edgar. Jim said he would.

For Jenny, the only dark cloud was Jim's excessive drinking when he was with her parents. Jim consistently denied he drank too much.

Harrison and Martha knew Jim was going to ask Jenny to marry him and while Martha was accepting of it, Harrison kept holding out for a breakup. Harrison told his wife he hoped Jenny would tire of Jim's drinking. On the day before Christmas Eve, Jim knew Jenny was shopping with a girlfriend in Columbus. He asked the Fowlers if he could stop by.

He told them he was going to ask Jenny to marry him, and he wanted their blessing. He knew their history was bumpy, but he hoped they knew he loved her and would always be good to her.

Harrison told him he knew the history was bumpy and he was partially responsible for it. "You are not the type of person I had in mind to marry my daughter. I had hoped she would marry into one of the families back in Boston. I think you drink too much and I hope you get it under control. But despite what I think, I know Jenny loves you. I won't stand in the way, so, you have my blessing to marry my daughter."

Jim didn't know whether to be pleased or pissed, so he simply said, "Thank you, Professor."

Martha beamed as her husband, albeit reluctantly, gave Jim his blessing. She knew how much Jenny loved Jim. She grabbed Jim by the arm and told Harrison she had private words for Jim. Taking him into the study, she told Jim she was very pleased to have him as her son-in-law. She handed him a small box. She told him the history of what was inside the box, saying, he had no obligation, but she would appreciate if he would consider using it.

Jim was astonished.

73

E arly on Christmas eve, Jim drove to Calvary Cemetery where he walked among the graves. A cold December wind blew through the trees and tombstones. *Snow might be coming for Christmas Eve,* Jim thought.

He stopped at Irene Dunn's grave. As he prayed, he silently thanked Irene for initially bringing the corruption to his attention. He walked over to Steve Hampton's grave. He knew not many people would stop there. Finally, he walked over to where he knew Maybelle was waiting. It wasn't his first trip to Haley's grave, but it was his first trip with Maybelle.

Together they cried, they laughed, and they cried again.

"You know, she saved my life, Maybelle. If she hadn't jumped into my lap, Slick would have had a clear shot at me. I told her to leave, but she refused.

"I know, Jimmy. I know she was a hero, but I still miss her so."

Jim and Maybelle embraced, and as they walked to their cars, Jim said,

"You know you are the closest person I have to a mother, so let me tell you something, at a time like this, I would be telling my mom. "Maybelle, I am going to ask Jenny to marry me this afternoon."

"Oh, Jimmy, that's wonderful, I am so happy for you. Now, make sure you invite me and Edgar to the weddin'. You promise?"

"Of course, I will Maybelle, I will reserve a seat for you next to my brother on my side of the church."

Arm in arm, they left the cemetery.

Jim told Jenny of his emotional walk through Calvary Cemetery and how it brought back bittersweet memories. Jim teared up when he told Jenny of his conversation with Maybelle. "Haley saved my life, but Maybelle lost her daughter forever. Maybelle is strong, and she is moving on. I have experienced so much death, I hope 1966 is going to be a great year.

"Speaking of 1966, why don't you get some ice and we can have a drink."

Jenny went to the kitchen to get glasses of ice water while Jim went to the bedroom and retrieved a small box up from its hiding place in a closet.

As Jenny came back, he had her sit down, and he went down to one knee and told her how much he loved her, then asked her to marry him. She immediately said yes and hugged him.

"Now, I know you didn't want a diamond, but I have a special one, and I would like you to wear it with pride." He opened the box and the diamond sparkled.

"My God, Jim, this looks like it is almost two carats. How in the world could you afford this? If Audrey gave you a bonus, and you spent it on this, I am going to be upset. This is beautiful, but I don't want you spending any money on me and a big diamond. But my goodness, it's gorgeous," Mary gushed.

"I think that's what Martha Fitzgibbon probably said when Patrick gave it to her almost eighty years ago," Jim said smiling.

Mary's mouth dropped open.

"When I asked your parents for their blessing, your mother took me into the study, gave me the ring and told me the story. Before Patrick died, he told your mother he wanted her to have it and perhaps her son or daughter could use it someday. She has kept it all these years and never told anyone about it, not even Harrison."

Jenny squealed, "Wait, you asked my parents for their blessing? Did they give it? Of course, they did, that's how you got the ring. Yes, I will wear it, Jim. I will wear it proudly. God love old Uncle Patrick."

Hugging Jim, Jenny whispered, "This is great, Jim, but you know we have to set a date and then solve some problems. What do you think about two weeks after my final exams this spring? I don't want to wait until I graduate.

"Mother is already working on a guest list. We can hold the reception at the Country Club or in our back yard. And of course, I will have to move back with Mom and Dad. We don't want to shock our Boston relatives, do we? Jenny said smiling.

"Wow how long have you been planning and thinking about this?"

"Oh, I started talking to Mother shortly after you got out of the hospital."

"Now, can't we just enjoy the evening and not talk about problems?" Jim pleaded.

"Well, one of us has to be practical. Have you thought about where we are going to get married?"

"No," Jim answered, then it dawned on him.

"Well, I am Presbyterian, and you are Catholic. My parents are going to insist that I get married at First Presbyterian, but I know you are Catholic and your church has strict rules, too."

"Well, we can figure it out," Jim said. "I know Msgr. Morris pretty well and he is creative, so we can work it out. But, speaking of problems, you better prepare your parents and your proper Boston relatives, there is going to be a Black man on the altar with me. My brother Hugh will be my best man, but Edgar is going to be a groomsman and Maybelle is sitting in the first row with my brother's family."

"Oh, I anticipated that. I told mother Edgar would be in the wedding and that Maybelle would probably be sitting with your family. She laughed and said the reactions of my father's family would be worth the price of admission. Mother is becoming quite the card."

"What? You mean you have already talked to your mother about Edgar and Maybelle?"

"Of course, I have. I knew you were going to ask me," Jenny laughed and said, "Wow, what an evening. Quite a Christmas, Jim Monaghan. Quite a Christmas. And what a life we are going to have together."

Thank you for reading THE INCIDENT.

I hope you enjoyed Jim Monaghan's story. Can't wait to find out what happens to him next?

One-click THE HOSTAGE Now!
A Prison Riot.

A reporter in over his head.
What happens when he's taken hostage by the prisoners?
Will he be able to escape with his life?

It's 1972. The last troops are withdrawn from Vietnam. Watergate is about to break.

Jim Monaghan's drinking is out of control. His marriage is on the rocks. His job is teetering on the brink. Then the story of a lifetime falls into his lap.

A riot breaks out at the Ohio State Penitentiary and he's the first journalist on the scene.

There's only one problem. Jim is taken hostage by the prisoners and now he has to do everything in his power to get out. But will that be enough?

One-click THE HOSTAGE Now!

BOOKS BY DF DORAN

AUTHOR'S NOTE

This is the first of the Jim Monaghan stories, a fictional series chronicling the trials and tribulations of a newspaper reporter for a midsize newspaper in the 1960s and 1970s.

Jim Monaghan is fictional and bears no relationship to anyone living or dead. All the characters in this novel and following novellas and novels are fictional but there are occasional references to historical figures and events.

There is a Lincoln, Ohio, a small community located near Columbus. My Lincoln, Ohio does not exist.

There is no Reid funeral home in Lincoln, Ohio. It exists only in my imagination and bears no relationship to any funeral home anywhere.

In my research, I never found any instance of a funeral home switching caskets.

There is a Donnellan Funeral Home in Illinois and it has existed for many decades and enjoys an excellent reputation. It is often found in the books of the late Andrew Greeley, one of my favorite authors.

ACKNOWLEDGMENTS

This novel could not have been written without the support and inspiration of my wife, Jan. My thanks to my son Kevin and his wife Kate, successful authors themselves, for their constant encouragement and editorial support.

A special thanks to Danya, Shannon, and Bryan for their editing, feedback, research and so many other assists.

ABOUT THE AUTHOR

D.F. Doran, when asked what he did for a living, always answers, "Which decade?" Mr. Doran has worked as a staff reporter and an editor for a daily newspaper, served in a senior position in the United States House of Representatives as chief of staff to a member of Congress, and for a Fortune 25 company as a vice-president.

He is married to his wife, Jan, for 50 years. Together, they have four married children and seven grandchildren.

The Dorans live in Highlands Ranch, Colorado.

Sign up for D. F. Doran's **newsletter** to find out when he has new books!

He loves to hear from his readers. You can reach him at **dfdoranauthor@gmail.com**

 facebook.com/DF-Doran-194785421384554